KADAKAS
IV

STEVEN P. WARR

KADAKAS IV

A novel

iUniverse, Inc.
New York Lincoln Shanghai

Kadakas IV

Copyright © 2006 by Steven P. Warr

All rights reserved. No part of this book may be used or reproduced by any means, graphic, electronic, or mechanical, including photocopying, recording, taping or by any information storage retrieval system without the written permission of the publisher except in the case of brief quotations embodied in critical articles and reviews.

iUniverse books may be ordered through booksellers or by contacting:

iUniverse
2021 Pine Lake Road, Suite 100
Lincoln, NE 68512
www.iuniverse.com
1-800-Authors (1-800-288-4677)

ISBN-13: 978-0-595-38296-5 (pbk)
ISBN-13: 978-0-595-82667-4 (ebk)
ISBN-10: 0-595-38296-7 (pbk)
ISBN-10: 0-595-82667-9 (ebk)

Printed in the United States of America

For my father Joseph Packer Warr. He loved to read science fiction. How I wish he could read this. Maybe he can?

I
BEGINNINGS

The drone of the huge engines of the starship *Columbia* had nearly lulled him to sleep as he reflected on the importance of tomorrow. He forced alertness back into his brain. The tedium of the past six years was about to pay off and the commander must be sharp. Tomorrow *Eagle II* would land on Kadakas IV, the fourth planet of Alpha Centauri A. The first of the Project *Icarus* probes had almost arrived.

Actually, Scott Armstrong and his crew had only been involved with the project for eighteen months, most of which had been spent on simulators. Now they were to embark on their most vital function.

Dwelling on the mission had been an attempt by Armstrong to clear his mind of the mixed feelings that rooted themselves to the back of his skull. It was, he knew, a dream come true for him; a dream for which he had worked ever since *Icarus* had been announced. But the unreasoning fear that something, in obedience to Murphy's Law, had to go wrong hung over him like a shroud. The landing craft had been tested, retested, and tested some more. Nothing could possibly go wrong.

Still…

Just then, Armstrong experienced a brief jolt of excitement during which the blood surged through his body making his head spin. It was instigated by the fleeting thought of the ancient dictum of the Chinese military genius Sun Tzu: *When you see the correct course, act; do not wait for orders.* The terrible result of that advice——one would nearly always be a hero or be dead in about equal proportion of probability——did not deter him when he had impulsively acted on that advice during the Russo-Iranian War. From that moment he had started his transformation from total obscurity to becoming the number one household name. He was the commander of humanity's first attempt to step foot on a totally alien planet. The high probability of death would not deter him now!

✳   ✳   ✳   ✳

2245 HOURS 26 FEBRUARY—CTOC (FWD) XVI CORPS, SOUTHERN IRAN. Armstrong had not seen so much activity in the Corps Tactical Operation Center since the first day of the ground war. A tired looking full colonel was attempting to explain the gravity of a very tense situation. Armstrong had gotten wind of trouble by eavesdropping on the 104th division intelligence radio net but was having trouble putting all the pieces together.

"Mac! What's going on?" *It was the Corps commander himself. He had just entered the tent and abruptly stopped by the large map displayed on the wall. He was addressing the colonel. The fifteen or so officers gathered around the G-2 rose abruptly from their squatting positions or stiffened to attention.*

"Relax gentleman!" *It was a command.* "I don't need everyone to talk——just the two and the three.——Go!" *The two and three in military parlance referred to the G-2 intelligence officer and the G3 operations officer.*

Colonel McDaniels, the G-2, picked up a pointer and thrust it indifferently toward a bold circle on the map labeled OBJECTIVE EAGLE.

"You know the one-hundred-fourth has established an airhead here and the French seventh division has gotten bogged down in some intermittent fighting here." *he began, then moved the pointer southwest about 50 kilometers.* "With the twenty-fourth, first and third divisions committed against enemy forces east around the Pakistani border, the one-oh-four is exposed here."

The general broke in. "We knew from the get-go that we were taking a risk there, but we don't see anything now to give them any problems. The Russian main force is trapped to the east."

When he was sure the CG had finished, McDaniels continued hurriedly. "Yes sir! That's what we thought, too, but..." He paused to take a breath. "BAI (battlefield air interdiction) and air recce (reconnaissance) has reported a large force, maybe as much as two tank divisions began moving out of positions about 40 klicks southwest of Tehran more than an hour ago. TAC AIR has diverted some sorties to the area, but our initial guess is they can be in contact with the 104th in eight to ten hours——worst case.

Combat power ratios heavily favor the enemy, because the 104th lacks significant tank killing capability. They could handle the older generation T-72, but my guess is these are T-80s and 90s judging by where they came from."

Armstrong felt his excitement grow. *This is the perfect place for the brigade to be deployed.* He knew that most of the aviation of both army and air force had already been committed. To turn them to a new threat in the kind of strength needed would expose the committed forces in the east. Bottom line. To truly defeat a force of that size, heavy ground forces are vital. <u>We are it</u>! He thought. His pulse began to race. With the brigade's heavy forces and M-1-A2 tanks, not even T-90s would stand a chance.

<u>We are the only ones the Corps has</u>.

Brigadier General Thornwald, the G-2 officer was now at the map, speaking to the group, and Armstrong forced himself to listen. "...TAC AIR and the Aviation Brigade," the one-star general was saying, "and maybe we'll have to pull the string on some divisional attack helicopter assets. But I see that as our only option. We can't pull the 104th out or the whole operation may go down the tube."

<u>What!!!</u> Armstrong felt his brief exuberance fade as he realized the brigade was not even being considered. *Have they forgotten about us, or do they just not have confidence in the guardsmen.* He felt the excitement ebb to a point just before resignation, when anger stepped in.

<u>Shit! This is no time to resurrect the reserve/active rivalry. Come on! Think!</u>

As indignation was building, Armstrong forced himself to clear his head and listen again. <u>Maybe they just haven't thought about us yet?</u>

Thornwald was finishing his briefing. "…about it, sir. It's a risk but we have no choice."

The Commanding General looked from face to face in the audience. When he spoke it was somber. "Looks like we're going to have to eat some casualties after all. But that's what war is all about. What's your best guess on casualties, One?" He nodded toward the G-1 personnel officer.

"There are a lot of variables, Sir, but worst case could be over a thousand."

"Do it Thorny, but leave the divisional birds where they are unless absolutely necessary to use them to support the one-oh-fourth."

Armstrong's anger had built until he felt himself near the point that Richards back in Adjutant Generals office had called three inches off the floor. *They are completely ignoring us!*

"GODDAMN IT! YOU STUPID FUCKERS CANNOT IGNORE 4,000 SUPREMELY TRAINED MEN AND A HUNDRED SIXTEEN M-1 TANKS AND OVER A HUNDRED BRADLEYS JUST BECAUSE OF A FUCKING SERVICE RIVALRY!"

His anger broke when he realized everyone in the place was looking at him. He hadn't intended to speak, but it just came out. As the Corps commander's eyes met his, he realized he didn't care. He knew this either meant instant oblivion or someone would listen to him. Either way, at that moment he knew he had done the right thing.

It didn't start well. The three stars on the general's collar seemed to bore deep into Armstrong's brain and he heard the strong voice say. "Who the hell are you?"

Lieutenant Colonel Brown, the assistant operations officer piped up then. "Sir, he's one of the reservists we got last week. His troops are pulling rear operations for the COSCOM."

"What kind of unit?" The CG addressed the question to Armstrong.

"Sir, Colonel Armstrong, commanding the 43rd Infantry Brigade Mechanized out of Texas. I have two tank and two mechanized task forces. We are ready!" His tone was clearly belligerent.

"In normal circumstances, you talk to me like that and you won't be ready. Someone else would be commanding your brigade. What can you do?"

"Sir, I can have the lead battalion moving in an hour. And we can close with the enemy in five." He was certain about the hour, but he hadn't looked much at the terrain so the five hours may have been optimistic." Everyone else in the room knew it was impossible.

The major representing the rear area operation center (RAOC) looked derisively Armstrong's direction. "You have troops scattered all over the rear area. It'll be impossible to get them through the traffic jams, especially at night."

"I only told you my troops were scattered. I actually have less than two companies scattered. My troops are heavy. We have to operate as a unit even in a rear OPS mission. To piecemeal them would be to emasculate them." Armstrong began enjoying the attention, but got impatient to get on with it.

The assistant operations officer spoke again in a whiny voice.

"You haven't had time to plan or allow planning time for your subordinate units."

"This operation along with three others have been planned in detail and rehearsed since 19 January. The one we will be using has been rehearsed six times in the last ten days, three of them at night. The only difference is compass point and location. We kicked Rip Roper's OPFOR butt with this plan on 24 January and again in February at the National Training Center."

Turning to the map, he slapped an area just south of OBJECTIVE EAGLE with an open palm. "One platoon of my cav troop is in contact with the 104th here already. Another platoon should link up with the French in the south soon. The third platoon has done a recon of the area between them. Here." Armstrong moved his hand over the big red arrow the G-2 had drawn indicating the Russian avenue of approach.

"We rehearsed this operation last night driving almost 20 klicks that direction before going through our meeting engagement drill."

It had actually been more than 40 kilometers south where they had run the practice. "We are ready! All I need is a few TAC AIR sorties and recce keeping us posted on the bad guys."

"Sir! Let us just do it!"

The officer from the RAOC had raised his eyebrows in surprise when Armstrong indicated the positions of his foxtrot troop. Now his tone became belligerent.

"Why did you have your cav troop posted there? You were supposed to be guarding the rear. How did you know where to send them?"

Armstrong almost went through a lengthy discourse about part of the commander's job being to analyze the situation continuously. He must anticipate many courses of action, and respond to the most likely. Scouts and cavalry must be out most of the time supporting those anticipations. More important, like a football team, if it does not routinely train, it will lose its edge.

"I guessed!" was the terse reply.

"What about fire support?"

The fire support officer was a full colonel and it seemed to Armstrong he would ask incomprehensible questions just to feel like he was part of the operation.

"I've got my own direct support 155mm battalion, but I could use some reinforcing fires if you can spare it."

They seemed to be accepting the fact that the 43rd would get a chance, and he was beginning to feel comfortable. He was feeling harassed by the questions, but knew the more questions asked the less likely something would be left out inadvertently.

Just when Armstrong thought he could stand no more, the CG raised his hand for silence and said matter-of-factly to Armstrong, "Tell me how you're going to do it."

Armstrong fished out his playbook, approached the map and briefly studied the open space between OBJECTIVE EAGLE and the 7th French Division. After no more than a few minutes he faced the general.

Folding back the playbook to the page labeled OFFENSE COLUMN and after hastily scribbling something on the page, Armstrong thrust the pamphlet toward the CG. The general took it from his hand and studied the open page.

Line one: Offense column 5850 mils or forearm west of Polaris.
Line two: INITIAL Travel on road 25 KPH white light (Headlights)
Line three: PREBATTLE travel overwatch—white light
Line four: DEPLOY bounding overwatch—blackout
Line five: 1/103 290100FEB 2/103 290130FEB" 1/115 290200FEB 2/115 290230FEB (the two armor heavy task forces—the 103——would lead the infantry)

"That's it, sir. The troops have been through it so often they could do it blindfolded."

Explanations of the lines were on the page in front of the general and as he leafed through subsequent pages the condensed information appeared to be quite adequate. "I don't know." he said hesitantly. "It seems too simple." I don't know." he repeated.

"Ah, what the hell. We need you. You say you're ready. Thorny, give him some air sorties, and a reinforcing artillery battalion." Turning back to Armstrong, he said simply,

"Don't screw it up."

*   *   *   *

Ironically, the war had turned Man's attention back to the stars. The Russians finally become convinced that their quest for world domination was futile. With that realization came the surplus of funds and Western cooperation in a mutual effort. That change in attitude was directly responsible for the development of the SP.[1] The Russians had developed the molecular transformation techniques and the Americans the transmission capability.

---

1. See Chapter II

*   *   *   *

Armstrong's coolness under fire had made him the logical choice to command the first landing on an alien planet. At least that's what the papers said. For three months now they had been close enough to Kadakas IV for detailed instrument analysis. Earth's best minds had ample opportunity to poke, probe and analyze the data. They had learned as much as possible without actually having stood on its surface.

Armstrong reviewed the brief in his hands. Kadakas IV was a paradise.

> G-2 type star as its primary sun (comparable to SOL in luminosity)
>
> Breathable atmosphere (after some acclimatization)
>
> Highly developed flora and fauna. (probably carbon based but not likely to be intelligent)
>
> Surface gravity .76 of Earth's
>
> Surface atmospheric pressure 11.9 P.S.I.
>
> Mean equatorial temperature 81.93 Fahrenheit
>
> Period of rotation 19.6 hours |

The proximity of *Alpha Centauri B*, the second star in the binary rotation, and of *Proxima Centauri* provided a "night" which would merely be a kind of twilight during the summer season. Kadakas IV appeared to be the perfect place for Man to begin his interstellar empire. The science boys had seen the "whites of their eyes." Now it was up to Scott and his fifteen-member team. It was their job to make the final test; survive six months on its surface.

With a jerk back to reality, he reminded himself that the mission would be far from the routine that he hoped his family believed. Because of the risk of some unknown infection spreading to Earth, there would be no rescue in the highly likely event of bacterial contamination. Doctors had estimated that there could be from 25 to 75 percent possibility that there existed on Kadakas IV some harmful microbe, even life threatening. It was true that there would be highly qualified scientists with the crew, and they would have almost instant access to equipment needed to combat the danger.

"Wake up, Skipper!"

The unexpected sound made Scott jump and look up like a startled deer at his second in command.

"Don't sneak up on me like that, Jimbo."

"Crew's waiting for you."

Armstrong remembered the final dry run. "Be right there."

"Have they found out what the hot spot is yet?" Lieutenant Colonel Jim Stark asked casually as he walked to the hatch.

Scanning had revealed an unusually hot area about fifty miles across on the planet's largest continent.

"No more than they knew before. Probably only geothermal."

Stark was a family man. His wife Laura and the kids had always been good about his prolonged absences, a fact of life for the military. He had many friends who hadn't been so lucky. A stable family is highly important to advancement. Ironically, work and long periods of separation usually produced the opposite. Jim Stark crammed so much togetherness into the limited family time that his had grown stronger. Sometimes he thought they were glad to see him leave for a while. This time he intended it to be even more so.

Armstrong, on the other hand, was still a bachelor. Nearing his mid-forties, he had still not found a soul mate. He was married to the Army.

The commander followed Stark into the tube that led up a few ladder rungs into the control compartment of the pod. The constant deceleration of the craft produced gravity slightly greater than that on the Earth's surface. The spacecraft never had a weightless interior. In fact, when there were no crewmen aboard it would increase to over 10 Gs. Because of the distance to the Centauri system, coasting would have taken a great deal of time.

Both Armstrong and Stark were above average in height and blond, although the elder's hair had already become tinged with gray. Stark was leaner than his companion. Not that Armstrong was overweight. He had always been ruggedly built. His size added to the commanding presence mainly attributed to his confident steel-gray eyes. The two men emerged on the upper deck and moved to their posts with the familiarity of long practice. Armstrong tapped some buttons on his console in the pilot's blister and spoke to the man already seated next to him.

"Are we ready for the final test, Jake?"

Air Force Major Jake Laird, the pod's pilot, studied his heads-up-display projected on the glass of the windshield and replied, "Ready, Colonel."

"Let's do it then, and get home."

Laird began the monotonous ticking off the pre-landing checklist.

"Trim?"

"Check."

"Tabs?"

"Check."

"Gyro-stabilizers?"

"Right…"

* * * *

The routine checks, which always seemed to go on interminably to Robert Benton, faded into the background as his thoughts turned inward. The realization this was the final test caused the nagging anxiety he always felt to grow in quantum leaps. *Tomorrow is the day, and there is no backing out now. But how can*

I do it? This thought repeated itself in rhythm with the checks and the drumming headache that always accompanied it. His fear continued to grow, until with sheer will power he forced it down and away, just short of complete panic. Benton reminded himself he did not have to be on this mission at all. It was completely voluntary, and there were so many volunteers that only the most highly qualified were selected. Why had they chosen a coward over the many heroes who could be here now?

Bob Benton knew the answer to that. On the surface, he was *not* a coward. In fact, he was a highly decorated *hero*. Only once had his true nature been allowed to surface. Luckily (or unluckily), he had been the only survivor then.

As a child in Roxbury, Massachusetts, he had been afraid to try out for his local hockey team. Despite being the best skater around, his fear kept him away. His father (dear old dad——rugged tavern brawler and longshoreman. If only he'd not been such a hero) refused to acknowledge that the fruit of his loins could possibly be afraid of anything. Dad had not believed in talking to children. He held to the long-out-of-date notion that children were to be seen and not heard. Bobby had ultimately been more afraid to oppose this tyrant, than to play, and became a star. He was so good that he played two years for Boston College and was hailed as the next Bobby Orr. It was assumed that he would go on to the National Hockey League (hopefully the Bruins). Mercifully (for him) in the first game of regional playoffs his sophomore year he sustained a massive knee injury. For three or four years there was talk of a miracle recovery, but Bob knew he would never play again.

His cowardice had surfaced during his hockey years in panic several times during games and once in practice. He had always been able to mask it with a feigned injury. Except once. In a game during his senior year in high school, after he had been viciously banged against the boards, it came again. When the player had come at him, consciousness left his mind, replaced by red folds of terror. After his reason returned, he learned he had beaten the boy into unconsciousness with his stick. Only the ensuing melee, when the benches cleared, hid the fact that two of his teammates had to remove the stick from his hands to prevent him from killing the boy.

Perhaps his unreasoning fear of his father had motivated him to volunteer for the commando raid into Tehran. More likely, it was an attempt by him to suppress his handicap. It was a mission to destroy a Russian surface-to-air missile site during the War.

Getting into the city had proved to be easier than expected, even with the stealth bomber used as the drop plane. That plane is nearly undetectable by radar, but with the number of overlapping radar receivers and observer stations the Russians had, there was more than a 95 percent probability they would be discovered. But with almost impossible luck, they had managed without being detected at all. They had arrived at the SAM site, emplaced the "standoff" munitions on surrounding trees and power poles, and departed without being seen. It was when they had stopped within range of the radio detonators that they had been discovered. And that was pure blind dumb luck. It takes about ten minutes to set up the detonation equipment, and Benton was posted as sentry. Less than five minutes passed before he saw the three BMP's coming toward him, one of which had the radio detection antenna atop it. They were making a house-to-house search.

If Benton had warned the others, they may have had time to move to a safer location. If they activated the detonator, the patrol would find them in seconds. There was no conscious decision on Benton's part. The familiar red veil once again obscured his reason. His only reaction was to find the nearest hiding place.

When sanity returned, Benton discovered the rest of his group was gone. He found out later that the SAM site had been destroyed, and that he, the only survivor, was acclaimed as a hero.

"Benton!"

He returned abruptly to the present, and realizing where he was, felt the panic begin to return, but he fought it off.

"Benton!" Armstrong's voice was edged with annoyance.

Benton pushed the remnants of the red curtain away and replied, certain he was not hiding his embarrassment.

"Yes sir? Sorry, I was thinking about tomorrow."

"We all are, but we cannot allow our attention to wander even in practice. We are within five minutes of touchdown phase. Are your men ready?"

Benton peered through the thick glass of the aft observation blister at the blackness filled with tiny points of light and said, "Yes sir. The real thing will go off tomorrow without a hitch."

Captain Bob Benton was the head of the security team. Their sole function was physical protection of the expedition.

The rest of the crew was eagerly alert, knowing that this would be the final practice. They were not the adventurous type for the most part, and they were aboard now for purely symbolic purposes. Chosen for their academic and scientific prowess, this group would not be aboard for the landing.

There was Hans Stauffer, a brilliant German microbiologist who had perfected a new technique for analyzing microbes, particularly viruses. More important for the crew was his uncanny ability to isolate and neutralize new forms of harmful bacteria.

His assistant was Susan Powell. She was a recent graduate of UCLA, and was already demonstrating similar prowess to her mentor. She sought the position by contacting Doctor Stauffer less than a week after the position was announced. He was so impressed with her interview that he passed over some seemingly more qualified applicants.

Boris Epilov was the Russian member of the expedition. His congenial nature had completely submerged the initial hostility that some of the war veterans harbored for Russians. Boris' natural way with words and humor had allowed even the mundane practice sessions to fly by. His real value to the mission was immeasurable.

He, and his Japanese assistant, Hiro Sakagowa were the sum of the expertise needed to return them from the mission when it was complete. They were the experts charged not only with keeping the electronic components of their vital equipment like helicopters and weapons, but their most important item, the SP, in working order.

The medical officer, Captain Kathleen Yeager, was responsible for treatment of injury and illness. She was not afforded assistants, because it was assumed that in an emergency the biologists could aid her. And if a really serious epidemic were to occur, policy called for the abandonment of the crew. Katy had been in the Air Force for two years, and was selected for the first landing of *Icarus* only six months after receiving her commission. As were the other members of the expedition, she was exemplary in her field. She had shown her ability to think under fire during her two-year tour as an emergency room physician at a Los Angeles hospital.

The remaining three crew members were Geologist George Barstow, his assistant Joni Hartley, and Sean Kelly the ecologist. Their jobs cornered most of their attention, and because they had only joined the crew three weeks before, they were not as familiar to the long time members.

"All right, folks. That does it! We're as trained as we are going to get. Tomorrow we'll know if that's enough. It goes without saying, you should be careful at home tonight. Tomorrow we'll face God-knows-what, and we'll all have to be sharp. Everything you've worked for will be on the line. Relax and get plenty of sleep. I don't want to hear about any of you observing the sailor's traditional last night in port routine. Anyone who returns tomorrow hung over will be a detriment to the rest of us. It is not too late to disqualify any of you. Remember there are a lot of people down there who'd give their eyeteeth to replace you."

Armstrong was aware that they knew, at this late date it would be extremely difficult to replace any of them. There were backups, but none had the specific two to three weeks of training for this particular planet. None of them would fit in as well as the present members. He knew the threats, therefore, were empty, but he hoped they would be impressed with the need to arrive in top form.

"I am extremely proud to be at the head of such a fine group of people," he continued, "and I am certain we will perform superbly. Okay! Boys and girls, let's go home."

Benton was the first to arrive at the stanisplummer. There waiting for them was pilot Terry Pratt, who would put the craft in orbit around Kadakas IV that night.

With a gallant sweep of his arm toward the gaping entrance to the SP, he said, "It's all yours, heroes."

Within five minutes the entire crew had crossed four and a third light years and was standing in front of the main SP in Houston.

The previous year and a half had been routine, almost monotonous. They were all ready for a break in that, but if they'd had any inkling of what they had in store, none would have been in the least anxious for a change.

‖
STANISPLUMMER

We all take for granted that wonderful machine which has so changed the world. If, however, one stopped to contemplate it, he would find it almost impossible to imagine life without it. So you are probably thinking right now: "What is this guy trying to do, teach me to walk, or talk?"

But bear with me; the stanisplummer is so intertwined with project Icarus, that it needs telling. If you can force yourself to imagine life without it…go one step farther and imagine you've never heard of a stanisplummer. If someone told you about it, you wouldn't believe it possible any more than the eighteenth century man would believe that man could fly. So let me teach you to walk and talk again. You may enjoy it. You may even learn to do it better.

It began during that time when the World was still breathing the collective sigh of relief that nuclear conflagration, so feared for sixty years, was not to be.

The month of August had held more fear than any month in the history of the world, and now it was over. On the tenth of that month, the Russian Union, spurred by the steadily moderating government in Iran, had decided to test the United States by striking deeply into the heart of the oil-rich country. The response from the West was so quick and devastating to the Russians, that they quickly sued for peace. Thousands on both sides had been killed and Iran was totally devastated. The terms of the hastily signed agreement included ideas and technology, and mutual observation to preclude future arms buildup.

* * * *

Most Americans on this snowy December day were skeptical about the cooperation pact. Viktor Stanislav, though he could hardly believe it, knew it was true. In fact, things had moved so fast, he was still fearful that he was the victim of a gigantic hoax. He half expected that the sign on the terminal building now coming into sight to read Vladivostok in Cyrillic script. He strained his neck to see the words that were just now becoming clear: John Foster Dulles International Airport, Washington, D.C. He would be here only long enough to go through customs and board another plane for Los Angeles. There he would do the last work of his life.

* * * *

Doctor John Plummer gazed out of his laboratory window irritably. He hated waiting, especially when something as exciting as this was about to happen. He had already dismantled all equipment not related to his Instantaneous Conductive Transmission (ICT) research and there was nothing for him to do until Stanislav arrived. Even if there had been something to do, he doubted he could concentrate on it. He felt like a little boy waiting impatiently for reindeer sounds on the roof.

From the first time he had heard of Viktor Stanislav, he had been intrigued with the idea of combining their research. Even the snatches of information about Stanislav's work that U.S. intelligence had managed to get had been enough to convince Plummer that it would be the ideal complement to his own research. Plummer had developed the dubbed Instantaneous Conductive Transmission, ICT. The ICT had proven impossible for the Russians to jam and was impervious to other interference like weather conditions. Long practice with computer network security enabled them to make the ICT nearly infinitely secure. It even passed through solid obstacles with no loss of power.

This new technique was a medium independent of radio waves. The conductive name was really a misnomer, because the technique consisted of the creation of artificial singularities (micro-miniature atomic bombs) in both the sender and receiver. Plummer had developed it based on the *Einstein-Rosen bridge* or *space warp theory*. The wormhole thus created connected the two instruments long enough to send a saved burst of digits through. Actually there had to be two transmissions—the first consisted of a sixteen bytes or 128 digits address that determined which receiver to connect with and the second contained the actual data or message. The address was much like a phone number or an Internet address except Internet addresses are only four bytes. Although the tunnel created was much too small (submicroscopic) to send a spaceship through, a digital message transmitted serially worked just fine. In fact, the signal was so reliable that it was almost unnecessary to worry about error checking. The standard error checking routines and check digits *were* included, however, from habit. Error checking turned out to be a good thing when objects and *people* began to be transported. The deep space probe *Shepherd* had been out three years now and was just about a light-year from Earth carrying an ICT. It demonstrated that there was no loss of power or delay in transmission with an ICT.

Plummer remembered, with pleasure, the day the ICT had worked for the first time, but now felt frustrated by his inability to carry it any further. He had constantly reminded himself that pure research rarely bore fruit in the near term. One engaged in it had to be content to work for the sake of work and the slim hope of success. But this time it was different. With Stanislav coming, he saw much more.

"Doctor Plummer." Mrs. Olson's scratchy voice jerked him abruptly out of his reverie. "Are you going to have anything to eat today? I believe you'd starve to death, if I wasn't here to look after you."

Her interruption increased his irritation, but he concealed it because he knew she was right.

"All right, Martha. I'll have something," he told his housekeeper quietly.

She moved in the direction of the kitchen, pausing momentarily, when he asked: "You haven't seen a taxi pull up on that side of the house, have you?"

She shook her head and disappeared through the door.

"What's taking him so long?" he asked himself aloud, despite the fact he knew the answer. No one in Los Angeles County gets anywhere fast between the hours of three and seven in the evening. It was for that reason he'd declined meeting Stanislav at the airport. He abhorred bumper-to-bumper traffic on the freeways. Time spent not working, to him, should be spent sleeping. Idle time was the largest detriment to progress.

The first thing he had done when he'd realized he'd attained sufficient stature, was to insist that Jet Propulsion Laboratory establish a special lab in his house to preclude the daily commute. The freeways, originally designed to speed the flow of traffic, now seemed to be the cause of slowdowns. The problem became worse every year, until the only solution seemed to be to pave every square inch of land. The world was ready for a new form of transportation. Maybe he and Stanislav could answer that need.

Finally, Plummer picked up the ream of computer printout paper, sat on a stool and began to pore over it eagerly, as if he'd never seen it before. These were his research notes, and he became so engrossed that when Mrs. Olson brought him soup and a sandwich, and the taxi pulled up simultaneously, he failed to notice either.

"Taxi's here." The screech again roused him from his stupor. Without a word, he was at the door.

The two men exchanged cursory greetings, both eager to begin work. They ritualistically exchanged notes, Stanislav's on molecular transformation and Plummer's on the ICT, and without another word settled down to study.

Stanislav was a caricature of the typical Russian. Five feet-six, he wore a rumpled black suit and a white shirt over his dumpy body. A bowling-ball head topped this. The metaphor held true for his features, except for the color. His face was white as a ghost, but the eyes and mouth were perfect copies of the finger holes, and the nose was insignificant. On top of this, gray wisps of hair stuck out from under the expected fur cap.

Plummer was Jeff to Stanislav's Mutt. He was six-feet four and seemed taller because of the way his wrists stuck out of his cuffs. It was difficult for him to get clothes off the rack to fit him, and because of his lack of interest in fashion, most of his shirts were too short. His bright blue eyes seemed almost hidden deep inside a mass of tangled beard, grown because of reluctance to spare work time to shave.

The two scientists remained nearly motionless for almost twelve hours, breaking their concentration only to obtain clarification on one point or other in the notes. Even Mrs. Olson's insistent pleas for them to eat were irritably waved away. The soup and sandwich she had brought earlier remained cold and untouched.

Finally they were ready to begin work. Together they forced themselves to eat something while discussing ways to start. Any observer would have been forced to the conclusion that either something great was about to happen or both men would die from sheer exhaustion within the next twenty-four hours. Thankfully, Mrs. Olson would not allow the latter, and the world has done a great disservice by not having raised a monument to her. Because of both men's past success and the promise of their project, they were afforded unlimited monetary and technical support. If any equipment they didn't already have was required, a mere phone call would have it there by the fastest transportation, whether it was from JPL or Moscow.

At the same time, inquisitive congressmen and members of the Russian congress were kept carefully away to prevent interruption. If either man had any desire for personal enrichment, he was in a position to take the two most powerful nations for the world's biggest caper.

It took a week for Stanislav's experiments, which had to be transported from Leningrad, to be reconstructed. While this was being accomplished, the two spent most of their time working with Plummer's apparatus. Already Stanislav had made some important modifications. The real effort, however, did not begin until Plummer had a chance to look at some of the molecular transformation experiments. Great discoveries, which elude scientists for centuries, are sometimes pieced together in an incredibly short time. Such was the case now. It was only eight days, almost to the minute, after Stanislav's arrival that the first breakthrough came. Plummer had, with the help of Jim Ames, one of his assistants, been trying Stanislav's technique on a synthetic molecule. The conversion of matter to energy had taken place without a hitch.

Scientists had for centuries been able to accomplish that. Indeed, one simple way to do it was by fire, but the energy produced was dispersed or consumed. It was necessary to contain the energy in a digital buffer so that it could be recombined into its original form without harm. Stanislav's method held the synthetic molecule into position in a fast bubble memory buffer. The theory was if the energy could be held in position long enough, the reverse reaction should reconstitute the matter. The problem was, there was too great a delay getting to the reconstitution chamber. They had tried many times with varying degrees of success. But they had never managed to hold it long enough to reconstitute more than a portion of it. This was hardly enough to be worthwhile transporting, especially if it were something you wanted to stay alive. Like yourself!

Suddenly a wild thought dispelled the musings in Plummer's brain. A look appeared on his face that gave Ames cause for alarm. "The solution is in the outcome!"

That statement was a thought, but he could contain his excitement no more. What came out was even more frightening to Ames than the look on Plummer's face had been.

"THAT'S IT! THAT'S IT! AMES QUICKLY, HELP ME DO IT! WHY ARE YOU STANDING THERE LIKE THAT? MOVE!"

"Do what, Sir?" Ames' face revealed grave concern.

"WHAT'S THE MATTER MAN? GET IT! WHILE I HOLD ON HERE!"

Ames was clearly at a loss, and Stanislav came in just then. Noticing Plummer's agitation, he felt his own excitement grow, and he asked the taller man in his slight accent, "What is it?"

"Don't you see it, Viktor!" His agitation was only slightly diminished. "It's not holding in place long enough to reconstitute it! Why can't we reconstitute it at the same precise instant we convert it to digits, thus reducing the need to hold it stable?"

"It is impossible. One cannot do both at the same time. There is always the delay to move it from the converter to the reconstituter.

Even if we could do both in the same location, electronic circuits are not quick enough to switch from one to another. That's no good anyway, because we haven't transmitted it anywhere."

"BUT WE CAN! Nearly, anyhow!"

Still excited, Plummer's hands moved like a boxer's when his opponent is on the ropes. We can convert in one location and *stream* the digits to the reconstituter using the ICT. Transmission time is instantaneous as far as we can tell. The problem has created the solution! We don't need the memory buffer!"

Now Stanislav's excitement was almost as great as his colleague's, but he did not waste time babbling. He moved directly to the laboratory ICT, grabbed the transmitter in one hand, and the receiver in the other. He moved his burden to where Plummer was waiting, shouldering the bewildered Ames out of the way in the process.

"We shall have to modify this equipment somewhat…Ames, get us someone capable of doing that."

Ames left the room, and both of the other occupants forgot he'd been there. They were on to the process that, ironically, solved all their problems at once.

One. Convert matter into digits.

Two. Stream the digits somewhere.

Three. Reconstitute that digits back to their original form on the fly.

Despite the pleas and cajoling of Mrs. Olson, the two scientists could not be pried from their work. They were at it non-stop for thirty-six hours, refusing rest until the machine was tested.

Their first try with the synthetic molecule worked, and they were both so ecstatic that neither could sleep for considerable time.

After finally succumbing to the housekeeper's demands, Plummer slept for not more than five hours, but by the time he returned to the lab, he discovered Stanislav already there. It was obvious that he'd been there for quite awhile, for he had a crew of assistants busily constructing a larger version of the successful apparatus.

"Good morning, John. I see you could not sleep, either. I came down early, only to discover there is really not much we can do until these men get finished. We might as well go somewhere comfortable and discuss it."

They left the laboratory deep in conversation about some of the possibilities of the new machine. If the industrial might of the world had known the implications of what was happening at that moment, it would be entirely possible that every hit man and terrorist organization would be moving with orders to kill these two men and destroy their discovery.

* * * *

Here are some of the organizations that had the most to fear because of the invention of the stanisplummer. The entire automobile industry. Can one imagine buying a car to travel congested freeways and streets, when all one had to do was to find the nearest SP, punch in a number, and be instantly transported anywhere he wished to go. Of course all the other forms of transport (except for pleasure) were doomed to obsolescence as well. Airlines, railroads, truck companies, all went broke. Indeed, they were the instruments of their own demise. The SPs had to be conventionally transported in order to be installed. The teamsters union did attempt to halt their spread briefly by refusing to carry them, but gave it up when it became clear the SP would proliferate, regardless.

The government, which held a monopoly on the SP, simply began using military transport and all too willing independent truckers. The union boys decided they'd better haul while there was still something to be hauled. The oil companies, and oil producing nations were logically the next to fall. This was especially true after SPs were placed on the gas giant planets like Jupiter and Saturn making liquid hydrogen the staple for generation of power. Finally the Telephone Company and its millions of miles of wire and satellite links became useless. It was easy to rig the SP to carry sound, and anyway, if one could simply step into a booth and be face-to-face with someone, why call? There was brief recession immediately after the institution of the SP when people in those doomed industries became unemployed, but it wasn't long before these workers were absorbed by the new SP related industries.

It did not solve the problems of the world immediately, and many of the third world countries were denied access to the SP for a while. World powers feared that the hungry masses would overwhelm them.

* * * *

Stanislav and Plummer took less than two months to perfect a full scale SP from the time they demonstrated it could be done.

Some of the early experiments had gone awry. For example, in some attempts to transmit inanimate objects, metal bars were reconstituted into powder because of nanoseconds delay. Even when timing was improved, and animals were used as subjects, some died because of small imperfections. But finally the cats, dogs and monkeys were being transmitted with seemingly no ill effects.

On March 2,…the SP was ready to be tested on a human being, Viktor Stanislav.

March had come in like the proverbial lion. There was a gale accompanied by a heavy rainfall, unusual in Los Angeles. The crew in the lab stood in anticipation and anxiety, clustered around the controls of the SP. Stanislav opened the door on the front of the machine and calmly stepped into the unknown. He turned and faced them, giving the characteristic little hand wave of his, indicating he was ready. All eyes were on the reconstituter booth as Plummer flipped the toggle. As quickly, Stanislav appeared there.

A quizzical mask had replaced the usual intelligent look on the Russian's face, and the door was quickly opened allowing him to step out. He hesitated. His glance darted from one assistant to another, seemingly without recognition. As he looked, his expression evolved into one of panic.

"What is it, Viktor?" Plummer voiced the concern he felt at that moment.

As if the sound had been a catalyst, Stanislav looked wildly at him and emitted a loud screech. He turned in fear, looking for a direction in which to escape. Although everyone was too startled to move when he bolted, he could not find his way out of the lab and he was eventually restrained.

It was later learned that he had not gone mad. His brain had simply been wiped clean of any memory. Within three years he had relearned enough to get along by himself, but he never regained his former brilliance.

Plummer and the rest of his staff, as you know, continued to work out the bugs, until the SP became what it is today. Incidentally, it has also become a valuable tool in the treatment of the mentally ill.

III

LAST NIGHT.

Jim Stark punched the familiar SP number and blinked in the bright sunlight streaming through the glass of the booth in front of his house. He had never gotten used to the rapid change of scene that SP trans sometimes produces, and was momentarily stunned.

As he fished for his house key, he became aware of a movement on the lawn behind him. He wheeled about to recognize John Tippington, anchorman of NBC, with his cameraman in tow.

"Oh, no!" He whistled through clenched teeth, "Can't they leave me alone on my last night? Goddamn Scott Armstrong is hiding from them again, so they come to me!"

But, after initial hesitation when he considered slugging the newsman and stomping him into the ground, he reluctantly smiled broadly at the well-known face, and stepped out of the booth onto the lawn.

Tippington got right to the point. "Colonel Stark, I know it's your last night to be with your family, so I'm only going to spend five or ten minutes with you. The American people want to know what you'll be doing on your last night, and they want to hear reactions from your family.

Millions of your countrymen wish they were going along with you in person. They can't of course, but as you know the historic moment will be broadcast from the sendoff ceremony tomorrow, until the far off planet Kadakas VI is declared safe for human colonization."

The camera was running through all this, but Stark doubted that this introduction would be used. He maintained his automatic smile, and replied.

"This is really an historic moment, John, and I'm honored to be chosen to lead it. I only wish everyone out there could share the excitement I'm feeling right now."

Jim started toward the house, but Tippington was not to be put off so easily.

"It would be wonderful, Colonel Stark, if we could share a few moments of your last night on Earth. Would it be presumptuous of us to invite ourselves in for a short chat with the people who mean the most to you; your family?

"You know damned well it is, you pushy bastard," he thought, while he heard himself say, "No Problem. Come right in." and led the way.

He had been flattered and filled with the euphoria of self-importance the first time he'd been interviewed by a major newsman, but the sheen had long-since worn off. The questions they asked had no substance, and they inevitably produced inaccuracies, simply because they cut the meat and exaggerated the flashy. Originally perceived as a way to foster one's views, Stark now knew that to get away from them without giving them something on which to hang a gigantic misconception or even scandal was an accomplishment.

That was his mission tonight. Give the news media enough that they didn't have to invent things, and do not say so much that they could blow an answer way out of proportion.

It took a few minutes (it seemed hours to Stark) of dragging cords through flower beds, chipping paint off walls with cameras and microphones, and rounding up of the family, before they were all settled in the modest living room. Some of the crew was still bustling around when Tippington began his interview.

"Good evening. John Tippington, NBC news.

We are honored to have been invited into the home of Lieutenant Colonel Jim Stark to share the feelings of those closest to a member of the group that will represent humanity by stepping foot on soil not a part of our solar system.

"Colonel Stark, It's really nice of you to invite us into your home on this most historic occasion. Would it be all right if we began with an interview of your family?"

"That sounds fine, John."

"Good, we'll begin with this pretty young lady." He pushed the microphone at Stark's daughter. "What is your name, sweetheart?"

"Sarah." She was twelve years old.

"Sarah! My what a pretty name! What do you think about all the hoopla that's made your dad the most famous man on Earth right now?"

"I think it's really great!" He went through the same ritual with fourteen-year-old Joey and Jim's wife, Laura. It seemed to Stark to go on for an eternity. He even thought Tippington was going to interview Plastic, the family's Irish setter, but he was content to say something inane about how the dog seemed to be so calm.

Tippington finally turned his attention back to the mission. Jim had been through the interview for print and broadcast journalists at least a hundred times before and he felt like he was reciting a script.

Tippington turned serious. "Well, the big day arrives tomorrow. How do you feel?"

Stark forced excitement into his voice and replied, "Great John! Just great!"

The newsman turned to the camera with a knowing look. "Does it look like anything can happen now to delay the trip?"

"No, nothing. It looks like we're a go for touchdown."

"How have your training sessions gone? Any problems there?"

Stark struggled to show delight. "Everything's great! I couldn't ask for a better crew."

"Are there any new developments in the study of Kadakas IV."

"No. Nothing of significance has been discovered for the last two weeks."

Tippington feigned concern and asked, "What about the hot spot they discovered? Does anyone have any better idea as to what it is?"

"No."

"What do *you* think it is?"

"Probably just geothermal activity."

Tippington terminated the interview with a happy look. "Well, Colonel Stark," he said, "I think it's time we left you alone with your family. We'll be with you on your adventure to Kadakas IV, fourth planet in the Alpha Centauri system. Good luck and may God speed."

It took another twenty minutes for them to wrap up their gear and clear the house.

When they were gone, Jim literally ran to the SP to lodge his complaint with the Project Icarus information officer. All of these interviews were supposed to be cleared through the IO and there weren't supposed to be any tonight. After he'd received assurances that he wouldn't be bothered any more, he turned his attention to the family. Whatever the IO did, the family wasn't bothered the rest of the night.

* * * *

Susan Powell stayed at the space center. The fact that her three-room flat was in Atlanta had no bearing on her decision. With the SP she could have been there in seconds. Susan knew she should have been following the commander's advice to get some rest, but she was so excited about the mission that she didn't think she could sleep. It was more important to her to be prepared. She had an intense drive to learn more about biology than anyone else. She'd had few boyfriends while growing up, being rather plain. Between her books and microscopes, she hadn't the time for a social life. The fact that she had been a late bloomer hadn't put distractions in her way. Her senior year she had developed into what Stark had jokingly termed a "great looking broad." There had been some advances then, but those were put off with a look of incredulity which most of the men interpreted as "stuck up." She simply did not understand.

* * * *

Devlin, Caglin and Miller, three members of Eagle II's security force went to the Moon also. Theirs was not to be a lover's retreat. They were looking for action! No sooner had the SP made it cheap and easy to get to the Moon, than had opportunists and vagabonds found a way to make money. Since no country owned the Moon, it followed that there were as yet no laws. The anarchy of the Old West returned. The Moon and some Earth orbiting satellites became centers for some base forms of entertainment. All sorts of weird things were going on. Naturally, they drew customers by the droves.

There were tourists bringing kids for their first low-weight experience, and dirty-old-men (and not-so-dirty-young-men) frequenting orbital cathouses. Here you really could get an "around the world." Little old ladies, who had heard that low weight could do wonders for sagging breasts, came. Everyone found something he could enjoy.

The crowds in the beginning were amazing. Because of the demand, men with few scruples got into the act. With the lack of laws to govern such conduct, and difficulty of apprehension, creativity went to the limit (or to the bottom). The tales of exploitation were numerous and frightening. More than a few hastily constructed domes on the lunar surface had burst, exposing their occupants to a hard vacuum.

One of the more common tales was of unsuspecting rubes being told they could experience low-weight for a ridiculously low fee. Once herded into a compact Moon-dome, they were forced to leave all their money and valuables, or have the air vented. It was a simple matter for those victims to be returned to Earth via public stan booths. Once on Earth, there was no way of knowing where on the Moon's surface they had been located.

There was even one highly publicized case in which the proprietors SPed whole groups of tourists into the open on the Moon's surface, robbed the corpses, and moved to a new location when the bodies piled too high.

It wasn't long, however, before regulation caught up with technology. The honest operators formed a sophisticated vigilance committee. It was realized that the tremendous potential for honest profits might simply evaporate were the fly-by-night operations not stopped. This group was dubbed the External Entertainment Commission (EEC). The commission frequently came under attack as being a kind of organized crime syndicate, which simply bullied petty criminals out of existence. The astronomical "membership" fee was denounced as being a modern protection racket and the strong-arm tactics compared to Nazism, but the EEC was effective in nearly eliminating the abuses.

As the three security team members stepped from the SP, Rob Caglin, the youngest, recognized the half-dozen scantily clad (even for the air-conditioned comfort of the casino) girls for what they were and let out a whoop. As he did so, he started to move directly toward the closest one, forgetting the one-sixth Moon gravity. Three of the girls and his two companions grinned involuntarily, as he did a graceful one-and-one-half flip, landing on his outstretched arms and nose. Mass being the same on the Moon as it is on the Earth, the effect was similar to falling on Earth.

Devlin and Miller each snagged an arm, righting the embarrassed young man. After a quick dusting off, they led him off in the direction of the gaming tables. They were more interested in gambling right now than in the ladies. Besides they both fancied themselves macho enough to attract girls who wouldn't ask for pay.

None of these three, nor Tony James, the fourth member of the security team was a green recruit. Chosen for their stability, they were career soldiers with considerable expertise among them. Staff Sergeant Jack Devlin had been in the army since the end of the war, and the least experienced, Sergeant Doug Miller, was a five-year veteran. They believed in working and playing hard. Tonight was to be no exception.

Miller, who considered himself quite a ladies man, spotted a cute little blond at one of the blackjack tables on the other side of the room and left the other two playing craps. They watched as he moved into position on the empty stool beside her and placed a small stack of chips on a numbered square. He played three hands, winning two until a waitress came by. He ordered a drink for himself and turned to the blond. "What're you drinking, sweet thing?" he asked, in his best Bogart imitation.

"Buzz off soldier!" He wasn't wearing a uniform, and it surprised him that they always seemed to know was in the army.

On his way back to the crap table, he touched the waitress' arm, saying: "Bring it over there."

"Bad breath." he muttered to no one in particular as he shouldered in next to Caglin.

Devlin had a mild run going, but had lost all his winnings in one roll when he'd let it ride. All three continued to play the game half-heartedly while a timid looking man crapped out and passed the dice to a middle aged woman with a huge bosom. As she shook the dice, her motion in the low gravity caused the men to be more interested in her than in the dice. She wore a very low-cut dress and Miller made a side bet with Devlin that she would come out of it. They were all disappointed when Miller lost.

The three lost interest in gambling shortly. They began wandering the room looking for something to do while they finished their drinks. Devlin spotted one of those large vacuum cleaners, apparently left out by some irresponsible custodian. On a lark he dragged it along with him.

"What're you going to do with that thing?" a suspicious Miller hissed. He had been with Devlin before when the two of them had barely managed to stay out of jail. Devlin had a way of attracting attention.

"I'll think of something." He imitated Groucho Marx, using the hose to the vacuum for a cigar.

"Tomorrow is not an ordinary day. Remember what the skipper said." This time it was Caglin who was nervous.

"Ah…ye-as, I remember it well.." Now he was W. C. Fields.

They found an empty row of seats in the back on an area reserved for Keno players. They settled in and Caglin went off for a runner and a waitress to get the free-while-you-play drinks. By the time he was back, Devlin had figured out a use for the vacuum. He reversed the hose so that it would blow air and wedged the end between two seats. The hose was pointed upward and across a highly used aisle. Two coats that happened to have been lying on a chair camouflaged the canister.

Devlin stationed himself near an electrical outlet with the long power cord in his hand. He began to take bets from the other two men.

"You guess the color, I pay double. For none, three to one. White is even."

Bets were eagerly placed and the three men faced the aisle from their vantage point expectantly. Miller couldn't believe his eyes. Their first "client" bouncing toward them in the low Moon gravity was the blond who had given him the brush off. She was wearing one of those loose-silky dresses that were so in style.

"Devlin! The one in the blue dress! You've got to get her! I'll pay twice what I bet." Miller was beside himself.

"I'll try. She's on the other side of the aisle. I don't know if she'll come close enough."

"Come on baby! Over to this side! Come on!"

Just when it seemed as though she would pass by too far away, a cocktail waitress stepped into her path, forcing her to come near the vacuum. Devlin plugged in the cord.

"HOOO HEE!" Miller fairly screamed it. With the aid of the low gravity the loose fitting gown billowed out like a parachute so quickly she had no chance to stop it. The men saw long-creamy legs, pubic bulge covered with brunette hair, and even her breasts before she had a chance to cover herself.

"Nothin'! She wasn't wearin' nothin'!" Caglin was exuberant.

Devlin calmly counted out some money and paid off. The girl was too embarrassed to search for the source of her humiliation and quickly walked off.

Though the vacuum was hidden carefully, other men soon discovered what was going on and eagerly began to place bets with Devlin. Careful not to turn it on too frequently, they continued to play Keno, socking down drink after drink on the house. The game had gone on for more than an hour and a half before the security people got suspicious. The three soldiers decided not to press their luck and abandoned the vacuum.

After only a short stay in the casino bar, buying their own drinks and listening to some obscure crooner, they became bored enough and drunk enough to try their luck again. Devlin led the way and re-established his station by the power cord. They had no sooner settled in and placed their bets, than a likely candidate came down the aisle. She was a big girl, with a kind of blocky figure. At this point in their evolution toward inebriation, looks had ceased to gain much importance. She was okay looking and she was wearing the right kind of a dress.

As soon as he had plugged in the cord, Devlin was instantly aware he'd won all bets. "Oh my God!" He hissed resignedly when he recognized her underwear. She was wearing Jockey shorts!

Things happened quickly then. The next thing any of them knew they were in the casino's holding cell, drunkenly trying to explain to their captors why they should not be held for twenty-four hours. Devlin had passed out, but somehow Miller had managed to call NASA. The duty officer verified their identities, and they were released in time to be present for the sendoff ceremonies.

*   *   *   *

Jake Laird was not interested in sowing any oats.

He was thirty-two, and fancied himself a man whose carousing days were over. His life had been his work, but this night had been planned for over six months. He was treating himself to a night in freefall in the Orbit Star Hilton. The cost was out of sight and the waiting list was full for a year in advance.

They had made an exception in his case. Last wish for the condemned, perhaps? His grand plan was to have two or three drinks in the bar and watch that exhibition basketball game between the Pacers and the Knicks. That should be interesting——someone had thought up the idea to play the game on the Moon with thirty-foot baskets. Then go to his room for the (as advertised) most relaxing sleep of his life.

The first part went according to plan. He was nursing his second scotch and water from a plastic, nippled container, when something happened which he instantly sensed would change his night.

A dream floated in.

Literally.

On some impulse he looked toward the door. There she was standing with the light at her back. Actually she was hovering about a foot off the floor. She wore a billowing white gown that barely concealed the most perfect body he had ever seen. The picture of an angel was complete. She moved gracefully toward him using the grips along the bar to propel herself. Her perfect poise clearly revealed that she was no stranger to weightlessness. Her braless breasts moved in that sensual way he had only heard about, and it was all he could do to force his gaze to her face. He was not disappointed in what he saw. The narrow lips had only a hint of color (he did not like the new fad which had many women using bright shade of lipstick). Her nose was delicate and slightly turned up. The cascade of blond hair floated in waves to her shoulders, and the cool blue eyes revealed a crisp intellect.

His mind was whirring as he mentally tested and discarded many asinine openers. Soon he noticed his neck was hurting and the girl and the bartender were giving him strange looks.

In his embarrassment he discovered that in his preoccupation he had released his handhold. He had drifted six feet from the bar and turned nearly upside down in relationship to them. His first reaction was to try, futilely, to stand up and walk back to his stool. That made his plight look even more awkward, and he tried to cover his embarrassment.

"Help, I can't swim," he said softly. The girl laughed the sound of tinkling bells and deftly hooked her right foot in one of the grips and reached her right hand for his.

He felt her touch clear to his toes as she pulled him to the bar. He couldn't speak and didn't even understand her first question.

"First time in orbit?" she repeated. Her voice was a choir of angels.

He heard his voice say, "No, I'm a NASA pilot."

His sanity returned when he realized how ludicrous the statement seemed. He had trained in a weightless environment little because lander pilots seldom have time to practice anything but their specialty.

Laird saw the interest flare in her immediately after his statement. She seemed to be honestly excited that he was pilot.

"My uncle was a pilot for Project Icarus. Well, not for the mission itself, but for the fuel runs to Jupiter and Saturn until he was killed on Jupiter nine years ago. I have always felt a great fascination for the project. In fact, I even took the tests for the pilot program myself. But my parents had not gotten over the grief of Uncle Jeff's death, and I couldn't see putting them through additional fear."

Jake was not really interested in talking about himself, or anything. His idea of heaven at the moment was to be allowed the pleasure of watching her expression changes, the movement of that exquisite body, the flow of her hair, and listening to her voice that was becoming more appealing with each moment. (He didn't dare hope to touch the smooth skin again.)

He reluctantly told her a little about the basic training of the pilots (the part many outsiders see as silly or the release for some cadre man's sadistic tendencies).

"In the beginning it is very difficult, especially for those who have been used to mother's protection. The independent ones fare the best. We graduates are compelled under oath not to reveal the actual techniques, for fear candidates who are not so sure of themselves, might practice resistance. Of course that would destroy the effectiveness of the program designed to weed out the unstable personalities."

He wanted to blurt out everything to her and physically restrain her from ever having to endure that ordeal.

"That phase of training lasted only for about three weeks, but candidates are subjected to psychological, sexual and physical torture. There is only one limitation. The test cannot result in permanent physical injury——although it often accidentally did. Rumor had it that more than one candidate had been psychologically destroyed."

He stopped talking and basked in the warmth of her reply. "I'm sure I could handle it. I think I am stronger than Uncle Jeff was and he went through it fine. The landing tomorrow," she said, changing the subject, " is fascinating to me. May I ask you a favor?"

He was ready to grant her all his worldly goods if she would only go on talking. She lifted her right arm slightly and her left breast did the captivating jiggle and came to rest with a perfect nipple yearning to come out through the snow white of her dress. He could imagine the pinkish-tan color underneath the clinging cloth. He could manage only a mute yes.

"Would you watch tomorrow's telecast of the landing with me and explain everything that's going on? I don't want to miss any part of it. You being a lander pilot could tell me so much more than the newsmen."

Laird glanced down at her breast, knowing that if it moved, he would be watching with her tomorrow, someone else would be piloting, and in two weeks he would be facing a General Court Martial for desertion. It didn't move and he was disappointed.

"I regret I can't. I will be piloting that craft tomorrow." He resolved right then to clear anything he did in future with her, prior to agreeing to it.

The excitement in her face seemed to double.

"You're the pilot tomorrow? How wonderful! Before you leave, I want to know everything about you! I want to hear everything about the mission! I know I've heard it all from the news reports, but somehow it's not as good as hearing it from someone who will be there. You don't mind, do you? I realize you have to get your sleep, so just tell me when you want to get to your room."

"I'd really enjoy telling you about it." He felt a warm glow of satisfaction, knowing that this girl was going to be there as long as he wanted her. The breast danced again. "I'm too excited to sleep anyway."

After about three hours in the bar, during which his fascination for her seemed to grow, he heard the exciting voice say: "We've got to get you to bed. You're responsible for more tomorrow than anyone has ever been."

He felt his emotions refuse to leave her. It would be more than six months before he'd get a chance to see her again. He knew she was right and that it was so late that unless he got some sleep now he may be next to worthless tomorrow. But he heard his voice say: "I'm fine, and I'm really enjoying this."

She reached for his hand (the breast jiggled for the three-hundred-twenty-first time). A warm glow surged through his veins. He felt himself moving along the handholds to the door like a little child following his mother. As they were caught by the gentle breeze that carried them through the lift tube toward the rooms of the hotel, she asked for his room number.

"422." Jake replied regretfully." But let me take you to yours. What is it?"

"422." She replied playfully. It took a few seconds for the impact of what she'd said to hit him. When it did, he let out a whoop and involuntarily his foot grazed the side of the tube, sending him into crazy loops. By the time she caught and steadied him he was a little dizzy from the motion and the effects of the drinks. They both laughed the rest of the way to the room. As soon as the door closed behind them and he realized it wasn't a dream, his excitement returned.

Seeing his interest, the girl led the way to the sleep net, a six foot diameter, webbed cylinder suspended midway between floor and ceiling, pausing only to remove her shoes. He did the same, zipped closed the entranceway and turned to her. She had already unfastened her dress and was working it down over her shoulder (three-hundred-twenty-two). The left breast was exposed, and the gown slid easily the rest of the way off. She wore nothing else and he was paralyzed as he realized her body was even more perfect than he had imagined. He focused his attention on her left breast again. Her movement enhanced its continued undulations (three-hundred-twenty-three, three-hundred-twenty-four, three-hundred-twenty-five…) until she was in his arms. She curled her body close to him and the excitement grew until the comber broke.

They clung to one another, enjoying a warm feeling meant to last for half a year and half a universe until his return. Just before he dozed, he heard her tinkle-bell voice say:

"My name's Holly Bell. What's yours?"

* * * *

Harvey Canton was a "Luddite". The group modeled itself after the original anti progress Luddites during the Industrial Revolution whose goal was to stop the production of machines. Their philosophy stemmed from the "natural order of God's universe" that also motivated the anti-Darwinists and to a similar extent the extreme anti-abortionists and environmentalists of the twentieth century. Their major premise was God created man "in his own image" in his garden (Earth) and anything unnatural like scattering atoms of God's creations into the cosmos had to be immoral. Although ostensibly adhering to the "thou shalt nots" in everything else, they saw potential destruction and deaths as unfortunate "collateral" damage in God's crusade. Recently they had stepped up the action by blowing up SPs all over the world. There had been thirty-four to date. The body count was 18 with more than two hundred injuries.

Enter Harvey. Harvey wasn't really a Luddite, he just liked to blow things up. At ten, he captured small animals like mice and rats (once a Great Dane) and repeatedly experimented with creative ways to attach firecrackers, bottle rockets and cherry bombs to them. It wasn't sadism, he knew. It just tickled him so to see the delicious explosions and watch as the blood and body parts splattered against walls and even on himself. The entire purpose was to watch those wonderful moments. Staying to watch, however, had produced some tense moments when he had almost been caught.

It was surprising, in fact, that he had not been caught, even to him. Harvey was not stupid and after one particularly close call, he forced himself to abstain from his passion. It lasted three months.

Harvey graduated to people when, in trying to finance his fun, he discovered a wonderful combination——the stanisplummer and the Moon.

Stanisplummers were easy to come by, especially the small ones. The government factories had produced them in much greater quantities than could be distributed and it had decided to give them away for free to anyone who would promise to install them in a remote location. The idea was to quickly increase the transportation grid. There were some rudimentary screening of those who would receive them, but there was no way to detect Harvey's propensity for explosives when he had never been caught.

Harvey was in ecstasy for more than six months before the pressure from the EEC toward other such "entrepreneurs" caused him to look to safer ventures.

Now he was a Luddite on the biggest mission thus far——the stanisplummers of NASA! He had already completed four missions and when the Luddites decided to go for a bigger target, Harvey was a natural choice. He worked alone, he was highly successful and he had not been caught.

He arrived at the *Icarus* building the old-fashioned way. He drove an old car and then walked the last three blocks carrying the tools of his trade in a small knapsack. He took advantage of the fact that even though it was the middle of a Wednesday afternoon, the streets were completely deserted—an unfortunate byproduct of the SP society. People seldom went outside any more.

The most difficult part of his mission was gaining access through a door, but Harvey was nothing if not inventive. His passion for explosives propelled him to expert status. It was trivial for him to plant a small explosive and blow the strongest door lock with no more noise than a sneeze. Inside, easily finding the nearest SP, he quickly rigged his first inconspicuous charge. Dressed in a workman's jumpsuit he attracted little attention. NASA workers were used to seeing men dressed in a similar manner, so he was ignored.

Except for one highly unlikely incident, it was probable he could have routinely set the rest of his charges unnoticed. If that had been the case, and all the SPs that could have dialed to *Columbia* were destroyed the landing on Kadakas IV would have been missed and it would be impossible to have ever landed unless another ship were sent.

Just as Harvey passed a restroom the door swung outward into his side hitting the pistol in his shoulder holster with a metallic thwack. Sue Powell came out of the bathroom behind the door concerned that she might have hurt the man. Before she could apologize, Harvey inexplicably panicked.

Frantically pulling the pistol out of its holster, he grabbed Sue by the arm and dragged her back into the restroom. Sue was immediately stunned into silence, but as the man dragged her, quick understanding of what was happening was revealed.

Harvey threatened, "I have a bomb in the back pack. You make a sound and I'll set it off."

Still unable to speak, Sue's thoughts ranged from that of a panicky little girl to that of the logical scientist she was. She had no choice at the present except to do exactly as Canton said and quickly. He was obviously in turmoil, and though she instinctively knew that was the best time to act, the fear kept her from doing anything. He said nothing for a long moment, he just held her in what seemed like a vise-like grip against the tile wall.

"What do you want?" Sue murmured when she finally had somewhat regained her composure.

Harvey's panic had abated until he was his own blast-loving self again and realized the opportunity that had presented itself to him. *This beautiful girl would be the center of the best explosion he had ever created.*

"You just keep yourself quiet and you won't be hurt at all, lady." he said in a voice that made it plain to her that she did need to be concerned. "I'll just go finish my job and everything will be all right."

With a roll of duct tape from his backpack, he securely bound and gagged Sue and left her in one of the bathroom stalls.

IV

PROJECT ICARUS

One of the first persons to recognize the benefits the SP could hold for aerospace was Colonel Frank Janakowski. As head of astronaut training program he had years of difficulty selling the program to Congress. This was especially true in recent years. The initial excitement of the first exploration of the Moon and nearby planets had become old hat to the public. Unemployment and other social problems had grabbed center ring. Congress was embroiled in bitter debates on how to solve those problems, and advocates of space initiatives were all but ignored. But now they had to listen!

Janakowski had been on vacation in Las Vegas, and two hours before he had been in the middle of the hottest streak he'd ever had at the tables. Fatigue had forced him to his room for a nap. The steady beep-beep of the little travel alarm forced its way into his unconsciousness. His first impulse was to fling the thing into a wall where it smashed into bits. Goddam new fangled contraption!

His disposition toward progress was identical to his grandfather's. He remembered the old gentleman's consistent refusal to even watch a color television, let alone get one for himself. The paradox totally escaped him. Janakowski himself was on the cutting edge of technology. Indeed, the space program that he was so fond of had pioneered the electronics that made possible the clock he'd so casually destroyed. The sound of the impact of the clock woke him enough that he remembered the beckoning casino. He climbed out of bed and clicked the remote switch for the television set.

As he dug for his razor, the face of John Plummer resolved from the random light on the tube. From the first half sentence he heard, Frank Janakowski forgot all thoughts of gambling, or even shaving. His hand was shaking as he reached for the telephone. The wait for the answer on the other end was interminable. He could hardly contain himself when he heard the click and the sleep-slowed voice came through.

"Hello?"

"George, get your fat ass out of the sack, and get a pencil! The biggest thing you can imagine has happened for us!"

"What the hell? Who is this?"

General George Norton was not used to being spoken to like that. Especially not at two-fifteen AM!

"Frank Janakowski, George! Sorry to wake you up, but this is big!" He had addressed his superior by his first name from long habit. They had been classmates at the academy together. Janakowski was slower on the promotion path because of his propensity for saying exactly what was on his mind.

"I should have known it was you, Frank. Do you know what time it is? You're supposed to be on leave. I thought I had two weeks free from you. Leave me alone and let me go back to sleep."

He took the receiver from his ear and placed it back on the cradle, an act he knew to be futile when the urgent ring again filled the bedroom. After it had rung five times Norton's wife, Karen, reached for the phone.

"Leave it alone. Maybe he'll give up."

"That's never worked before. What makes you think he's softened now?"

Knowing the validity of her comment, Norton groaned and stretched out his arm to the instrument that threatened to bore a hole in the table. He allowed it to ring one more time, and reluctantly picked it up.

"Frank why can't you leave me alone? I've had a rough night and a big day tomorrow. You know we're fighting for NASA's life in Congress. Tomorrow is the most important. Call me back in two days and I'll give..."

Why he had wasted his breath with that statement, he didn't know. He almost felt Janakowski's grin coming over the line.

* * * *

It was only 10:32 A.M. Washington time, as the F-22 lowered its nose for the descent into Dulles. How his boss had managed to get the craft to Las Vegas so quickly was a mystery to Janakowski, but it had already been waiting for him by the time he arrived at the airport. He hadn't even had time for a short breakfast.

The PA in the lobby had droned insistently on and on: "Colonel Frank Janakowski...meet your party at gate fifteen...Colonel Frank Janakowski..."

Janakowski could clearly see the dome of the Capitol, where he would be spending the remainder of that day and tomorrow. He was normally a little nervous before he had to present any kind of a briefing, especially before congressmen. They were civilians and not so easy to predict as his military colleagues. If you presented military bearing, and kept your voice crisp and filled with resonance, it didn't matter much what you said. But congressmen actually listened to the words much of the time, and interrupted to ask questions at awkward moments.

This time, Frank mused, *the closer they listen the better.*

He knew there were no holes anywhere in his presentation, even though he'd had less time to prepare than normal. Oh, there were some of the idiot types on the committee, like Jonathon Bellamy, who, despite being from one of the wealthiest families in New York, opposed anything that did not give money away in some program or other to the oppressed, and who was dogmatically opposed to anyone who wore a military uniform. But Janakowski knew there would be more than enough votes on his side today. He was dragged back to the present by the jar of the gear on the runway and saw the flashing lights of the staff car that was to take him to the Capitol. No sooner had the plane stopped on the runway, than he was speeding through the traffic of Washington, D.C., without any regard for the fascination that usually held him spellbound while on the streets of this city.

Chairman Daniel J. Brosterman had already gaveled the House committee on Science and Astronautics to order, when he arrived. The wizened Republican had a great shock of snow-white hair that threatened to blind the careless soul who allowed his gaze to rest on it too long. He was speaking in his clipped, precise accent, which reminded Janakowski of FDR. Frank worked his way up the aisle where General Norton had left a chair vacant. He stumbled as he was trying to sit down, almost knocking the chair over. Any other time it would have embarrassed him but today he ignored the titters and amused looks and leaned toward Norton.

"Have you said anything yet, sir?" Today he felt he should be formal, as if familiarity with his boss could erase some of the magic from his presentation.

"Hearing's just convened." the general hissed back. "Brosterman is reminding everyone what a great fount of wisdom he is."

The committee chairman chose that moment to address Norton, and Janakowski thought he caught a trace of a blush under the stern features of his boss.

"General Norton, are you ready to continue your testimony?"

The general paused for a moment, pretended to gather his notes, and slowly and deliberately rose to his feet. He had always prided himself on a flair for the dramatic. Clearing his throat, he tried to gain eye contact with all twenty-one members of the committee at once, before he began to speak.

"I am, Mr. Chairman. Today, however, a development of great moment has caused me to abandon my arguments of previous days entirely."

There was a commotion in the gallery and among the press, which betrayed their sudden interest, and Norton paused to let it subside. Frank also noticed that most of the committee members had suddenly become more alert.

"Are you telling us, General, that all our work from the previous two days is worthless?" The chairman looked incredulous. He had been about to endorse NASA's arguments and recommend the agency be given all it had asked for.

"That is correct, sir but hear me out." He paused again and Frank thought he would never get to the point, but this time no voice or random noise rose to fill the vacant air, and Norton spoke again. "Today, gentlemen, you are about to hear the most adventurous plan ever devised by man. A plan that will provide the absolute solution for every problem humans have ever encountered in the history of the world. Poverty, pollution, waste disposal, unemployment, famine, over-population, crime and even war!

"*All* will disappear as if they never existed!"

This time the commotion in the gallery was greater, and some of the reporters began to edge toward the phones in the hallway. Even Frank Janakowski, who already knew what he was going to say, was surprised. He hadn't expected this kind of a buildup, and he wasn't sure it was the answer to all those scourges. Especially crime.

The noise level was still so high that Brosterman had to wield his gavel and a stern look before Norton could continue.

"That pronouncement made me as skeptical as you gentlemen look right now, but I assure you, it is true. I have had Colonel Frank Janakowski flown here from the west this morning on a specially diverted aircraft to explain the project in detail to you." Even though the plan was simple to understand, it was so fantastic that the general didn't trust himself to relate it. Norton was afraid that his attempt to bungle his way through it would somehow burst the bubble, and it would vanish before their eyes. He was visibly relieved when he saw Janakowski rise to his feet.

Every eye in the hearing room was riveted to Janakowski, and he knew he should keep them dangling on a string, but he was too eager, and the words seemed to tumble out before he was even standing erect.

"I am sure you gentlemen are aware of the announcement made by Professor Plummer last night about the development of his new matter transmission machine," he began. "Well, that exciting new discovery is the heart of the project we have dubbed Icarus...

What we propose, Gentlemen, is interstellar travel and colonization of habitable planets."

The uproar in the gallery began again, but Janakowski plunged right on, and it quickly hushed. "Combining this new discovery with the technology we have at NASA right now, we can have a colony on a new planet within ten years. This will be a colony with none of the hardships or loneliness of our historical models, because transportation to and from it will be cheap and instantaneous. Plummer's new gadget uses instantaneous conductive transmitters. We already know that there is no time lag between us and the deep space probe *Shepherd* almost a quarter of the way to Alpha Centauri with the ICT."

"Think of it gentlemen! Your own imagination can reveal the extraordinary benefits this capability can bring! Think of the farmland waiting to be plowed! The industry that can be transplanted! The living space! The resources! With the imagination and resourcefulness of today's leaders, we can eliminate most of the world's problems."

"But that part will be your job, Gentlemen. Ours will be to make it possible. Here is how it will work. The first step is to place in orbit a stanisplummer, or actually eighteen initially, with our space shuttles. In orbit we construct the actual interstellar vessels, which will have a main component, headed by a larger landing module or pod. Both sections will contain their own stanisplummers, which will be utilized to transport personnel, materials, equipment, and even fuel to the ships. The last is the most important. One of our continuing problems had been the inability to carry enough fuel."

"Now we don't have to carry any at all, or only a small amount in reserve. The discoveries of Doctor Plummer have solved most of our problems. Crew fatigue——everyone works a six to eight hour shift, and then simply goes home. Sleeping quarters on the craft are unnecessary, as are food storage, and sanitary concerns. If an astronaut feels one of the natural urges, he simply goes to the cafeteria or lavatory in Houston. Even radiation, the once insurmountable objection to close to light-speed flight is removed. This radiation, which is generated by the collision with intra-spatial particles, can be shielded partially, but during those high speeds, the craft remains unmanned except when crucial maneuvers are necessary, and then it is manned for short periods of time only——our conventional shielding can protect the astronaut enough that he will receive only a minimal dosage. Of course the craft will have to be decontaminated before he gets there; a simple matter with stanisplummers."

"Once the construction in orbit is completed, we simply point the ship in the desired direction and accelerate to about .7c——seventy percent of the speed of light, which, with current technology, will take slightly over a year. At that speed we coast——unless someone can prove Dr. Einstein wrong and allows us to go faster——until we want to slow down again. At that point we detach the lander and send the main ship on its merry way never to slow down again, but to drop off more landers each time it gets close to a friendly star. The landing module takes a downhill trip with the brakes on all the way and lands a crew on a new colony."

Frank was beginning to enjoy himself immensely, as he realized he had them eating out of his hand. He rubbed his palms together to relieve the itch that he always got when he was excited. His ex-wife had been the only one who knew about that, and she probably thought it was from being greedy. Lord knows, he gave her more than she deserved. He allowed himself the pause he had passed up in the beginning, before he continued. The room was deathly quiet.

"Well, Gentlemen, I have given you an extremely cursory look at Project Icarus. May I have your questions?"

At least half of the committee members tried to gain recognition from the chairman at once, and the gallery exploded with newsmen charging out the doors. It took at least ten minutes before Brosterman with his animated gavel could regain order. At one point when the pandemonium was greatest, he shrugged expansively and put the gavel down, leaning back in his chair until it subsided. When silence returned the gravelly voice began.

"How do you know...Colonel...uh...Sorry, what was your name again?"

"Frank Janakowski, sir."

"Uh, yes, Colonel Janakowski. How do you know that this gadget even works, or even if it does, whether it transmits instantaneously? It seems to me that one could be very uncomfortable if the transmission were say only twice or three times the speed of light. I would not like to take a trip of four and one half light years, which I believe is the distance to our nearest star, Alpha Centauri, dissolved. The trip would take more than a year."

Laughter filled the hall, and the stately congressman had to bring his gavel into play once again. After a moment Janakowski replied.

"Professor Plummer made his discovery by utilizing the best research money and facilities the U.S. and the Russian Union could provide. He was, as you know, the inventor of the ICT. This device has been thoroughly tested and documented——It works, and because it does, the transmission has to be instantaneous. If it were as slow as you suggest, reconstitution could never be made. Part of the energy would be consumed, and the rest would be hopelessly jumbled. In addition, you know about the deep space probe *Shepherd*? Right now it is more than a light year away from us carrying an ICT. Coordinators have not been able to detect even a nanosecond delay in transmission to it."

Although Brosterman clearly would have liked to ignore him, he caught Jonathon Bellamy's frenetic motions far to his left. With a shrug he obviously had decided he might as well give him his say now. Besides, Brosterman could think of nothing else to say. He was overwhelmed. This seemed to be the solution to everything he'd ever stood for. But it seemed so easy...Bellamy would tie up the floor forever, but the chairman did not want to talk now or even listen. He wanted to think.

"Congressman Bellamy," he said tiredly.

Bellamy turned to the colonel. "Colonel Janakowski?" He almost spat the title out. "It seems to me, that you're just seizing upon this thing to pour more millions of dollars down the bottomless military pit. You and your henchmen have already soaked up too much of the World's most precious resources. Many times before, you people have come to this committee, telling very convincing stories. This country will go to the Russians, or they have got a new weapon which will destroy us if we don't come up with one just like it——soon.' All of these things cost more money than the one before. Bellamy made speeches, rather than asking simple questions, and he was good at laying on the hearts and flowers. "For decades you have managed to cloud the issues, and convince the majority of this committee that you are right. And we have dumped more money into the pit."

"What has been the result of this military gluttony? What will become of this Project Icarus? Probably the same as its namesake: Fly too close to the Sun and melt.

In the past, that is what has happened. The result is just the opposite of what you promise. In the past it has only ended in more war and killing. In the past it has ignored poverty and hunger! In the past it has been American boys spilling their blood on foreign battlefields!"

"And for what?"

"*More of the same!*"

"Colonel Janakowski, if we of this body had more sense fifty or a hundred years ago…If we had allowed ourselves to follow our hearts instead of our so-called rationality, which was actually fear, those problems mentioned by General Norton earlier, would not be problems! Or, at least we'd be a lot closer to their solutions."

"If, instead of dumping our hard-earned gold into your military, which has brought only death and destruction, we had acted with compassion, and directed those funds toward fighting POLLUTION…POVERTY…RACISM…HUNGER…and INJUSTICE, I say they would be licked."

The last phrase was a whisper. Bellamy paused and ran his tongue over his lips before continuing.

"Colonel Janakowski, I'm opposed to your venture. Since the end of the Iranian war, some of us have gotten a little sense. We've begun many programs to solve those problems. I think we have a better chance at that now than we ever had before. Your program is going to take a lot of money. Money that we cannot afford to divert at this time."

Janakowski had never been much of a speaker, and while Bellamy railed on he began to sweat. One point the congressman had made rang true. Congress was not willing to fund military programs now. The wind-down period after wars had always been times of disarmament, and this was no exception. This was especially true since the Russians seemed so willing to work together with the U. S.

He had to force his hand away from his itchy left palm as he reached for the microphone.

"Congressman Bellamy, I don't pretend to be a historian of congressional spending, nor of social reform programs. I am simply offering you a program that will work."

He wanted to tell Bellamy that military spending generally coincided with an increase in social outlay. When there were cutbacks, there were usually cuts in both areas. The big depression in the nineteen-thirties was an excellent example of that. In fact, its final solution had been the increase of military spending necessary to subsidize the Lend-Lease program. But it wouldn't do at this point, he knew, to get the rest of the committee against him for attacking one of their colleagues, even one as out-to-lunch as Bellamy.

The verbal congressman was visibly disappointed with Janakowski's answer. He would have liked to have begun a fiery exchange, at which, he thought, he was unmatched. He didn't give up yet. He addressed Janakowski again.

"If this SP does what you and others say it does, then why do we need NASA at all? Why not just set up one of those things and aim it at the nearest star? That way we could instantly put explorers on another planet."

That answer was easy for Frank.

"The SP works much like a telephone or radio. There must be a transmitter *and* a receiver. Even if it didn't require a receiver, the distances covered are so great that there are no instruments, mathematics, or computers precise enough to calculate the stopping point. Vectors figured to say, fifty decimal places, could only be accurate within a few thousand miles or so. Quite a drop for a human landing party! Besides, with our most sophisticated instruments, we still have not been able to find many planets around stars. We're pretty sure they are there, because we've seen some stars wobble like Barnard's star. That could indicate a large gravitational field circling them. We just haven't gotten close enough to see them all yet, let alone determine which are habitable for humans."

Members of the committee stirred and some of them were nodding their heads knowingly, as if they had already figured all that out for themselves. Janakowski knew that he'd neutralized Bellamy at that moment. Nevertheless, the argumentative congressman continued to ask questions for more than an hour, unwilling to admit defeat.

The other committee members were, in turn, afforded opportunity to question Janakowski and General Norton. None returned to the attacking posture of Bellamy, they were, for the most part, intrigued and anxious to gain information. The Democratic congressman from Florida (Janakowski couldn't read his nameplate from across the room) asked one of the more valid questions.

"What if the planet turns out to be uninhabitable, or even dangerous? Would the equipment and space ships be a total loss?"

Janakowski reached eagerly for the microphone to respond.

"The landing craft would probably have to be abandoned if the new environment proved to be dangerous, but remember there is an SP aboard. If there were no toxic danger to Earth that craft could be dismantled and transported back. Or better yet, we could build a larger SP on the planet and transport it back whole. Most likely, however, we would not bring it back to here even if the mission were not successful. We would probably be better served to send it to its original ship or any of the other ships. Remember those crafts are continuing on to other systems and will eventually need landing vehicles. This would eliminate the need to construct new ones. Those ships will be on eternal missions. If an engine fails, transport up a new one. If the ship absorbs too much radiation to be safe, replace it piece-by-piece. If someone invents a new-more powerful engine, replace the old one on board. The only really vital piece of equipment is the SP. We would always make certain there was a backup or two on board."

"Colonel Janakowski?" The inquiry came from Lawrence Macklin, the lanky Democrat from Kentucky. Janakowski mused: put a stovepipe hat on him and there stands Abe Lincoln.

"Congressman Macklin?"

"I seem to remember from my school days, or from some'ere else, that gittin' a rocketship to go that fast, requires a huge load of fuel." He paused but not long enough for Janakowski to break in. He took out his handkerchief and mopped his brow as he spoke. "It seems to me, it was some'in' tremendous——on the order of twice the fuel that's available on Earth, and that's just gettin' up to speed, not to mention slowin' it down ag'in. You say you're goin' to do that with eighteen ships. How you gonna do that?"

While he listened to Macklin's question, Janakowski couldn't help a sidelong glance at General Norton's face. His imagination made him almost hear the thoughts written on the general's face. *That Goddam Frank Janakowski's done it to me again, and I fell for it hook, line and sinker.* It took a long time for the relief to show even when it was clear Janakowski had the answer.

"Hydrogen." Said Janakowski softly. "Hydrogen from Jupiter and Saturn. We have plenty of fuel to place a SP into the almost pure hydrogen atmospheres of those planets. We can transfer fuel directly to the spacecraft by SP. With them and other gas giants we encounter in the stars we truly have an unlimited fuel supply."

V

JOVIAN NIGHTMARE

Jeff Graham shook the cobwebs from the back of his brain as sleep slowly seeped away and he finally came fully awake. It was unusual for him to be anything but completely alert, but now was an unusual moment. He had slept for only three hours and his last waking period had been for more than thirty-six. The lack of sleep had not been from necessity, but from choice. Graham would descend into Jupiter's lethal atmosphere within the next four hours.

Tall and confident, Graham exuded that indefinable quality that labeled him successful at any task. Few men possess only slight touches of that quality, but he demonstrated it from the top of his sandy head to the toes of his well-polished flight boots. Flight boots were not normally worn aboard spacecraft, but Graham had grown so accustomed to them, that he refused to be without them. He had worn the same boots throughout the Iranian war, in which he had been an ace pilot, and during his two-year tour with the Air Force's Thunderbirds precision flying team. Incredible reflexes and split-second judgment, his flight experience and uncanny ability to remain alert under G forces which would cause ordinary men to black out had qualified him for the impending mission. He would need it all.

Project Icarus was ultimately as dependent upon Jeff Graham and others like him, as it was on Stanislav and Plummer. Making eighteen spacecraft fly at incredible speeds between stars requires a great deal of fuel. More than Earth could possibly produce would be required for only one. But on the planet Jupiter swirled huge amounts of almost pure hydrogen——the fuel of the stars themselves——there for the taking.

Getting the fuel sounds easy, but it would have to surmount formidable obstacles. Although it would seem simple to descend to the liquid surface of the behemoth planet where the fuel could be taken, there remained three problems: the temperature, the pressure and the weather. At thirty one hundred degrees Fahrenheit, and a pressure four and a half times that on Earth, the more than three hundred mile per hour wind created an eternal hurricane which no earthly vehicle could survive——save one. *Faust*, aptly named, for it would descend into a Hell, was extremely well insulated, entirely for the comfort of its human baggage, but not well enough to keep out the extreme heat for more than the ten or so minutes necessary to ensure the stabilization of the craft in the hydrogen soup. Graham would have considerable computer aid, but at the end he would be essentially a barnstormer, flying literally by the seat of his pants. He alone could maneuver the craft to lightly set down on the raging sea.

The door slid softly into the wall and Jeff stepped out of the SP booth into the long hallway, which led to the nerve center of project *Icarus*. As he walked that direction he acknowledged the many back slaps and calls of "good luck" from the technicians he passed with a characteristic grin and slight wave of his hand. Once in the big room, however his features fell into a mask of seriousness. He was ready to go, and any distraction annoyed him. His initial survey of the room told him that General Janakowski had already arrived, and Graham scarcely paused before he moved directly to where the general was having an animated conversation with a rather tall man.

"Good morning, sir. Nothing wrong I hope?"

"Hello, Graham. Nothing serious. Hadley here is just discussing some of the finer details of the *Faust*. Seems like he turned up something unusual on yesterday's tests. Tell him about it, Hadley."

Hadley was one of the scientists who'd helped develop and conduct wind tunnel tests of the Jupiter lander. A problem there could cause considerable delay, so Graham watched and listened closely to the man.

"Right on top, let me tell you it is not really anything to be much concerned about, and there's probably no problem at all; just data errors. The model we used was slightly different than usual, because we want to check all angles. Anyway, at the equivalent speed of about three hundred miles per hour, the model began to vibrate intensely, and it took more time than usual to bring it under control. We think we know what the problem was and are now modifying the model accordingly. We should be able to test again in about ten minutes."

"You want to watch?"

Neither Jeff nor Janakowski was much concerned about the problem. After years with NASA they had become used to over-cautious techs, but Jeff still had some time to kill, so he accepted Hadley's invitation. The twenty-foot long, one-tenth scale model in the tunnel looked exactly like the irreverent nickname it had been given——the pregnant stick. Long and streamlined the *Faust* was built to provide cushioning from the heavy turbulence on Jupiter. The "sticks" fore and aft of the bubble that was the actual craft, employed computer controlled countermotion engines. Before a strong gust hit the craft, they would actually sense it and swing, providing counter motion to absorb the brunt of the shock. They were absolutely vital to preventing the pilot from being smashed all over the side of the cabin.

He had watched the test before, but had never ceased to marvel at some of the gyrations the stick would go through. Sometimes they would be almost perpendicular to their original plane. The turbulence in the tunnel was awesome and Jeff thought they must have been exaggerating the relative wind, because even with the sophisticated technology, the cabin whipped violently. Intellectually he knew he would be safe, but a primitive prickly feeling at the nape of his neck was aroused while he watched. He was glad when the sergeant called him out of the room.

"Time to go, sir."

Eager and reluctant at the same time, Graham followed the man, who had worked with Graham before and knew enough to be silent at this moment. All that could be heard in the walk to the control room was the sound of flight boots on concrete. Had it not been for that, Graham was sure the sound of his rapidly beating heart would have been audible. They arrived at the main stanisplummer, and without a pause the astronaut stepped inside and punched the button that would seal the door and send him into adventure. He forced the butterflies from his stomach by emitting a high screech from between tightly clenched lips. Just then he felt the queasiness that accompanied stanning, and the door slid back into the wall.

He moved out of the cubicle, as usual feeling no discomfort in a null gravity environment. The two men already in the ship were the captain and first officer. They had worked aboard the Jupiter orbiter for more than six months, helping to construct the actual *Faust*. Through the transparent port between the two men Graham could see the spindly Jovian lander posed against the background of brilliant, fiery red; the color of Jupiter.

"Hi, Greg." He addressed the greeting to the elder of the pair.

Although no more than thirty-five, Commander Gregory Nielsen had prematurely grayed, and with his command presence, he looked much more mature. He acknowledged the greeting with a mere lifting of an eyebrow, the friendliest gesture Jeff had ever seen him bestow.

"Graham, we're a little behind schedule. Right now we're at seventy-eight minutes and counting to launch. I know you've been through briefing after briefing for the last month, but I'm a firm believer in Murphy's Law, and we've got to be sure nothing is left to chance. I originally set aside fifteen minutes for the final brief. This will be a dialogue, if you wish. You, of course, have the most on the line, but Jack and I have ultimate responsibility for the success of this portion of the mission. If something does go wrong, you will not be here to explain it, but we *will*. I know that sound callous, but I want to re-emphasize the risks of the mission."

"Let's start with Jack reading the checklist. Feel free to interrupt with questions or comments at any time. This is being recorded for further reference."

Jack Peterson, the first officer, was a young and brilliant engineer who preferred being a military man to the more lucrative and boring private industry. He spoke with a slight lisp.

"Seal and check heat resistant suit…to also be checked twice at all possible leak points, prior to entry into the atmosphere."

The commander broke in. "You know the problems they've had with those suits leaking. Not critical before, and the designers have made some modifications which should help, but cabin temperatures will reach almost a thousand degrees at the end, so *triple* check those seals."

Jeff was aware from his military training that the smallest detail neglected could cause failure of a mission. He had been through all this at least six times, but he forced himself to be alert.

Peterson went on to the next item. "Pilot boards the lander. Instrument and communications check…Seal hatches to both mother craft and lander…pressure check the seals…Third instrument and communications check…"

The commander again interrupted him. "Jack. I think you can skip the instrument and commo checks from here on in the interest of time. We're all aware that they must be performed on a regular basis. Any failure there is grounds for immediate abort."

"Yes sir…Disengagement of lander from mother ship, and visual check to ensure all explosive bolts have severed…Comm…Uh…separation of the two craft…After a separation of one kilometer, firing of the retro-rockets to take the lander out of orbit."

"The timing of the retro fire is automatic, but be sure to monitor it yourself. A few seconds one way or the other won't make much difference, but we don't want you entering the atmosphere too fast and burning away a lot of the insulation prematurely."

Graham grunted acknowledgement, and Peterson again turned to the list.

"Entry into the outer reaches of Jupiter's atmosphere, approximately eighty-seven kilometers above the surface at ten point two-one minutes after retro-fire…Twenty-eight hundredths of a minute later you reach the cloud tops, something over seventy kilometers high…"

Nielsen interrupted again. "Here's where the communications checks become extremely critical, Jeff. The planet's magnetosphere produces so much radiation that's the only way we can track you under the clouds. If we get a negative, we go back to square one and try again in about six months."

This was one point that Graham was not ready to concede. He was determined to go through with the entire mission today, regardless, but he merely nodded his head and Peterson went on.

"At an elevation of about thirty-five kilometers, entry speed will have been reduced by friction to about two hundred kilometers per hour, where it will remain until the landing rockets are fired. At this time the viewing ports may be opened because friction heat will be gone, and the temperature will drop to about zero. You probably won't be able to see much, even with lights. Atmospheric pressure will be fairly high at this point, so you will begin to feel some turbulence. Do not leave the viewing ports open for more than forty-five seconds. They are not as impervious to radiation as the hull. "Seven minutes later comes the real test. If it turns out instruments cannot be monitored from here, and that will probably be the case, you will have to open the viewing ports and land the craft manually. Any impact of greater than seven or eight KPH will probably destroy the main stanisplummer, and the mission. Timing is critical. From the time the view ports are open, you have only eight and a half minutes to land and return here, or be roasted. We can deploy the floats from here."

Graham nodded his head, and Nielsen opened his mouth to speak. "Jeff, are there any questions?"

When the negative was indicated he continued. "Look over the list again, and be sure there is nothing left to chance. I cannot over emphasize the need for thoroughness. We can always replace the *Faust*, but not you."

"There's nothing, Commander. At this point it's too late to second-guess the experts. I'm ready, let's get on with it."

There was no live television coverage of the event for two reasons. There was a high possibility of failure, and no one wanted the public to witness that. A series of problems had already put the project behind schedule and dampened public opinion somewhat, and the liberals were becoming more and more vocal in their demands to solve poverty and hunger with the funds that, from their point of view, were being swallowed up in the bottom-less gullet of *Project Icarus*. The other reason was to prevent the distraction of the participants.

Now the time was here, Jeff felt the butterflies returning. He zipped himself into the protective sheath of the suit, and before the nervousness could magnify he pushed open the hatch between the two craft. Sealing it behind him, he floated into the cocoon of the lander and began tightening the restraining straps. The thickly padded head and body shells, composed of high impact Kevlar were next, making Jeff feel as if he were in an extremely tight body cast. He heard the hiss that indicated the empty spaces in the cabin were being filled with the hardening foam, which would provide further protection, not only from the jolting but also as insulation from the heat and radiation. Only a small bubble around his hands and face, and the heads up display and control panel, so he could see and manipulate the instruments would remain empty. He was actually part of the spacecraft now. On the completion of his mission he would be stanned back to Houston where a crew was standing by to remove him from the foam and suit, ready to treat him for heat, radiation, or broken body.

"Faust, this is Mother. How do you hear me?"

The question reminded him that he had already forgotten the first communication check. The first one was not critical, but it served to remind him of how easy it would be to make a mistake. That realization brought the butterflies back in force, but he successfully fought them down.

"Roger, Mother. You're loud and clear. Stand by. I'll give you visual…"

"Houston, this is Faust. How do you hear?"

"This is Houston. We've got you loud and clear", came the voice that sounded closer to Graham than Mother. He supposed that was due to more space for better equipment. "We've got clear audio and visual. You're a go for separation. Good luck."

"Roger, Houston. I'm strapped in, sealed and checked here. Mother, anytime you're ready, kick me loose."

"Roger, Faust. Audio and visual are clear...Stand by for separation in ten seconds.. mark...nine...eight...seven...six...five...four...three..."

Graham braced himself for the expected jolt, even though he knew he was so bound in, the minor bump of the explosive bolts would be nothing compared to what he'd feel in the next half hour.

"Two...one...separation...Well you're on your own, Jeff, go get 'em."

The bolts did their job well. He could see that he had already drifted more than ten meters from the mother ship.

"Clean separation, Mother. I'm gonna put some distance between us." His left little finger was on the button that would give impetus to the rocket that would move Faust from the bigger ship. He pressed hard, feeling the whiteness of his knuckles, and immediately felt the slight acceleration. His eyes found the digital readout that would show him his distance from Mother. When the number reached one thousand he wiggled his left hand ring finger. Simultaneously he felt the acceleration of the retro-rockets and a pang that had him almost wishing he could call it off.

"Mother, this is Faust. Here I go." His eyes found the view screen that revealed the planet, huge and menacing. At first it didn't seem to be getting any larger, and he harbored a brief feeling of relief that the rocket hadn't worked and he wouldn't have to go after all. But presently the screen showed he was getting closer, and after two or three minutes he could not see the horizon without adjusting the camera.

The awesome sight had a hypnotic effect on him. He could no more force his eyes from the spectacle, than he could will his heart to stop beating. It was a scene out of a movie about Hell. The dominant color was red, but the diagonal upper-right to lower-left of his view screen bands of color bled into each other like raspberry ripple ice cream with brown, green and blue all blended together. But the dominant feature where his eyes seemed to automatically settle was the huge red spot in the lower-left of his screen. With the tremendous turbulence he expected in another, calmer area where he would land, he could not imagine what it would be like in the spot.

He remained mesmerized by the spectacle until the slight buffeting and movement of the compensating shafts on the craft signaled his arrival into the atmosphere. Fifteen seconds later he braced himself involuntarily, expecting an impact as the clouds rushed to it and then swallowed him in the misty void. All he could see then was the projections of his own craft.

"Houston, this is Faust. I just went under and the road is getting a little bumpy."

"Roger, Faust. We've still got a line on you. We'll let you know when we can't see you anymore."

There was not much either could say or do at this point. It was a matter of wait and see. He could see nothing now and assumed it was the heat of entry that would probably obscure transmission from Houston for a while anyway. He began to get used to the constant bouncing and was almost enjoying the ride now that the initial vertigo had dissipated.

Less than three minutes after disappearing under the clouds he hit the first of many big "air" pockets. He could see again, a little, just in time to watch a compensator arm fly wildly to his right. He felt as if he'd been hit simultaneously with about two hundred paddles. He hadn't expected it so soon and was preoccupied with trying to pierce the gelatinous mass outside, so it surprised him all the more. The second and third jolts came in quick succession, feeling if anything, worse than the first. The experts were wrong. It was going to be a wilder ride than they thought.

"Houston, this is Faust. The real bumps have already begun, and they are tough…"

He stopped to ride out another.

"…but I should be okay."

The huge jolts came closer together now, and with them came the noise. The constant rush of the wind was overwhelming. It rose to the pitch of a thousand banshees, even through the heavy insulation of the craft. When the strongest gusts hit, perhaps because of a warping of the hull and reverberation along the shafts, it was like being inside a huge steel ball, with which giants with sledgehammers for racquets were playing tennis. As it got worse, it felt to Graham like someone had gotten inside his brain with a jackhammer. At the same time the vibration grew in leaps and bounds. Communications with mission control were almost totally gone. The only way they could make him understand was by repeating each word three times, and the technicians had great difficulty sorting his voice from the background, even with sophisticated filters and equipment. The vibration had either destroyed the cameras or was so great as to prevent focus, so there was no video. Contact was lost entirely then, but it wouldn't have mattered anyway. Express train noise seemed to permeate every tissue of Graham's body, and it began to drive sanity out.

He struggled to cover his ears with his hands, knowing full well they were fixed in position, and couldn't be moved. The index finger of his right hand longed to apply the pressure on the button it was poised over. That would activate the stanisplummer and remove him from this raging Hell. Had he been fully rational, that is almost certainly what he would have done, but the only thought that would surface from his tortured mind was:

"noise…noise…My God!…Got to!…Cover my ears!…"

Then blackness drew a merciful blanket over him as he fell away into unconsciousness. The frantic calls from Houston and Mother could not have been heard over the din, even had Graham been conscious to hear.

    *   *   *   *

The voice of "Houston" at that moment, General Frank Janakowski himself quavered in its quest to pierce that awful clatter which poured from speakers even with the volume turned way down, but he already knew it was futile.

To him this was a disaster which would not only rob him of a man he'd come to consider almost as a son, but also threatened to rob him of *Project Icarus*. He knew *Icarus* was dead at that moment. This was worse than the *Columbia* disaster, because they had realized the risk and gone way beyond the minimum to negate it. A Congress which was plainly promised complete success would simply not provide funds for another mission. Oh, maybe ten years from now, but by then it would be too late for him and thousands of people.

The silence in the room could have been cut with a knife, someone had turned off the sound of Jupiter completely or the vibration had destroyed the equipment on *Faust*. The technicians seemed too tired to move, and many simply lay their heads down on consoles, and slumped in chairs. The minutes seemed to drag interminably.

"Houston, this is Mother," The sound echoed hollowly in the room, "I've got a ready light on the stanisplummer!"

*   *   *   *

Jeff felt the violent shaking, and his first thought was that somehow he had gone back in time, and his mother was shaking the bed to wake him. "Okay Mom, I'm…" He stopped, puzzled. The insistent shaking, shaking was still there, but something was wrong.

"I CAN'T HEAR MYSELF!"

The noise had deafened him completely, and the absence of noise had allowed him to revive. It all came back to him in a rush, and his eyes found the digital readout. *Less than three minutes to impact*! His first reaction was to try to press the SP button with his index finger and escape, but he fought off the panic with the realization he still had time to land the craft. The wild fluctuations of the digits, which were the altimeter, told him he would have to land visually, if he could see anything. The readout below the altimeter told him the outside temperature was twenty-six-hundred degrees. At least that was working.

He watched the timer digits change, at nine point five minutes elapsed time he would open the view port and try to find a horizon. If he couldn't find one, the procedure was simple——punch the lander rockets with his right hand middle finger and hope the rocket got down in time for him to deploy the float before he turned into a lump of charcoal. He was already uncomfortable inside his suit, but he knew it would become much hotter.

Now! He jabbed his finger at the button and the view ports rolled back, revealing the forward stabilizer whipping so violently it reminded Jeff of the ribbon he'd tied to the mast of his bicycle when he was a kid. The sight enhanced the shaking of the craft, and Graham realized that it was only with great difficulty that he was able to read the digits on the display. Outside the craft he could see nothing but the indistinct compensator arms, but the mere fact that he could see them reassured him that he would be able to see the surface within a couple hundred meters or so. If he could make an educated guess as to when to hit the rockets, he should be able to land in time. He took a chance and gave slight pressure to the landing rockets, feeling his descent slow slightly, and strained to see through the mist.

His eyes flashed back and forth from the timer to the swirling clouds outside. Ten minutes thirty seconds…forty…At ten fifty he gave the rocket full thrust and watched the vertical speed indicator drop. 170…160…150…140…130…

He was already past the expected landing time and strained his eyes for a glimpse of the ocean below.

Nothing!…100…90…80…70…He was now at a speed that he could stop the craft within one hundred fifty meters, so he eased the pressure on the button and tried to stabilize at sixty kilometers per hour but the violent wrenching of the craft prevented him from maintaining an even pressure, and the speed varied between one hundred and thirty. He hoped he wasn't going a hundred when the surface appeared. The heat inside his suit was oppressive now like the inside of a sauna. He glanced at the temperature display. Outside thirty-one hundred, as expected, but inside it was already five hundred twenty-five that meant he had to get out soon. The readout next to the temperature indicated it had been over seven minutes since he had opened the ports.

Seven point twelve…seven point twenty. His mind began to tick of the elapsed time. Seven point twenty-eight.

"WHERE IS THE SURFACE?"

"There? Yes! I see it!" His fingers longed to give full thrust.

"No! Make sure!" There was no longer any doubt, and he pressed both his middle and index fingers and felt himself sink into the cushioning of the seat. He could see it clearer now, closer than he had expected. Not more than fifty meters below was the wildest raging storm that any human had ever witnessed. Waves fragmented and climbed seemingly almost to the height of the craft itself. The sight was awe inspiring to Graham, and for an instant he sat transfixed. He had to maneuver the craft to set down on the crest of one of the massive swells. Fifty meters high, if he were to miss and drop between two, a wave, with its hundred kilometer per hour speed would probably crush the craft like an egg. At first he didn't think he'd be able to bring the craft under control in time, and in fact the speed of descent had carried him below the crest of an oncoming swell. Only by maintaining full thrust was he able to rise above, just before it went flashing underneath. Now it remained to provide lateral thrust, to match the speed of the waves, land, unfold the huge stanisplummer which would accept the massive pumps, and press the button which would allow him to escape this raging Hell. Compared with what he'd already been through, Jeff thought the actual landing simple, but when he touched the liquid hydrogen he almost wished for the relative calm of the atmosphere. Every seam of the craft seemed ready to burst as he maneuvered it so the raft could be deployed in its lee. He was inside an enormous cement mixer running crazily at five hundred times normal speed. He could literally feel his brains bouncing around in his skull. What kept him conscious as he watched the spreading frame of the stanisplummer he didn't know, and he had only time for the fleeting pleasurable thought that he had succeeded.

Jeff Graham felt himself sink into a calm of relief, through which not even the raging storm could penetrate, and just before the final black curtain covered him forever, he thought serenely:

It was worth it!

VI

GRAFITTI

Hans Stauffer was sentimental. He was fifty-three years old and more interested in spending this night in Frankfurt than anywhere in the fancy new resorts. He could hardly contain himself in his eagerness to depart from the sterile modernness of the Space Center. He was frustrated in that desire by the line waiting for the stanisplummer. After fifteen minutes it was finally his turn, and he was standing in the entryway to his two hundred year old town house. Hans had been well known in science circles for almost three decades. He loved the amenities that came with that fame. He had descended from Frederick the Great and also enjoyed the considerable wealth still concentrated in the family. There were few members of the family left because many of them, like Hans, had chosen not to marry. Helga, his housekeeper, met him at the door. He brushed past her somewhat rudely in his haste to dress for the elaborate meal he'd had prepared for this occasion. Not much later he was clad in an elaborate dinner jacket, in time to greet his first guest..................

* * * *

Half a world away, the Watts night hanging over him like a dark shroud, Sergeant Tony James stepped from the public SP booth. He walked the block to the cottage that had been his home since the base housing had been closed six months ago. He had been raised in Watts, and his mother-in-law lived across the street, so it had been a natural selection. Besides, although more than the base housing had been, it was the cheapest rent he could find——$1,967 a month. He walked on without noticing the spray-painted graffiti that marred the ugly walls on the street.

He could still not understand why they had closed base housing; his family had been doing so well until then. The official reason had been——old substandard units, and with the price of resources rising, and the burgeoning demand for space for the ever-growing world population, they were razed to make room for more economical apartment units (There turned out to be less apartments, each of which charged higher rent than anyone he knew could afford to pay.)

A child's wail filled the air as he neared his house, and James quickened his step as he recognized it as being from his youngest son Bobby. He had four other children, all under the age of ten. Bobby was four, and seemed to be sick almost all of the time. Tony thought it was probably from the poor diet they were forced to feed him, even with the food stamp supplement. The sergeant entered his house, letting the door slam behind him. He went directly to the room in which he knew Bobby lay, pausing only to put the six-pack of beer he'd bought in the refrigerator. As soon as Bobby saw his daddy, he reached his arms toward him, and James took the boy from his wife.

"It's okay, Bobby. Daddy's right here. Don' cry now baby."

The boy stopped crying and put his head on his father's shoulder. Tony had always been able to calm him down when no one else could. Soon the regular breathing told him the boy was asleep. He laid the boy gently on the bed he shared with his two brothers, and tiptoed from the room.

"Tony, I still wish you weren't goin' away tomorrow. With Bobby so sick, and all, can't you tell them you'll be goin' on the next mission, when he gets well?"

They had been through this at least fifty times before, and he was afraid any answer now would only weaken his resolve, so he did not reply. This would be the only mission he could hope to make for at least six years. It wouldn't be until then that the next landing would take place. It was more than likely that he wouldn't be chosen to be on it, so this was his last chance.

They needed the bonus that would be paid for hazardous duty to all *Project Icarus* members. Five thousand dollars was more than enough to pay the homestead fee and for a few supplies to begin construction of a house and a new life on Kadakas IV. James looked in on his other children, and joined his wife in the kitchen, where he finally got the nerve to speak to her.

"Nadine honey, it's goin' to be alright. We' goin' to get our new home when I come back. I'm only goin' to be gone for a month; then life will be great ag'in. You'll see."

The rest of the evening, the woman was content to sip the beer he'd bought to celebrate their impending prosperity. James thought she was either hiding her feelings to make his last night at home more pleasant, or she'd finally accepted. At last they went to the small living room, which did double duty as their bedroom and enjoyed the last pleasure they would share.

* * * *

Boris Epilov arrived at his Moscow apartment, and immediately regretted his decision to come home. The man seated so comfortably in his living room was Sergei Klepsemev, a mid level agent for the KGB (the Russian version of the FBI. CIA, and military intelligence all rolled into one——although the political climate in the Russian Union initially had moderated, it had swung back toward communism. Even during the moderate years the name of the agency remained.) He shouldn't have been surprised, because the man's subordinates had interviewed him several times in the last year and a half. He was sure it was Klepsemev who'd had him followed almost continuously. The KGB agent was a product of the revived communist party machine that was still in place despite the disappointment of the Iranian war.

Klepsemev was old enough to have advanced through the hierarchy, methodically beginning with the *Komsomol*. Nothing had escaped from his mouth that was not strictly party line, and he was fanatical about it. Having been conditioned to spout anti-west slogans from birth, he was steeped in that dogmatism, but now a new threat to his beliefs was formidable. The softening of tensions with the capitalists had thrown his mind into turmoil. He would not accept the loss. The discovery that Boris Epilov resided within his jurisdiction became the embodiment of that loss. He saw his duty clearly. He must protect the Motherland from this

American-imperialist plot, which was so insidious this time that even the congress had been fooled. Tonight was his last chance to expose the plot. He must waste no effort getting Epilov to talk. He reminded himself that it was still a possibility that Epilov was an unsuspecting victim, so he resolved to go slowly at first until he determined his degree of involvement. Of course, if it were not determined, that would be okay, too. He would willingly forego the rights of the individual for the good of the state. At any rate, he knew it would be easy to trip up this unsuspecting man. It was too late to back out of the apartment now.

Boris raised his right arm to shake hands with the other.

"Comrade Kleptemev. To what do I owe the honor of this visit?"

"Just using my official position to wish you well, and satisfy my curiosity about some points of little importance." He stared into Epilov's eyes.

Boris felt a chill course through the nape of his neck, with a sudden recollection of a long-forgotten horror. He'd developed his aversion to secret service men, since that day long ago, when he'd had a first hand observation of their methods. At eleven or twelve years old, he had been a close friend of Sacha Feinstein. The boy had lived in the large house about two blocks from his own apartment. He remembered the fine old house well. Sacha's father had been a doctor who used the bottom floor for an office and clinic. The two boys loved to play in the attic and upstairs during the day, finding numerous hiding places.

That fateful winter night they were playing later than usual, when a heavy knock sounded on the door. Agents came storming in and rounded up the family. Allowed to take only a few belongings, they were herded into the snowy streets. Boris had been terrified and remained in his hiding place until well after they had gone. He had heard no more from the Feinsteins and the house had since been converted into apartments to ease the housing shortage.

Boris had not forgotten this incident. Later research revealed they had disappeared during the time when Jews were being denied exit visas to Israel in the nineteen-seventies and eighties. It took only simple deduction to assume they had been involved in that, probably aiding others to escape Russia.

The amenities out of the way, the KGB agent began to ask more pointed questions, making Boris begin to feel the direction they were going. At that moment Anna entered the room. She walked directly to Boris, kissing him lightly on the cheek as she sat next to him on the couch.

"Comrade Klepsemev is here to add his best wishes for Project *Icarus*, Anna." He had a slim hope that he could dissuade the other man from his probing, but it was futile.

Klepsemev continued the interrogation, ignoring the woman entirely.

"Comrade, how do you feel working so closely with the capitalists?"

"It is a great pleasure to serve the Motherland in so noble a project. It matters not who our glorious leaders have chosen for me to work with." Boris had to be sure to spice each answer with evidence that he was duly loyal to the state.

"How have you found the equipment to be on the mission."

"Of course, comrade, no tool or equipment produced in the Imperialist West approaches the quality of that made by the proletariat of the Russian Union working in harmony. The capitalist exploitation of the people robs them of their productivity, and the equipment is merely adequate."

The KGB man began to aim at the core. "I'm sure you were being alert to locate signs of the capitalist plot, so that you could aid us in the inevitable demise of the capitalist system. I'm sure you were saving your observations for a moment such as this when you could reveal them all to the proper authorities. What signs have you observed?"

"The Capitalists are extremely clever. Their plot against the Motherland was shielded from these untrained eyes. I *have* observed some things, which could be pieces of the plot, and I'm afraid I have been reticent in my duty to report these out of a lack of certainty, and the great involvement in my work. Would that I had the trained mind of comrades such as you and could obtain the insight that you so easily reach." He hoped the flattery would put the agent off the track, but he could see that it wasn't working and he dredged his mind to remember an incident that Klepsemev would interpret as revisionist.

"Tell me what you have observed, comrade. I should be able to interpret it for you."

Epilov spent the next half hour describing every incident he could think of that could be considered marginally demeaning to the Russian Union, and his responses to them. Most of the incidents were simply invented, but some were embellishments of actual events. For example, Sergeant Devlin, who had been involved in some of the heaviest fighting in the Russian War had called him a "fucking Russky" the first time they met and the two had almost come to blows. Epilov described the encounter as an attempt to intimidate him——probably hatched by warmonger American high command——and thus discredit the Motherland. His refusal to back down had been real.

Epilov concluded his narrative by saying, "The Capitalists are clever, comrade, but the glorious Motherland shall prevail as long as we poor citizens are vigilant, and you excellent gentlemen continue your excellent work."

He wasn't sure if Klepsemev was buying the dissertation, but he would continue as long as he could.

During the discussion Klepsemev felt himself believing Boris because his answers were good. His belief that the space project was only a Capitalist plot began to loosen, and was almost gone when a thought saved him.

Of course his answers are good! They're too good!

The American Imperialists were clever, and they'd almost fooled him. But no Russian citizen could possibly follow the party line that closely, unless he was *rehearsed*.

He reached in his pocket for the remote stanisplummer switch and suddenly there were two more KGB agents pounding for admittance into the room.

Boris gave a resigned sigh. He hadn't really expected it to work.

"The door's not locked, tell your men to come in."

The two entered and Kleptemev began to gloat. He was so pleased with himself for having trapped Epilov that he wanted to enjoy every moment of it.

"You were clever, but not nearly so clever as I."

"No, comrade, I guess not." Boris was calm.

The KGB Chief directed his attention to the muscleman—"Take them away," he commanded shortly.

Before the two could reach the couch, Boris fingered the remote button in his own pocket. He and Anna disappeared along with the couch.

Klepsemev heard "Good…"

"…bye." The word echoed strangely in the almost empty storeroom in Houston. Boris felt a dissipating twinge of sadness. He would never be able to return to his homeland. The stanisplummers, which he had rigged to make his escape had been in place for more than a year, but he had wanted to wait until after the mission to prevent complications. He reached for Anna, who had already begun to unpack their valuables from the couch. He pulled her to him in a lingering embrace.

*   *   *   *

Scott Armstrong's inkling that it would not be wise to go home to his apartment turned out to be prophetic, judging from Stark's reception by the news media. Because of his position as commander of the mission, he had been given his choice of offices at the space center. Although he could have had the most opulent suite in the building, he chose a small unwindowed room with a lockable door. It had room for his small army-issue gray metal desk and a bunk that he had surreptitiously slipped in the previous week. On the desk lay all the paperwork about the mission in two rather untidy heaps. He hated paperwork, but he had been through the two piles over and over—unwilling to allow any possibility of error to slip by unnoticed. He intended to go through the stacks another two or three times before the morning.

He finally got the solitude he desperately wanted. He also wanted a slug of Jim Beam, but his sense of duty (no hangover tomorrow) stifled that urge and settled for black coffee from the vending machine. Two years before, his sister Mary had dug out all of his military awards and photos and displayed them on the walls. Though he publicly feigned disinterest in the past, his gaze fell on some of the memorabilia from the Iranian war. The photos of his staff and subordinate commanders, some of whom had died there, garnered the greater amount of his attention.

Armstrong still had nightmares about the actual fighting of war. He remembered it as if he were inside a frosted glass globe in the heart of a raging furnace. He did not recall making any conscious decisions in the heat of battle. It was true that they had been meticulously planned, but when the first round was fired, everything changed. The fighting seemed to unfold of its own accord. It was as if battle was itself a living, devilish being; dragging all the combatants into its maw. So chaotic had it been, that it was impossible to distinguish friend from foe. He had just forced himself to continue moving forward true to Sun Tsu's dictum, *attack him when he does not expect it; avoid his strength and strike his emptiness, and like water, none can oppose you.*

*   *   *   *

Armstrong felt grim satisfaction as he ducked out of the briefing tent. He looked up briefly to reassure himself about the weather. Never had he seen the sky quite so large as it was in the desert. Perfect! No moon, and stars clear and bright. They should have no trouble navigating, particularly with the help of the Air Force. At the HMMWV (or "hum-vee", the modern version of the jeep) he took the porkchop microphone off the hook and announced: "ALPHA-FOX, THIS IS YANKEE SIX-SIX, BLUEBONNET——OVER."

In quick succession all major subordinate commands responded.

"KAY-BECK-SIX-SIX——OVER." *Stanton of the 1/103rd Armor (First tank) had fit right in to Armstrong's scheme.*

"XRAY-SIX-SIX——OVER." *The 1/130 field artillery battalion had to be ready to move with the 1/103 so that maximum fire would be forward. There would be no* other indirect fire support except mortars. All the rest were supporting the lead divisions.

"NOVEMBA-SIX-SIX——OVER." 1/115 Mech (First Mech) was Armstrong's biggest worry. Dalton had been commander for a long time. Although he knew his troops, he was not very flexible. A petty politician in Texas, he felt he wielded considerable power. He had already tested Armstrong on two or three occasions. So far the tests had only irritated and the man had retreated quickly, but he bore watching.

"LEEMA-SIX-SIX——OVER." Matthews of 2/103rd Armor (Second tank) was green. A junior major, he had little staff experience, but Armstrong had selected him because he was aggressive. He could turn the whole battalion from a fast moving column of companies 90 degrees left or right within 30 minutes.

"ROMEO-ONE-ZERO——OVER."

He felt brief satisfaction in the contrast of the first such call he'd made more than two months ago. Then, it had taken more than two hours just to get all the battalion commanders on the radio. Although the net control station answered for 2/115 (Second Mech) rather than the commander, Armstrong knew it was because that battalion was spread out the farthest. It had been given the unglamorous job of scattering troops for the dummy rear area protection/security mission and Lieutenant Colonel Fox was probably out of radio range. The battalion had a follow-on mission, and he idly hoped Fox had gotten the subtle message Armstrong had given him. It was ludicrous to split a heavy combat unit into small units throughout the Corps. The RAOC commander had wanted the unit split so that every ammo point or shower stall had their own tank or Bradley for protection. He wouldn't listen to reason. Armstrong had used two companies to provide a token force. He hoped Fox had a plan that would reunite his force in minimal time.

Part of the reason for the improvement was the BLUEBONNET code word indicated that this one was for real. Another big part was that Armstrong had predicted something would happen and had given the battalion commanders a warning order before he went to the corps TOC.

The Foxtrot Cavalry troop had not responded because of the need to maintain security. Although they were more than forty kilometers away, the lack of terrain features should have enabled them to monitor the transmission. At least Armstrong hoped so.

Most of the cav troop's transmission would come over their remote terminals, actually laptop computers in the maneuver control system (MCS) net. The MCS is a sophisticated computer system linked by satellite for communication among headquarters. It includes a video graphics screen that overlays military symbols (icons) on a videodisk generated map-image. Enemy and friendly units locations and movements were updated almost instantaneously among Air Force and army units. Communication would come in burst of data relayed by satellite.

As soon as the last response was made, he rattled off the list from the playbook finishing with "ACKNOWLEDGE——OVER."

"Go Charlie!" He directed the command to Specialist Charles Nelson, his driver. Nelson was ready, so the vehicle was immediately thrust into motion. The voices sounded calm as they each in turn repeated his instructions line by line. Armstrong recognized the voice of the battalion commander himself in each case. They sounded calm, but he could imagine the turmoil in the respective assembly areas. He knew all company commanders and platoon leaders were already assembling for quick briefings.

Armstrong looked at the radium dial of his watch. 0017 hours. He was confident they would be ready to kick it off. Starting fast was critical. They had to contact the enemy before first light. With our night vision devices the advantage would be marked. The enemy vehicles did have night vision capability, he reminded himself, but it depended on active infrared illumination and the range was probably less than 1,000 meters. The Russians probably would be better off not to use their searchlights at all; at least not until the range was significantly shorter. Those infrared searchlights would be beacons to the 43rd's passive thermal sights. He thumbed the button on the microphone again and waited for the cooling fan to whine to its full revolutions.

"YANKEE-THREE-THREE——THIS IS YANKEE-SIX-SIX——OVER."

The amber light on the radio glowed almost immediately as if the brigade operations officer had anticipated his call. Major Jack Thompkins had been the S-3 throughout the NTC training. He had been invaluable to Armstrong in assessing the character of the four battalions.

"THREE-THREE——OVER."

"I'M INCOMING——ECHO-TANGO-ALPHA ONE-FIVE MIKES. BE READY TO ROLL. I WANT YOU, THE FOX-SIERRA AND BLUE AIR WITH ME. WE'LL HAVE LESS THAN A HALF HOUR TO GET WITH KAY-BEK, SO HAVE THEM READY. BREAK. YANKEE-TWO-TWO, THIS IS SIX-SIX OVER."

"TWO-TWO——GO."

"DID YOU COPY MY TRANSMISSION TO THREE-THREE? OVER."

The brigade intelligence officer, Major Mike McCormick was colorful and clearly outstanding at what he did. The most important benefit was his ability to read Armstrong's mind. It was unnerving sometimes and caught the senior officer by surprise. This time it was welcome.

"ROGER, SIX. OUR ROUTE SHOULD BE CLEAR SAILING. NO MAJOR OBSTACLES OTHER THAN A SMALL ESCARPMENT VICINITY CHARLIE-PAPA ALPHA-THREE-ONE. IF WE USE WHITE LIGHT THERE, IT WILL BE NO HINDRANCE. I'LL KEEP AN EYE ON THE BAD GUYS. AIR FORCE RECCE HAS A PRETTY GOOD FIX ON THEM AND WE GET DOWNLINKS DIRECTLY NOW. IT'S ALMOST LIKE WATCHING A VIDEO GAME ON THE MIKE-CHARLIE-SIERRA. WE'RE DUMPING THAT INFO TO LOWER EVERY CHANCE WE GET."

The mike-charlie-sierra (MCS) to which McCormick referred is the maneuver control system. Armstrong had worried that the system might produce information overload to the humans who had to interpret it. So far however, it had worked well with one exception. Someone who understood the usefulness of the information had to constantly monitor the system. Initially, that had to be a primary staff officer. Then First Lieutenant Jim Merkel, and assistant operations officer (S-3) had taken it on himself to learn it. Not only did he train the junior officers in the brigade TOC to sort the information correctly, but in his position as liaison officer to the battalions he had most of the personnel there on track.

"ROGER, TWO. GOOD JOB. KEEP ME POSTED. BREAK. YANKEE-EIGHT-EIGHT——THIS IS YANKEE-SIX-SIX——OVER."

Armstrong knew his air liaison officer (ALO) Major John Peters would be a key to success. He was depending on the air force to guide them rapidly to the Russians, more important, to guide them to the weak flanks and rear. The ALO had a tendency to talk on the radio like the pilots do. The familiar tone and lapses of proper radio-telephone procedures rankled some NCOs and junior officers, who wrongly assumed Peters to have a callous attitude. This time Peters answered correctly.

"THIS IS YANKEE-EIGHT-EIGHT——OVER."

"THIS IS SIX. WE'RE GOING WHITE LIGHT THROUGH PHASES ONE AND TWO. I'M COUNTING ON YOU TO KEEP US ON TRACK."

"WILL DO SIX."

Armstrong looked at his watch again. 0031 hours. God, the time is flying! He reached over the seat and turned the dials of the radio to a preset position. He was satisfied everyone knew what to do and would not be calling him for a while. If they did, he could check in at the tactical operation center (TOC) when he arrived for messages. Meantime, he would better be served by eavesdropping on the 1/103d armor battalion net. Not that he needed to check up on the lead battalion, he knew their training was kicking in and the troops were up and moving. Rather, he found it useful to keep himself apprised of the situation by listening to company commanders and particularly to scout platoon leaders. Sometimes, like gossip, relayed messages lost their accuracy. Decay of value over time was another factor. That does not imply that information analyzed by the brigade staff is valueless. On the contrary, to appreciate the beauty of a painting one must step back from it.

Another frequency he often monitored was the fire support net. While a soldier in combat will usually be so busy fighting to report to headquarters, he will seldom forget to call for artillery or air cover.

"…ATHENTICATE PAPA-ROMEO——OVER"

"THIS IS ALPHA-FOX-KAY-BEC THUREE-THUREE, I AUTHENTICATE WHISKEY——OVER."

"THIS IS ALPHA-FOXTROT-KAY-BEC-ONE-ZERO. ROGER. OUT."

Several other stations requested permission to enter the radio net and were challenged by the net control station while he listened. Armstrong just blocked the transmissions from his mind. He propped his right foot on the dashboard and leaned back into the seat——looking up at the stars. The last time he had seen the sky so full was when he had been in California, at Fort Hunter-Liggett. It had startled him then. He loved the stars and their patterns, but the view in Houston was subdued. Whether from the damping of city lights or the humidity, he didn't know. Even at Irwin they were less bright. Here, now they were spectacular. He found Polaris (The North Star) with Ursa Major (the Little Dipper) reaching out to the right. Cassiopea, the sideways "W" immersed in the lacy diagonal of the Milky Way was about the direction he'd ordered his forces to head. He did not order direction based on that constellation, because some junior commanders could not get the hang of recognition, and in four hours Cassiopea would be south of Polaris. The only constant was Polaris itself. Reading a compass near masses of steel in gun and tank and low light was nearly impossible. Since they had not been issued the global positioning systems (GPS) the ancient art of navigation by stars was the solution. The forearm extended parallel to the ground gave them general direction. Precise direction would be provided by the air force once they got closer to the Russians.

The HMMWV lurched unexpectedly in the ruts as Nelson recognized the glowing green arrow formed of glow-in-the-dark plastic chemical light capsules. The arrow signaled their arrival at the brigade tactical operation center (TOC). Armstrong left the vehicle before it stopped moving, taking only time to glance at his watch. 0044 hours. It had taken him longer than he'd expected to get back.

He ducked his head to clear the camouflage netting and was halted by a sentry. He was impatient with the security procedures, but gratified the soldier was so concerned about his duty. Moving through the canvas flap of the huge tarpaulin that covered the space between the four M-577 command and control vehicles, he caught his protective mask case on the edge of the opening. He irritably jerked at it, knowing it probably would have come free easier if he had checked what was caught.

Inside he blinked in the bright light. Not waiting for his vision to clear he moved his eyes around the plastic covered map sheets lining the interior until he found Thompson engaged in discussion at the map with McCormick. Since they would not speak face to face until after the operation, but almost had to know what the other was thinking, they were doing some last minute coordination.

"Let's go, Jack," Armstrong said evenly to Thompson. Then as an afterthought he turned to the intelligence officer. "Anything new, Mac?"

"Not much. John says TAC AIR is turning up the heat, but there are so many of them, they're barely making a dent."

Armstrong and Thompkins left the TOC through the same opening Armstrong had entered. Outside they walked twenty-five meters and ducked through the rear hatch of an idling M-2 Bradley fighting vehicle. In the eerie red glow they could make out Sergeant Ray Lewis as he slipped quietly from the track commander's (TC) hatch to the driver's seat. There were two other people seated in the crew compartment: air force Major John Peters the ALO and Major Will Sternan the fire support officer (FSO).

Sternan was the main cog in the TACFIRE network. From his computer screen in the command track he could monitor and cancel fire missions sent over the net by the FIST teams at company level who had similar equipment. That action ensured artillery fire support would go the highest priority target and most importantly prevented errors that might result in fratricide, the killing of friendly troops with our own weapons.

Armstrong took his place in the TC's hatch and wriggled the combat vehicle crewman (CVC) helmet over his ears. Pushing the toggle switch below his left ear to the rear locked position, he announced, "Move out, Ray. You know where first tank is. We've got ten minutes to get there. Use white light"

"Holy shit, Sir! No way we gonna get there by then. Twenty minutes, at least. Unless I beat the hell out of ya'all."

"Just do it, Sergeant Lewis." The track moved off with a lurch. The sergeant was right. They were almost five miles from the first tank. They would have to move faster than thirty miles an hour to make it. The M-2 Bradley was not particularly rough riding as armored vehicles go, but there were no roads; only a line of the phosphorescent glowing markers. When they reached the glowing red arrow that indicated first tank's assembly area Armstrong's watch showed 0101 hours. Pretty good time!

Headlights showed everywhere converging to a vague column as the battalion moved out. Right on time.

"ALPHA-FOXTROT-YANKEE THIS IS KAY-BEK SIX-SIX, SIERRA PAPA NOW——OVER!"

Armstrong acknowledged the start point report and clicked the switch on his helmet to the intercom position.

"Ray, try to mix in with the second tank company in the column. Don't bother trying to find Colonel Stanton."

Armstrong moved down inside the crew compartment where his staff members were, stretching the coiled cord.

"John, your people got anything different?"

Thompkins answered for him, shining the beam of the flashlight on his map. "They're picking them off at about the same rate they did before. Our guess is that they will be about right on schedule. Second platoon of Foxtrot troop has moved about eight miles north of where they were. They're going to give us a kind of weak screen. They can only watch about six klicks though, ten at the outside. Maybe we ought to get first and third platoon to break contact with friendlies and get to the middle to support."

"Tell Mark to move his third platoon to the west to try a link up." *Armstrong replied.* "They've already made contact with the 104th Division. But let's have Fox Troop make sure they contact the French division before they come in. I don't want to get a surprise from there."

Thompkins opened the lid to the olive drab box on the seat next to him and typed the message to the Fox troop commander on the small computer it enclosed."

* * * *

The Air Force pilots had kept them apprised of the Russian forces and contact was expected within an hour. Armstrong had given the order to go to blackout conditions, but not before ordering the lead battalion to go to prebattle formation. The sight was impressive as the lights fanned out away from them to the right and left flickering as the dust clouds obscured the light from time to time, appearing like a slowly bursting rocket. Suddenly the night had grown black except for the faint glow of the stars that would become brighter as his eyes adjusted, until they had reestablished their rightful ancient domain over the night sky. Now for the first time he noticed the flashes of light on the horizon. These flashes, he knew were the TAC AIR strikes on the Russian divisions.

Kill bunches, guys, but don't slow them down too much. I want to make contact before first light. Forward, right and left on the ground the myriad of red specks gathered brightness. These were the "cat's eyes" lights on the rear of vehicles that prevented them from crashing into one another. The drivers looking through thermal viewers, gunners looking through their sights and commanders with night vision goggles perceived these red specks as green. They could still actually see the outlines of the vehicles that housed them, but in ghostly perspective as the heat that projected the images wavered. There was no depth of vision.

The weight of the "Goggles", really miniature television monitors, hurt Armstrong's nose, so he kept them off and just watched the "cat's eyes," occasionally looking to the rear to see the misty patches of white blackout drive in front of each vehicle. One by one these links to the reality of the battlefield were swallowed up as drivers felt their eyes had adjusted enough to go completely black. Within a half hour, the only hooks that Armstrong had to prevent himself from feeling totally abandoned on the Iranian desert was the occasional change in the sound of an engine in the distance which had to struggle over some minor obstacle and intermittent flashes on the horizon which enabled glimpses of vague outlines. The sound managed to intrude on the steady thrum of the Bradley in which he was riding. Armstrong had learned if he looked hard enough he could see the slight difference in the black void that indicated the presence of a vehicle. He didn't know if this was some kind of sixth sense or actual sight, but it had always worked for him.

Even so he risked the sharpness of his vision and dropped down slightly to look through the thermal sight of the Bradley's 25-millimeter chain gun to confirm it again. As he traversed the turret he could clearly see the ghostly shapes of the nearer vehicles, but those 2,000 meters away were merely dim "hot spots". Although the FLIR (Forward Looking InfraRed) sights "saw" heat the dust clouds diffused it somewhat causing the decay of sharpness.

Where are they? Almost 0400 hours! We should make contact any time. Focus! Are the troops ready? We'll know soon. We've got to make contact before first light. We have the advantage at night unless they have some new vision devices. What if they do? Nah, there has been no contact with anything unexpected yet, so why would there be now? This is like the National Training Center. Are we in the Valley of Death, and over there is just the sham "Samaran" army which is good, but their kills are not really kills? We "won" all but one battle against them, but always lost more than thirty-five vehicles in doing so. Thirty-five times four equals one-hundred-forty men who would have been dead or wounded. But those were only pretend casualties. Would these be real?

The OPFOR(opposing force) at the NTC, Fort Irwin, California were supposed to be the "best Russian motorized rifle regiment in the world." But we are not facing only a regiment here. It could be almost two divisions! Where were they? The Fox troop reported them to be only twenty klicks out more than a half hour ago. First tank should have been getting reports from their scouts by now.

Mike! Come on! Give me a spot report!

One of the reasons Mike Stanton's Task Force 1/103rd armor battalion had been given the lead was because he had always been the most responsive in reporting to brigade on contact. The other had been his responsiveness in going for the throat immediately. His task force had always taken the most casualties, but he had maneuvered his companies with a swiftness and overwhelming authority that the enemy had no choice but to focus his entire attention on him.

The remainder of the brigade had always been able to maneuver unseen to a vulnerable flank and the battle would be over within a half hour. Now Armstrong was waiting for that first spot report and immediate assessment of which enemy flank would be the most vulnerable. The supporting pilots had already suggested the left flank was the way to go, but timing was everything. Armstrong learned from experience waiting for the lead battalion contact prevented the enemy from receiving early warning of the direction of rotation and prevented the enveloping force from losing contact with the main body. Armstrong hoped that the vulnerable flank was wide enough early enough that the entire remainder of the brigade could be thrown the same direction, each battalion with a subsequently deeper penetration.

The flashes from the airstrikes had increased in brightness, and Armstrong thought he could hear the sound of the detonations over the roar of the engine. First tank was probably guiding solely on the flashes.

What if the Air Force has not located all the Russians and they are right now on our flank ready to roll us up. Don't think about that shit. It's too late now. My only function now is to tell them to rotate right or left. Even if we do get Russians on our flank, the companies or battalions will have to handle that.

Come on Mike! Where are they?

Maybe if I switch to his battalion push?

As the thought struck him, Armstrong was already fumbling with the radio controls, adjusting them to the preset frequency.

He had barely straightened in the hatch, when almost simultaneously at least fifteen M-1 tanks on line no more than 1,000 meters forward of him blossomed with white-orange flame.

"…OLY SHIT!——THERE THEY ARE," *came across the radio pouring into Armstrong's ears. He flinched at the sound, pausing involuntarily for a moment before switching back to the brigade frequency, just in time to hear the now unnecessary report.*

"…THIS IS KAY-BEC-SIX-SIX, SPOT REPORT. WE ARE ENGAGING MORE THAN A REGIMENT OF TANGO-EIGHT-ZERO TANKS. TAC AIR WAS RIGHT. THE OPENING IS ON THE LEFT. LOOKS LIKE AT LEAST ANOTHER REGIMENT OFF TO OUR RIGHT.""

TELL TAC AIR TO GET THEIR ASSES OUT OF HERE, I DON'T WANT THEM SHOOTING UP MY GUYS. OUT."

No response was necessary and Armstrong heard John Peters calling off the Air Force. There was but one useful function of the brigade commander and Armstrong didn't think even that was necessary. The other battalions would have heard Mike Stanton's transmission. As he keyed the microphone, he pulled the night vision goggles to his eyes and looked to the rear to see the numerous "hot spots" that were the other battalions already moving toward the southwest at top speed. He made the obligatory transmission anyway. He waited until he was certain that the radio's cooling fan was a full speed to be certain everyone heard the entire transmission.

"ALPHA-FOXTROT, THIS IS ALPHA-FOXTROT-YANKEE-SIX-SIX. EXECUTE ROTATE LEFT, EXECUTE ROTATE LEFT. ACKNOWLEDGE."

The replies came in swift sequence, almost as soon as he released the push-to-talk button.

"THIS IS LEEMA-SIX-SIX. I ACKNOWLEDGE—EXECUTE ROTATE LEFT. OVER."

"THIS IS NOVEMBA-SIX-SIX. I ACKNOWLEDGE—EXECUTE ROTATE LEFT. OVER."

"THIS IS ROMEO-SIX-SIX. I ACKNOWLEDGE—EXECUTE ROTATE LEFT. OVER."

"THIS IS XRAY-SIX-SIX. I ACKNOWLEDGE—EXECUTE ROTATE LEFT. OVER."

"THIS IS YANKEE-NINER-NINER. I ACKNOWLEDGE—EXECUTE ROTATE LEFT. OVER."

The last acknowledgement suprised Armstrong. He hadn't expected Mark Pickens' F troop, 43rd cavalry to be in radio range, but as flat as it was he guessed he should have. He'd wished that his brigade had been supplied with the ICT so that he could maintain contact with F troop. This seemed just as good.

"YANKEE-SIX-SIX——BREAK-BREAK——YANKEE-NINER-NINER THIS IS YANKEE-SIX-SIX, OVER."

"THIS IS YANKEE-NINER-NINER, OVER."

"THIS IS SIX——AH——DO YOU HAVE CONTACT WITH ALL OF YOUR ELEMENTS?"

"THIS IS NINER. NEGATIVE, MY THREE ELEMENT IS TOO FAR AWAY. OVER."

"SIX. I'M GOING TO CUT YOUR THREE ELEMENT FROM YOU AND GIVE ALPHA-FOXTROT-LEEMA MORE EYES AND EARS ON THE SOUTH. MAINTAIN CONTACT WITH THE ENEMY WHERE YOU ARE AND KEEP THEM BUSY WITH TAC AIR. WE'LL DEAL WITH THEM WHEN WE ARE THROUGH HERE. DO YOU COPY OVER?"

"THIS IS NINER. ROGER OVER."

"THIS IS SIX. HOW ARE YOU DOING UP THERE?"

"THIS IS NINER. GREAT! THE BAD GUYS DON'T EVEN SEEM TO KNOW WE'RE HERE. WE STAY ABOUT THREE OR FOUR KLICKS AWAY FROM THEM AND IT'S LIKE WATCHING A PARADE. IT'S WEIRD. THEY'RE LINED UP ONE BEHIND THE OTHER LIKE THEY ARE ON A ROAD MARCH. THE ONLY TIME THEY GO OFF THE ROAD IS WHEN THEY HAVE TO PASS A TANK HIT BY OUR TAC AIR. OVER."

"THIS IS SIX. ROGER, MAKE SURE YOU KEEP THAT DISTANCE. WHEN IT GETS LIGHT THEY WILL PROBABLY BE ABLE TO SEE YOU, BUT THEY WON'T HAVE THE RANGE TO HIT YOU. OUT."

Forward now, Armstrong could see all the M-1s were firing as fast as they could reload. The Bradley fighting vehicle 25-millimeter chain guns had joined in the chorus, and Armstrong could hear the occasional rippling noise of the 155-millimeter projectiles fired by the field artillery battalion as they passed overhead. None of the vehicles appeared to have been hit by enemy fire, at least they were all still moving at combat speed and in their irregular zigzag patterns. Armstrong's own Bradley had closed to within 400 meters of the tanks, when the deafening sounds of battle changed almost imperceptivity.

Incoming! The Russians were firing their own field artillery. Armstrong saw the impact of six or eight rounds within a half a kilometer from his position. One of them exploded almost on top of the nearest M-1 tank and it lurched to a stop.

"Ray, go over to that tank. Now!"

Armstrong didn't know what he could do but perhaps he could be of help. The Bradley moved to the left with a lurch at more than forty miles an hour. The light of the continuous explosions served as a constant beacon. The big fighting vehicle stopped behind the tank offering protection from enemy fire and Armstrong moved out the rear exit of the vehicle as quickly as the ramp lowered. He immediately scrambled over the fender of the tank using the rear sprocket as a step ladder; not usually an acceptable way to mount a tank because you don't have the driver's attention and he could begin moving, rolling you up in the track, but this wasn't peacetime.

From the tank's back-deck he could see the silhouette of slumped figure half out of the tank commander's hatch. The hatch was fully open, not in popped hatch mode, and a soldier was struggling to pull the figure completely out of the hatch.

"What happened?" Armstrong knew already, but the question was automatic.

"He was hit in the face with shrapnel. I think he's dead. What do I do with him?"

Armstrong did not reply but helped him remove the body from the hatch and carry him to the back deck where he was lifted down to the waiting arms of Jack Tompkins and John Peters. Armstrong yelled above the din of battle,

"Jack, you've got the track. I'm going to fight this tank."

Turning abruptly to the crewman on the deck, he said, "Let's go, son. What tank is this?"

"Alpha-Three-Three, sir. I'm the loader, and Sergeant Kyle was the TC."

Armstrong climbed into the TC position, pulled the hatch to the half-closed "popped hatch" configuration, and slid the combat vehicle crewman's (CVC) helmet over his head. It was wet and slippery; the cause of which Armstrong tried to banish *from his mind.* He checked the intercom switch on the back left of the helmet to see if it was in intercom mode and spoke into the microphone,

"DRIVER, MOVE OUT! GUNNER? GOT ANY TARGETS?"

"WHO THE HELL ARE YOU?" came a tinny voice as the tank lurched into motion.

"I'M YOUR TANK COMMANDER. ANSWER MY QUESTION!"

"THE ONES I SEE HERE HAVE ALREADY BEEN FIRED UP." came the not so defiant voice of the gunner.

"KEEP SCANNING. FASTER DRIVER. THE WAR'LL BE OVER BEFORE WE HAVE A CHANCE TO GET OUR SHARE."

Armstrong leaned down to look through the commander sight and watched the horizon as the gunner slowly traversed the turret from side to side. Satisfied he lifted his head out the opening in the top of the turret. Forward and to his right and left destroyed Russian tanks burned. He raised the night vision goggles to his eyes. *Maybe the soldiers are right in their riddle: What is the difference between a T-72 tank and a T-80? Answer: the T-80 burns brighter.*

The rest of this battle is mine and my crew's. I cannot help the rest of the brigade fight. Their training will have to carry them through. Don't look at the burning tanks. Concentrate on those still alive that can kill me. The burning tanks are too bright! Will I be able to see the live ones when they come? Where are the friendlies? Most of them on the left! There is only one M-1 on the right that I can see. How far away is he? Goddam goggles, no depth vision! Where'd he go?

"SON OF A BITCH! THERE MUST BE A HUNDRED OF THEM! I NEED HELP NOW!"

The sudden transmission startled Armstrong slightly, but he knew instinctively it had come from the lone tank on his right. It had disappeared from view, and so must have gone over an escarpment.

"DRIVER, GO RIGHT! NOW! GUNNER GET READY!" he pulled the switch on his helmet forward and yelled,

"ANY STATION THIS IS ALPHA-THREE-THREE. BE ADVISED THAT LAST TRANSMISSION CAME FROM MY RIGHT. MOVING TO CHECK IT OUT!" Just as he pressed the toggle on his helmet back to the intercom position, the tank crested the escarpment. What Armstrong saw there forced the disciplined GUNNER, SABOT, TANK fire command he had thought he was ready to say from his brain. Without counting, Armstrong knew there were well over two hundred "hot spots" in his field of vision. Instinctively he pressed the commander's override and slewed the turret slightly to the right and simply announced,

"THERE THEY ARE! DO YOU SEE THEM?"

"NO! WHERE?"

"HOLY SHIT!——ON THE WAY!"

The huge steel monster bucked violently and the 120-millimeter main gun spit a depleted uranium dart down range more than two kilometers in a split second. The burning tracer element on the base of the round made it look like a science fiction ray gun that burned a green streak across the darkness. It culminated in a huge fountain of sparks. Even from this distance Armstrong could see the toylike turret of the Russian tank rise slowly and arc to the desert floor.

"TARGET! GET THE ONE ON THE RIGHT."

"UP!" The loader was good. He had another round in the breach already.

"ON THE WAY!"

"TARGET! GUNNER CHOOSE YOUR TARGET."

"UP!"

"ON THE WAY."

At about the tenth round and the tenth destroyed Russian tank Armstrong noticed more green tracer streaks coming from his left. After the gunner fired one more round, he pressed the override again and slewed the turret about twenty degrees right before releasing it.

"GUNNER, WE MIGHT AS WELL TAKE THESE ON THE RIGHT. NO SENSE FIRING UP THE SAME TARGETS AS OUR BUDDIES. THEY NEED TO GET INTO THE ACT."

The gunner just said, "ON THE WAY!" and the tank bucked again. The driver had kept the vehicle moving at combat speed and they had closed to within 1,200 meters of the Russians. Armstrong left the gunner to fire the main gun and opened fire on personnel carriers like BMPs, and BRDMs with the commander's caliber .50 machinegun with bursts of fifteen rounds. Invariably it took two burst or less before the vehicle exploded.

The whole scene began to take on a surreal atmosphere as the adrenalin charge began to wear off. Armstrong felt himself go almost totally calm. For the first time he felt no fear. His body automatically went through the motions of aiming, holding the butterfly trigger for a count of five, pulling back the charging handle after a stoppage. His perception encompassed the entire scene of the battlefield. It was almost an out-of-body experience. Next to his tank, a Bradley fired its chain gun, the methodical thump-thump-thump produced a smaller tracer lead that drew Armstrong's eyes to its target, a T-80 tank. The Russian tank lurched to a stop and began to burn.

It was just then that he heard the sharp thwacking sound that he knew was the sound a fast moving slug makes as it passes close by. Just then, some instinct made him glance to the right. What he saw froze him.

There, not three hundred meters away, just behind a berm was a Russian T-80 tank. They had just cleared the edge of the dirt mound and by some happenstance the Russian commander had his 125-millimeter main gun aimed precisely in their direction. Armstrong could see clearly from his distance the movements of the big gun as it homed precisely on its target. Then its muzzle belched smoke and flame and its deadly projectile. Armstrong was now completely absorbed by the scene as the metal dart, its four fins as clearly seen as if he were holding it in his hand, slowly moved toward him. He could tell immediately that its trajectory would impact his M-1 tank at the turret ring, the most vulnerable part of the tank. He urged his frozen hand toward the com-

mander's override, but it was stuck in a thick molasses. He tried to issue a fire command to the gunner but all that came out was, "NOOOOOOOOO!"

※　※　※　※

Scott Armstrong sat bolt upright at the little gray desk with such a start that his right arm swept the cold half-cup of coffee all over the papers he had been poring through when he dozed off. He hardly noticed the spilled liquid. At first he thought it was simply a recurrence of the trauma he'd suffered through the dream reliving the war. That had been real enough and he had often had that very same dream. He had been terribly wounded in the left leg and two crewmembers had been killed. The battle had been nearly over by then; a decisive victory that had often been cited as the turning point that quickly let to American victory.

It was not the dream, however; something was happening here and now. *Something was wrong! All his combat instincts knew that was true.* And never more than at this moment! He could not say precisely *what* it was, but he knew it as well as he knew his own name. Along with the heightening alert came a terrible sense of dread. Not only was something wrong, there was a grave threat to someone he cared a great deal about. His first thought was Sue Powell. He had more than a passing interest in the pretty biologist. He had denied it and forced himself to renounce the thoughts as totally inappropriate. He was the commander and she worked for him. Not only that, there was the age difference, him pushing forty and her in her mid-twenties.

All of that went out of the window now. She was in trouble and he knew it. *Had he heard a scream?* Maybe, but he knew it was her.

He wanted to go bolting down the outside hallway toward the labs at a dead run but his training took over. He cautiously opened the door to his office and moved silently into the hall, carefully staying near the left wall. It was not enough to know that there was trouble; he needed to find out what and where it was quickly. He stopped periodically to listen intently at the small noises that all buildings produced, air conditioning fans, water running in pipes, and creaking of minute settling. It was vital to isolate anything out of the ordinary to home on.

Ahead was the cross hallway that led to the labs to the left and the building entrance right. He stopped to listen again before moving down the left branch. Nothing. He had a fleeting thought that he was being foolish, and almost stepped boldly around the corner, but the doubt passed quickly. He peered cautiously around the corner. The only thing there was a full-length portable mirror angled so that he could see through the lab doors and into the biology lab 15 meters away. What he could see looked empty and the thought that he was being foolish recurred, but he remained cautious. When he was about three meters from the lab doors a low-growling voice froze him in place for just a second.

"It won't be long now, my beauty."

Then he could hear scraping noises and muffled groans like someone was struggling to get free of bonds. He moved to a position low on his hands and knees and looked through the glass doors. What he saw was perplexing. A man on the far side of the lab with his back to the door was using a roll of duct tape to secure several small tan colored boxes to a woman lying bound on a lab work bench. The mirror in the hall had not been positioned quite right for him to see the man back in the hall. He recognized in an instant that the boxes were military issue explosive C7 and the woman was Sue Powell, but he had no recognition of the man.

Suppressing the immediate urge to bolt into the room to her rescue, Armstrong realized that the man might have already rigged the detonator and that any rash action might trigger it. He stayed where he was for the moment to assess the situation.

The man, apparently finished, straightened and took a step back, pausing to admire his work and said, "Perfect. This is going to be so great."

Even though it was semi-dark in the lab, Armstrong could see Sue's face now. She had stopped struggling against the bonds, realizing the futility. Her eyes were wide, but Armstrong could see placidity in them that revealed her great character. Although she had to be struggling with abject terror, the eyes appeared calm and level.

Armstrong decided the most prudent course of action would be to retreat to the cross hallway and wait until the man left the building. His assumption was that the bomber would want to get far away from the building before igniting the bombs, giving him time to disarm at least the ones attached to Sue. He had no doubt that there were more bombs placed in the building and that Sue's surprising him in his process of setting them was forcing him to eliminate her as a witness. He would have to work quickly to get her free and escape the building, but it still seemed the safest course. He hoped there would be no difficulty in defusing the bombs, but decided they probably had few, if any, anti-tampering devices because the bomber could have reasonably expected to have no one detect their presence. If they were on a simple timer or radio controlled they would be easy to disarm.

As he slipped around the corner into the cross hall, a strong sense of foreboding overcame him and he stopped and waited, listening briefly before continuing to the first open room. He waited there listening.

Within a few moments he could hear light footfalls in the adjacent hall with the killer presumably proceeding exactly as Armstrong expected. However the sound stopped near the intersection of the two halls. This puzzled Armstrong a little. *Why hadn't he continued on out of the building? Was he just walking more softly and his footfalls could not be heard?*

Armstrong could not stand the anxiety, so he quietly opened the door slightly and looked into the hall in the direction of the intersection. There, peering around the corner back toward the lab was the bomber with his back to Armstrong. He seemed intent on something down the hallway near the lab. Just then Armstrong heard him mutter, "Not quite right. I need to turn it a little more to the left so I can see her better." And the bomber disappeared from his view down the hall the way he'd come.

Total understanding hit Armstrong so hard that his knees buckled and he almost lost his balance. *The bomber wanted to watch the girl explode!* That was the reason for the mirror, and he was just now adjusting it so he could get a better view.

Instinct and training took over. Armstrong silently reached the corner before the bomber. Harvey may have been an explosives expert, but he was no match for this superbly trained killer. In less than a half second after he returned to the corner, Armstrong had stripped the detonator from his grasp, had the gun and used it to viciously hammer Harvey's face into pulp. Before the fifth blow had landed, the world had been relieved of another of God's experiments gone wrong. Harvey Canton was no more.

Armstrong had no memory of removing the duct tape that bound Sue, but it seemed she was magically in his arms. They stood and held each other for a long time before Armstrong recovered his composure long enough that he realized they needed to report the situation. Before he did, however he turned to Sue and asked, "Have you had dinner?"

* * * *

It took perhaps an hour for the security forces of NASA to locate and neutralize all the bombs that had been placed by Harvey. Armstrong had been right that none had been booby trapped, nor especially hidden. The bomber had expected to be able to detonate them all by radio as soon as he left the building. Sue Powell had been understandably shaken up by the threat, but it took little effort to convince her to accompany him to dinner on the moon.

As the two gazed at the Earth-lit plain and the full-beautiful globe as it hung just above the horizon, conversation came easy. Despite their reluctance to discuss the mission—it first gravitated to the Luddites.

"I do not understand," said Sue, "how that man can believe that destroying SP's could ever be good for mankind. How can they possibly not understand that the Earth is just not big enough for all of us to continue to exist?"

Armstrong simply shrugged and said, "That man didn't believe it. He was simply an insanely sadistic man who was only interested in blowing things up. I suppose the others are just misguided fanatics. I've read about similar groups throughout history who were totally convinced that violence of any sort is justified as long as it supports their cause."

Thereafter, the conversation turned more personal and Armstrong was pleased to discover how easy it was for them to discuss their mutual affection. Despite that, they ended the night with an agreement to put it on hold after tonight until the mission was complete.

VII

WHERE TO GO

April 16,…. PROJECT ICARUS CONVENTION TERMED OVERWHELMING SUCCESS NEW YORK (INA)——One hundred fifty-eight of the world's most prestigious astronomers and astrophysicists wound up their convention today.

The meeting, which lasted more than a month, was termed an overwhelming success by Dr. Abdul Kadakas, pre-eminent astrophysicist. He went on to say that although there was some "friendly infighting that delayed the proceedings considerably" the outcome was "agreeable to the overwhelming majority of the delegates."

The main task of the convention was to assign destinations to the eighteen *Project Icarus* ships.

The first ship, *Columbia* is scheduled to blast off from its orbit around the Earth in May of next year. Although the ships' courses will be somewhat flexible after their first stop, it is highly unlikely they will be altered before then. Changes will only be made if a method to determine whether a star system has habitable planets from farther away than is now possible is discovered. At present, it is not expected that planets will be seen from any distance farther away than three or four light years. In view of the vast cosmic distances involved, that short a distance is considered to be "in the neighborhood," and one may as well drop in for a visit.

In addition, a lander will have to be committed to stopping much farther away than that in order to have room to brake to a stop."

We may waste some rockets," said Kadakas, "but in my opinion, we are going to find planets around every star."

The ships in the order of their arrival at the first destination, are as follows:

COLUMBIA——Alpha Centauri system (4.3 light years), CC 658 (15.8 light years). The first lander should arrive in 6 to 7 years after leaving orbit.

CONSTITUTION——Barnard's Star (5.9 LY), 70 Ophluchi (16.7 LY). The first lander will arrive nine years after leaving orbit. Barnard's star is especially interesting to astronomers because they think it is probable there are habitable planets around this wobbling star.

PRESIDENT——Wolf 359 (7.6 LY) and Ross 128 (10.8 LY) arrival about 11.4 years.

CONSTELLATION——Lalande 21185 (8.1LY and BD+20ø2465 (15.8 LY) arrival 12.2 years.

CONGRESS——Sirius (8.6 LY) and Ross 614 (13.1 LY) arrival 12.9 years.

KREMLIN——Luyten 726-8 (8.9 LY) and Tau Ceti (11.6 LY) arrival 13.3 Years.

SENATE——Ross 154 (9.4 LY). CD44ø11909 (15.3 LY) arrival 14 years.

ENTERPRISE——Ross 245 (10.3 LY) and Kruger 60 (12.8 LY) arrival 15.3years.

WASHINGTON——Epsilon Eridani (10.7 LY) and Omicron Eridani (15.9 LY)arrival 15.9 years.

WHERE TO GO 99

LENIN——Luyten 789 (10.8 LY), BD-15ø6290 (15.8 LY) arrival 16 years.

KENNEDY——Epsilon Indi (11.2 LY), CDD-49ø13515 (15.2 LY) arrival 16. 6years.

GORBECHEV——6l Cygni (11.2 LY), BD+43ø4305 (16.5 LY) arrival 16.6 years.

CHURCHILL——Procyon dual stars (11.4 LY), BD+5ø1668 (13. 1 LY) arrival 16.9 years.

ROOSEVELT——Sigma 2398 (11.5 LY), AOE 17416-6 (15.7 LY) arrival 17 years.

VOYAGER——Groombridge 34 (11.6 LY) arrival 17.2 years.

PIONEER——Lacaille 9352 (11.7 LY), CD-37ø1549 (14.5 LY) arrival17.3 years.

PARLIAMENT——Lacaille 8760 (12.5 LY) arrival 18.5 years.

CHALLENGER——Kapteyn' Star (12.7 LY) arrival 18.8 years.

Kadakas said the decision to go to the nearest stars rather than choosing those most likely to contain habitable planets was one of expedience. Any planets encountered are likely to be useful. The directions chosen will eventually lead us to the other good prospects. Aiming solely at the likely prospects would require us to wait as much as a hundred years for results, whereas the local stars, although not as romantic as black boles and quasars, are ultimately more attainable. In the other major decision made by the convention, Doctor Kadakas was given first choice of a time to use the shipboard observatories of *Columbia* and its lander, and he was quick to reserve the three week period when they are expected to be close enough to first see planets in the Alpha Centauri system.

"I am extremely honored to have that choice, and I don't feel at all selfish in taking that time," said the sixty-seven year old scientist. "If I don't take that time, I may not be around when the next ship gets close enough. But I will live long enough to see this one." All the other assignments of observatory time were made by lottery. (The complete Calendar appears on page 16)

* * * *

August 7,...PLANET DISCOVERED IN ALPHA CENTAURI SYSTEM

HOUSTON (INA) A tremendous discovery has been made aboard the spacecraft, *Columbia* yesterday. Only three days after his assigned time aboard the observatory began, Dr. Abdul Kadakas had his eye to the telescope at two thirty seven Eastern Standard time. Using a heavy filter and a mask for the star (Alpha Centauri A) he made out a small speck, which has subsequently been confirmed as a gas giant, probably as large as our own planet Jupiter. The noted astrophysicist, although extremely frail, fullfilled a prediction he made more than eight years ago that he would be alive to see the first known planet in another system.

Elated at the discovery, the doctor's health has taken a turn for the worse. According to those attending him, it's just from over-exertion and he is expected to recover. Despite his weakened state, he continues to ask for news of the planet, dubbed *Kadakas I* by his colleagues.

The discovery of the planet raises to great heights the morale and optimism of *Project Icarus* officials. According to a spokesman, the planet's position, more than a billion kilometers from Alpha Centauri A, probably means that it inscribes a figure-eight orbit about both stars of the binary system. The distance also carries more reason for optimism, because it would seem to indicate the existence of inner planets more suitable for human habitation. Dr. Kadakas' assistants will continue a round-the-clock observation of the system for more than two weeks.

* * * *

October 22,...EARTHLIKE PLANET DISCOVERED

HOUSTON (INA) The fourth planet thus far discovered in the Alpha Centauri system holds great probability of being similar to Earth, a NASA spokesman said today. The right distance from its sun Alpha Centauri A, observers have detected an aura that appears to be an atmosphere. It will probably be another month before that will be confirmed, but officials are described as "elated" at the possibility. The planet was named Kadakas IV in honor of the late Doctor Abdul Kadakas.

Kadakas was one of the prime figures in *Project Icarus*. He died in August, only one day after he discovered *Kadakas I*, the first planet in the Alpha Centauri system. The other three planets discovered in the system to date have already been shown to be incapable of supporting life similar to that on Earth. Two are gas giants like Jupiter and Saturn, and the third is just a barren ball of rock. If the planet does prove to be Earth-like, a landing is scheduled for June of next year. This will be the payoff for the millions of dollars spent on *Project Icarus* thus far.

VIII

SENDOFF

Frank Janakowski had aged well, and was proud of the three stars, which now adorned each of his epaulets. George Norton had retired and left the direction of *Icarus* to Janakowski, who would never retire if he had his way. The staff car in which he was riding lurched to the left, as his driver tried, unsuccessfully to avoid one of the numerous chuck holes which now dotted the once-well maintained Gulf Freeway in Houston.

He cursed under his breath, a reflex ingrained from years of driving, but relaxed and enjoyed the rest of the ride. He knew some of his colleagues and subordinates laughed at his penchant for the car, but he loved the fifteen-minute drive, and only made the trip by stanisplummer if he was in a hurry.

This is it! he thought nervously, *in six hours and thirty-three minutes, Eagle II would land.* Despite the fact that there were seventeen other ships boring their own individual holes in the fabric of space, and there may even be others launched in the future, the *Columbia* would signal the success or failure of *Project Icarus* for General Janakowski and many others. The landing and subsequent exploration of Kadakas IV would end it for him.

He wished he were among the members of the crew. It seemed to be a fitting way to end his love affair with the space program. He would gladly have traded places with any one of them, even knowing that the craft might crash. A fiery death on a distant planet seemed a fitting end for a tired old spaceman.

He broke off his reverie and spoke to his driver. "Gary, do you wish you could go along with them today?"

"Sir?"

"Would you like to be landing on Kadakas IV tomorrow?"

"Yes, *sir!* I've had my application in for about six months. . Oh, I suppose there's really no chance that I'd be chosen from all the others who are so qualified, but I dream about it."

"So do I!…So do I." That was to himself.

He told his driver, "Maybe you will…"

They finished the trip in silence, except for the occasional screech of poorly maintained brakes, and finally stopped in front a huge amphitheater. There were already men dragging around the huge power cables, although the ceremony was still three hours away. The general moved briskly past them and into the spacious room that housed the technicians who are the heart and soul of the space program. He allowed himself a misty eyed moment as he took in the details of the place which had become so familiar to, not only him and other NASA officials, but the whole world through the medium of television. The banks of keyboards and screens were like home to him. The historical events this room had seen ticked themselves off in his mind, flushing him with great pleasure.

Alan Sheppard's first ride.

John Glenn's first orbit.

Neil Armstrong's small step.

Jeff Graham's insertion of the first siphon on Jupiter, and his death on the teeming surface of that planet.

Launch of the *Columbia* (Was that really almost seven years ago?).

Separation of the landing craft *Eagle II*, from the *Columbia* for its coast to Alpha Centauri.

And tomorrow the greatest event of all, the first human would touch soil outside our solar system.

He forced himself back to the present and walked deliberately into the smaller adjoining room, which was slightly higher than the console room. There was a huge window allowing easy observation over the proceedings. This was his command post for the mission. He remained there studying his speech until it was time for the ceremony to begin.

Three hours later the auditorium was jammed with congressmen, industrial giants, foreign dignitaries and anyone else who could somehow wheedle an invitation. Newsmen conspicuous by their earphones, antennas and microphones swarmed throughout, gathering in clumps about anyone remotely connected with NASA. Red lights on the front of nearly thirty cameras signified that the long awaited show was already underway.

Momentarily, the din subsided as the audience discerned something was happening, and the cameras swung as if controlled with one mind. Then vigorous applause erupted, sounding much like the roar of shuttle rockets at a launch. The landing party had entered the room and was making its way to the front. Scott Armstrong led, followed by the other four men who would actually be in the landing craft when it touched down. For safety reasons the other crewmen would come up after the craft was on the ground. They followed him immediately behind, and when they'd all reached the stage they faced the crowd and acknowledged the applause.

When the noise had finally dropped off, Janakowski made his way to the podium, and unlike that day almost ten years before, he forced himself to make the dramatic pause before he began speaking. Not that he was any less eager to begin. On the contrary, this would be a moment that would make history. His speech would be replayed for decades, and he wanted it to be perfect.

"Fellow humans," he began, "today will mark the end of the beginning. For millennia, mankind has forced himself to the pinnacle of everything on Earth. He was, however, locked to this ball of rock and dust to fulfill his destiny. Today he is free! Today he is finally divorced from the muck and slime that begat him. Today, he will step into the real destiny."

The stars!"

"Think of it!"

"Man with his puny strength, at the mercy of the beasts of the wild, and the whims of nature, has defeated all that. Yes, this day is the end of the beginning.

But it is *not* the beginning of the end. It is the beginning of eternity! Here is the real heaven that the righteous will inherit. Here is the heaven, which will finally grant us freedom from fear and want."

He paused and drank from the tumbler at his elbow. He looked over the audience, savoring the moment.

"This afternoon a second Colonel Armstrong will take a small step. A step that will be *more* than a giant leap! These sixteen people seated before you are the best we could find for the mission. If you asked each of them what he or she were feeling right now, they would all place *fear* high on the list, but the highest of all will be *PRIDE* in their accomplishments. These brave people are stepping forth without hesitation into the unknown in order that the rest of us might live."

"NEVER has such a small group of humans, been willing to do so much for so many. The rest of us will owe more to them than we can possibly repay in a lifetime."

"This is THEIR sendoff and I'll leave the rest to them."

Applause rose to a crescendo as the crew once again rose to their feet. Devlin, still nursing a headache, thought the ceremony would never end.

The president was next. He was brief, mainly there to present everyone the freedom award. It was thought more prudent to award it ahead of time in the event that some might not return.

Fifteen minutes later the landing party left the auditorium followed by cameras every step of the way. When they reached the main stanisplummer, only the official NASA camera was permitted, because of space considerations and the press of bodies was much less. Even so, the networks were afforded excellent coverage of the president and General Janakowski was shaking hands with the five men who stepped inside. The door slid closed and while the men were out of sight, though this part was routine, the world collectively held its breath. The men reappeared on the television screen, with the interior of the lander for a backdrop.

The five moved weightlessly to their stations for the pre-landing checks. They were extremely meticulous, taking at least twice as long to complete the list as they had in practices. Armstrong was reluctant to leave anything to chance. Laird slid into his pilot seat and double-checked the belts.

"We're about to do it gentlemen." Armstrong's voice sounded hollow to him, but he continued, "Check your belts and let me know when you're ready."

The report always went clockwise, so Devlin was first. He checked his seat position in the observation blister, so that he would have a clear view of the landing pad he was responsible for getting on firm ground, and snapped, "Starboard OB, ready."

Benton and James then reported in sequence." Aft OB, check."

"Port OB, A-okay."

Armstrong turned to the pilot and quipped, "Kick it in gear, whenever you're ready, Jake." He had scarcely finished the sentence when Laird punched some buttons on his console and weight returned to their bodies as they felt the powerful engines sputter and catch. Retrofire slowed them in orbit and they dropped toward the marbled blue-white ball that was Kadakas IV.

It seemed like an hour before the stream of smoke and the slight added weight signaled the beginning of the atmosphere. The smoke increased as the tiles of the heat shield burned, until view of the surface below was totally obscured. Although he'd been through thirty-two landings just like this one promised to be, Jake was terrified. This time there would be no ground observers or chase planes, in case he made a mistake. He had never made an error significant enough to endanger the craft, but that didn't seem reassuring to him now.

"Altitude?"

The question was directed at Armstrong, who glanced at the altimeter, which had been calibrated for Kadakas IV.

"Eighty-eight thousand." He would continue to report altitude at ten thousand meter intervals, and when Laird requested. He kept his eyes on the digits, which were changing so fast in the lower places he couldn't read them.

"Seventy-eight."

The drop seemed just about right, so Laird relaxed and just let the gravity and the braking effect of the atmosphere do their work.

"Sixty-eight."

"Right on schedule, Skipper." Laird displayed lightness he really didn't feel, and he knew he was speaking more for the benefit of Holly Graham than Scott Armstrong.

"Fifty-eight." The intervals were noticeably longer now and it seemed like the smoke outside the craft was slackening.

Laird glanced at the hull temperature readout, and what he saw caused him to exclaim: "*Ten thousand degrees!* That's much higher than it should be, and it's rising fast."

At that rate, the whole bottom of the lander would melt if something weren't done quickly. He hit the main drive controls and felt the power surge beneath him. Armstrong looked at him with wild surprise, and he was quick to explain.

"Hull temperature is way too high. We must have lost some tiles. He followed the commander's gaze to the hull temperature gauge.

"Think you hit the power in time?" Armstrong queried, straining to read the gauge.

"Eagle II? This is Houston. Do we copy you have a problem?"

"That's affirmative, Houston. Let you know in a minute how serious."

"Altitude?" Jake had momentarily forgotten to keep track. Armstrong looked back at the altimeter and reported.

"Fifty-one."

The report surprised Armstrong. He expected that surge of power would have slowed the craft more than it had.

"Houston, this is Eagle II. We've had an overheating of the hull, and subsequent retro-firing has not slowed us as much as it should have." Armstrong looked at the altimeter again, and reported.

"Forty-nine thousand five hundred and dropping about two hundred meters per second. I'll let you know in a minute how effective the engines are."

He entered the data into the computer and waited for the display. When the data was displayed, he spoke again.

"Now at forty-eight thousand meters, with vertical speed one hundred seventy-three point eight-four meters per second. Slowing at point three-two meters per second. That will slow us to zero in nine point zero-five-seven minutes at an altitude of seven hundred eighty point seven-one meters."

Laird emitted a low whistle." I sure hope we're not over an eight hundred meter hill."

"Eagle II, we're working on the reason for your loss of thrust. Be assured we'll make sure you land well below the eight hundred meter elevation. Even if we can't fix the problem, you should be okay, but you'd better blow your heat shields and get a visual on those engines."

"Roger, Houston."

"Forty-three." Armstrong resumed the count and punched the computer again.

"Eject the heat shields, Jake."

Laird thumbed a control, and the walls to their front and below fell away, leaving them an unobstructed view of the planet. Armstrong leaned across his console until his head rested against the thick glass bubble and strained his eyes to see below.

"Looks like one and two are functioning normally." His eyes fixed on the twin torches, which seemed to extend to the surface itself.

"Aft OB? What about yours?" Benton had already done the same as Armstrong as soon as the heat shield had fallen away, but he was not rewarded with the familiar finger of flame. He looked again, trying to will its appearance.

"No dice, Skipper. Not a thing."

"Houston, Eagle II. We have a non-functioning engine."

Armstrong was agonizing and that last pronouncement did nothing to ease his mind. Right then it seemed that the only solution would be to stan the whole crew back and abort, which would mean scratching Kadakas IV as a colony. Without all three engines functioning, he knew there would be no way to set the craft down. It would drop like a rock to the surface. Oh, they might be able to generate enough thrust to slow momentarily to landing speed, but because of impurities in the fuel, precision enough for a soft landing would be impossible. Even if by some miracle the fuel remained completely pure, the engines could maintain full thrust for only a few minutes. Wear on the nozzles would rapidly reduce their power. The men might be able to survive such a crash landing, but the sensitive stanisplummers aboard certainly would not.

"Thirty-three."

"Eagle II, this is Houston. The only thing we can come up with is that when the hull overheated, the hinges to the heat shield over engine three fused, and has not allowed the shield to be ejected. Try to eject it manually by refiring the engine."

"Roger, Houston." Laird was already working the controls. If any part of the heat shield were still in place over the outlet, it would not function on automatic, but he could fire it manually unless it were completely covered. He felt a sinking feeling as the touch of the button did not produce any change in thrust.

"No luck, Houston." The craft was vibrating heavily now, and they knew the movement would increase as the vertical speed was reduced. Without the third engine, control would become sluggish and it would take great skill just to keep the craft from flipping, even with the massive gyrostabilizers.

"Twenty-three thousand. What's the hull temperature now, Jake?"

"Only a couple hundred degrees. Why?"

Armstrong ignored the query, and removed the seat belt. As he moved to the central tube Laird looked at him quizzically.

"Where are you going?"

"We've got to get that engine going, and it's obvious we're not going to get it done from here. Be alert and ready to do what I tell you."

The commander dropped through the hatchway into the engine room. He didn't know what he was going to do but he knew he had to do something. As his eyes rested on the circular hatch in the floor, it hit him.

"Jake, have them send me up a cutting torch, crowbar, ten meters of half-inch cable and a two by two sheet of asbestos, quick."

Laird had no more than complied with his wish, when Armstrong's head appeared through the hatch, looking the direction of the stanisplummer, expectantly.

The next transmission from Houston told Armstrong the director had guessed what he was planning to do. "Scott, this Frank Janakowski. I won't let you do it. It's foolhardy. I want you and your crew to abort right now. Get out of there. The mission has failed; no sense losing men over it."

"No way, General. I've come too far to fail now. The crew is on its way down, but I stay. Now send me the torch, or I try to land this thing by the seat of my pants."

"Colonel Armstrong, this is an order. I want you down, now."

"No disrespect intended, General, but you know this mission is more important to mankind than losing one man, or even two hundred. I signed on to do this job because I believe in it. I haven't even started it, and I don't intend to quit now, so I must respectfully decline to obey your order. Do I get the torch?"

"Yeah! That, a court martial, and the Congressional Medal of Honor, if you pull this thing off."

The material he'd requested appeared in the stanisplummer, and he stepped forward to pick it up, but was shouldered out of the way by James and Devlin, who hefted the equipment and followed Armstrong down to the engine room.

"What's our altitude now Jake?" He fastened the air mask around his neck and motioned for the others to go back up into the control compartment. He would open the hatch to the raw environment of Kadakas IV momentarily, and if they were exposed they wouldn't be able to return to Earth.

"Fourteen thousand," came the reply over the intercom.

James and Devlin had made no move to leave, and Armstrong gestured irritably at them.

"Jake, stabilize this thing as best you can, then you get out of here." He turned his attention to the two sergeants and glared.

"The rest of you get out of here, NOW!"

"Skipper." James shot back. "You just disobeyed a direct order from the high mucky-muck of this whole shootin' match. What makes you think I'm going to obey a mere Colonel? You need help down there, and this thing is not going to stay stable by itself. I'm staying. We need at least one other. Who'll it be?"

The other three answered in an affirmative chorus. The two sergeants put on oxygen masks and James began to undog the hatch, while Devlin checked out the acetylene torch.

Laird continued. "All right, Benton. You stay put so you can help me watch for drift. You other two give the Skipper a hand in the engine room." Armstrong continued his preparation and felt the sudden drop in pressure and increase in engine noise that signaled the hatch opening. He held his hand over his eyes to cut the glare and looped the cable around his hips. James already had the other end secured, and the two sergeants were working the asbestos sheet down through the hatch rolled into a tube. Devlin secured the upper edge of the sheet to the hinge of the hatch with a short length of twine and motioned that it was ready.

Just then they heard Laird's voice. "Ten thousand meters, Skipper, and the instruments show that the engine tubes have already worn to the point that we will not be able stop, even at sea level."

"I'm going out now, Jake. Maneuver us to the lowest place you can find to land this crate."

They were low enough now for Laird to get a vaguely familiar breathtakingly beautiful view of the landscape. On his right the ground was a beautiful blue-green that faded gradually to a yellowish tint on the horizon. To the left he could see a vast ocean and the brilliant white line, which sharply divided water from land. The white, he assumed, was beach, and he maneuvered for it.

"Nine thousand."

Armstrong took the torch from James and slung the crowbar, sword-like in his belt, and sat on the edge of the hatch, feet dangling out. The two men pulled the slack out of the cable, and without thinking of the danger, the colonel slid though the opening, feeling a slight pain in his legs as his weight shifted entirely to the cable. He was lowered out of the hatch slowly. As soon as be was out, he could see that the assessment made by mission control was correct. The hinge was fused. All he had to do was cut it free with the torch and they could fire the engine for a safe landing. His elation was short lived, however as he realized he couldn't reach the engine from his sling. The hinge was more than three meters from him. His first thought was to leave the sling and get to it hand over hand, but rationality told him that though there were handholds designed for working outside in null gravity, and though his gravity would be only some eighty-five percent of Earth normal, there would be no way he could hold on to the heavily vibrating craft with one hand long enough to cut the hinge. Not and make a clear-cut in time. He wracked his brain and could come up with nothing. He almost decided to try anyway, when he thought of a better way——if there was time.

He motioned for the two sergeants to hoist him back into the craft.

"I need some kind of metal hook, maybe a meter in length. One end will hook to the cable at my waist and the other through the handhold. Jake, tell them to send up something like that."

"Roger." They heard him repeat the request, and he again addressed the commander.

"We're below six thousand meters, vertical speed of about twelve meters a second and picking up speed. At that rate we have only about eight minutes until impact. I can give emergency thrust, but only for a couple minutes. That should give us an additional minute or so, but I'm not sure I can control the craft with only two engines."

"Put on your mask, Jake. We're coming up to get the hook now. Can you use the emergency thrust now?"

"If I do it will make regular thrust less efficient afterward because of the wear it will cause. I'd better wait until the end to lessen impact."

Armstrong had already gotten the hook and was being lowered into the open hatch again, and he yelled over the roar of the engines. "Use your own judge…" The rest of what he said could not be heard.

Armstrong reached for the handholds as soon as he was clear of the hatch and careful not to slip from the cable loop, began pulling himself toward the non-functioning engine. He was halfway there when the torch he had stuck in his belt suddenly pulled loose and fell free. The instinctive reaction of his left hand was to retrieve it, and the motion pulled his other hand off the rung, and he fell after the torch. The cable slipped and held fast, but he immediately realized the danger he was in. He was dangling below the asbestos heat shield, exposed to the full fury of the other two engines. The sergeants had reacted quickly in hauling him up, but not before he felt his face burn while the mask on his face begin to melt. He flung the mask from him as if it were poisonous and pulled himself through the hatch. Though his clothes hadn't caught fire, they had scorched. Seeing the condition of his commander, James began trying to remove the cable from his waist, but Armstrong pushed his hand away.

"I'm okay," he snapped.

"Let me go, Colonel. You're all burned." James was insistent, but the commander waved him aside and sat back in the hatch.

"How' we doing, Jake?"

"Under five minutes…vertical speed 14 meters per second."

Armstrong didn't hear the speed. He was outside again, swinging from hand to hand like a monkey, this time the torch secured in his belt. When he reached the hinge to the heat shield, he pulled the steel rod out of his belt and hooked one end to the nearest handhold and hooked the other through the loop in the cable around his hips. He bounced twice hard on the rig before letting go with his hand. With both hands free, Armstrong was able to grasp the torch and get a precise flame adjusted, so that he could cut the metal. He directed the spear of fire at the hinge. It was difficult with the wind turbulence and the increasing vibration of the landing craft to keep the focus of the flame on the same point to allow it to eat the metal. James, hanging his head through the hatch thought he'd never get it cut through. It was especially nerve wracking for him, because he could hear Laird's periodic reports of their altitude and vertical speed. Worse, his eyes were drawn irresistibly to the surface below, and his imagination made it seem to fairly leap up at him.

"Two minutes thirty seconds to impact, speed five meters per second. How's it going down there, James? I'm going to have to hit the emergency thrust pretty soon." His voice was strained, and he was hoping for a miracle.

James stuck his head back through the hatch and reported, "He's got a ways to go."

"We'll probably be going over fifty if he doesn't get it fixed. The landing gear will break like matchsticks and the engines will explode like an atomic bomb. When there are only forty seconds to go, pull the torch away from the colonel giving him time to crawl back into the craft and save him from being crushed underneath."

"One minute twenty-six seconds, speed seventeen meters per second. I'm going to hit the emergency power."

James felt a feeble boost in the thrust that supported them and Laird's voice went on. "Didn't do much good. We slowed to fourteen for a bit, but we're already back to sixteen; no seventeen. ONE MINUTE. Better get the colonel back inside."

James stuck his head back out to look. Armstrong was in the same posture, so he withdrew his head, almost feeling the ground less than a thousand meters below.

"Forty seconds and twenty meters per second. "Armstrong's fingers seemed to be the size of hams, and the vibrations of the craft doubled his lack of dexterity. He had to hold the torch with both hands and brace his left arm against the hull to get the flame to burn through the metal. It would eat a little, and a particularly strong shake would throw it out of the grooves again. It seemed hours before he'd even gotten halfway through the hinge. His wrists and arms ached, and he wanted to force the hinge with physical brute strength, but all he could do was patiently wait until the flame ate slowly through the metal. It seemed that any moment the cover should fall away. The gash the torch had made was nearly through. Just then he felt a tentative tug at the hose, and though he tried to hold on his tortured fingers would not obey and the torch fell free again.

True to his word, James jerked the hose, saw the torch fall and leaned his head out again, to see if he could help the commander into the craft. He was shocked to see the colonel still feverishly working on the engine, now with the crowbar. *My God! Is he crazy?* He thought. Then he yelled. "Colonel, you've got to come in. Though he knew the sound was swallowed up in the roar of the engine.

Resigned, he pulled his head back in just as Laird was making the report. "Twenty seconds."

James looked around startled, as Devlin bumped him out of the way to see the commanders head emerge from the hatch. He was stunned for only a second, and he leapt to help pull Armstrong inside.

"FIRE THE AFT ENGINE, JAKE!" Armstrong's yell had barely died when they felt the additional weight that told them it was working. But was it in time?

Laird worked the controls as if they had been remotely linked to Armstrong's voice. He glanced at the computer display that had been counting down the seconds to impact, and he saw that it had bottomed out at five seconds before the engine fired, but was now up twenty seconds. Maybe time to land it, he thought as he fought the controls to compensate for the overbalance of thrust. He would not be able to slow the descent to zero and have the luxury of finding another landing site if the primary was no good. Engines one and two were too worn for that, but the beach should be okay. The craft was swaying wildly, but Laird felt he had it under control.

"Come on baby!"

Armstrong came up behind him, and quickly strapped himself in next to the pilot. The display read eight seconds, and five meters per second. If it got down to three they would land softly, but he'd have to get the swaying under control.

Armstrong watched the numbers change."…five…four…three…" The speed indicator changed to four."…two…One, Brace…"

The bone-crushing jolt prevented him from completing the phrase. The craft rocked to port a little and then settled nearly vertical. Neither man was able to talk at the moment, but they both knew they had won. All they could do was lean back and bask in the glow of achievement, not to mention, allow considerably shaken nerves to settle.

"Eagle II? This is Houston."

They still couldn't talk. The call was repeated three more times with concern mounting noticeably in the voice. Finally Armstrong thumbed the switch.

"Serenity base here. Eagle II has landed."

They had already earned their money, but they would soon have much more to prove.

IX

EXPLORATION

Of course it wasn't as simple as that. The jolt was more than they had bargained for, and no one knew if the jar had damaged the stanisplummer. That would have to be thoroughly checked, and it would have been foolhardy to subject more people to the untested atmosphere on Kadakas IV. The tests would take less than three hours after the site had cooled sufficiently to go outside. The stanisplummer checked out okay, as Armstrong had predicted it would, and all of the testing equipment was ready within the twenty-five minute cool down period.

The honor of setting the first human foot on the new planet belonged of course to the commander, and Armstrong felt the same as he had on that day long ago, when he'd gone through the turnstile at Disneyland with his parents. Here, too was an adventureland; one in which the dangers were very real. This would be a step into the unknown. True. There had been many landings on other planets within the solar system, but on all those there was little chance that the astronauts would encounter life. Here, they not only had assurances that there would be life, the lush green vegetation that lined the beach gave ample evidence of that, but that vegetation was so thick, it had been impossible to explore for animals from orbit. Armstrong personally felt the landmasses were so large that they must support some form of fauna. With all the variety that existed on Earth from dinosaur to grizzly bear, he knew they could be stepping out to be a meal.

Benton had kept half an eye out the window during the preparation for disembarkation and created a stir among the crew when his voice shrilled over the intercom.

"Something moved out there! Right over there by those bushes."

This pronouncement drew the attention of all the crewmembers to the nearest observation port and riveted millions of eyes to their television sets. Of course, the audience on Earth could see nothing because none of the crew thought to direct the cameras. One had been pointed at the wood line, but nowhere near where Benton had seen the movement. The talk inside the craft was excited and reminded Armstrong of the times when he was a small boy riding in the countryside and someone pointed out a cow or a train.

"What did it look like, Captain?" Sergeant James asked.

Laird's voice interrupted before he could answer. "Over there! . . No just the wind."

"I really didn't see what it was. Just a glimpse of movement——really quick. Sort of like a shadow. Or a big bird. Something like that. Fairly large like a big dog or a deer." Benton's voice trailed off as his mind caused the creature to grow with his fear. He had to force himself not to believe the thing he saw was six feet high at the shoulder, and was all cruel fangs and talons. Reason told him something that large could not have possibly moved that fast.

"Eagle II? This is Houston. Position the cameras so we can see the wood line better."

Armstrong realized then that mission control had been trying to raise them for the last three or four minutes, so he finally touched the toggle and replied.

"Roger, Houston." And to Benton, "Bob, deploy all the cameras in the general vicinity of your movement. That will undoubtedly give them a better show than the final prep here will."

The calm statement put an immediate damper on the excitement. Although everyone remained tuned in anticipation that any moment could bring the discovery of animal life. The view outside was stark contrast depending on the direction you looked. The craft was perched squarely in the center of a glistening white sandy beach three hundred meters wide. The beach stretched nearly straight to the north and south. The surf and deep blue ocean was familiar but not quite the right color to those familiar with Earth beaches. Just a little too much greenish tint. The cloudless sky looked normal, but as the eye carried over to the line of the wood, there was a subtle hint of not quite rightness there as well. It was as if a little blue had been taken from the water and added to the trees. The artist had not mixed his color right. The view outside was breathtaking, but it seemed to be too neat and orderly. The beach ended abruptly with the quick rise of the land into what seemed to be the same type of bushes growing in a thicket. Further inland they could see individual plants of three or four meters in height, with a few reaching as high as ten or twelve. There didn't seem to be any breaks in the undergrowth like animal trails, and the lack of footprints in the sand disappointed them.

Laird broke the silence. "This looks a lot like the Oregon coast near my home town. Look, that tree looks kind of like a spruce with its scaly needles, but not quite. The only differences are the lack of driftwood on the beach and maybe the trees are a different-lighter shade of green. The waves are a little bigger, maybe because of the lower gravity? There's something missing that I really can't put my finger on…" He trailed off absorbing the view.

The crew turned back to the pre-disembarkment preparations, most of which could have probably been deferred until later, but there was one unexpected pressing task: measurement of the tide. Being forced to land at the lowest point possible had placed them squarely in the middle of a predicament, called a beach. With two stars exerting great force on the planet, not to mention a moon more than twice the size of Earth's, the tides had to be tremendous. Someone in the control room in Houston checked the positions of the stars and the satellites, as soon as he heard they would have to land on the beach, and made a startling discovery. The three would be almost in line later today and if they didn't move, they would probably have to swim. But they were going to check, and Armstrong took the task for himself.

The atmosphere was still a big question mark. Even though they had been forced to breathe the air during the descent, they would have to take precautions. The craft had already been resealed and purged of the local air. When the crew ventured outside they would be required to wear protective suits and a portable air supply for a full two weeks. After they were settled a little more, two rhesus monkeys would be placed outside and observed closely as part of the tests.

Finally the twenty-five minutes cooling period had elapsed and they were poised to go outside. All they had to do now was a final show for the home crowd, so they gathered in the engine room for that. They still had about a minute before the cameras would be turned on again, and Armstrong took advantage of the time to talk to them.

"Check your suits once more." he commanded solemnly. They had undoubtedly been checked innumerable times before, but so had the landing engines.

"It may seem like only a routine day for you because it is so like all our practices…No, actually I think we can say it looks better. This looks like a picnic spot. I want you all to remember no one has ever been here before. *EVER*! There could be anything out there, so take the security precautions seriously. Anyone who violates one of the pickiest rules, places the whole group in danger, and I will not hesitate to inflict the harshest penalty. The rules require you to remain within ten meters of your designated partner. Don't ever let me see you eleven meters apart!"

"Check and *triple* check everything! A slight mistake here could cost us our lives."

The red light on the camera in front of him went on and Armstrong knew it was activated. He stopped and looked at it expectantly. When he heard nothing, he pressed the switch on the side of the mask that was hanging around his neck and spoke into it.

"Houston? This is Serenity Base. We're ready at this end to wow you with song and dance, and amazing feats of daring do."

"Roger, Serenity. We have you go for egress from the landing craft. Anything new up there?"

"Nothing." Armstrong grew impatient at the talk, and anxious to get on with it.

"Don't forget our first worry is the tide. Look to that as soon as you're out." They could tell from the studies made when high tide would be, but there was no way of knowing how high it would get without physically measuring its advance.

"We wouldn't forget that, Houston. Let's get on with the show."

"Roger. You are now connected live."

"Colonel Armstrong," came the rumbling voice of anchorman John Tippington. "the world is waiting to hear your feelings and thoughts on this most historic occasion, but first I'd like you to fill us in on how the mission is progressing. Are there any surprises, other than the near crash landing?"

"None but those you already know about. Mainly the tide."

"Yes. We've already been briefed on that. What will you do if the tide comes too high?"

"Get a bulldozer up here and tow the lander to high ground."

"Why can't you just fly it?"

"The lander was meant to do just that——land. It can generate enough thrust for a short period of time to lift it, but it would be extremely unstable. We can't even think about that with ours. Not without a complete refitting of engines one and two. They had to fire too long in landing, and we had to use emergency thrust almost to its limit. The most thrust we could get would be out of number three, and that would only tip us on our side."

"Is moving it with a bulldozer going to present any problems?"

"It might. The lander was never intended to move on land, and the landing struts will not be strong enough for the lateral stress, so we'll have to beef them up. We also have to design some sort of skids for them so they won't just dig in and topple over. We should be all right, if we get enough time."

"Well I'm sure you'll have no difficulty with the move, if it becomes necessary. Let me direct the next question to Captain Benton."

"Go ahead, sir. I'm listening." It was clear that Benton knew what the question was going to be, and he was not sure how he was going to answer it. The gargoyle-like creature!

"Captain, tell us about the creature you saw. If that's what it was."

"Really not much to tell. I didn't see more than a quick movement out of the corner of my eye——not enough to describe the creature, or even that it was a creature."

"Could it have been a natural movement of the bushes, like wind or something like that? Sometimes our imagination plays tricks on us in stressful situations. Could it have been that?"

"I've thought about that, and maybe it was, but I have a distinct impression that something was there. My interpretation of its size…" Armstrong cut him off.

"Gentlemen. I'm going to break in here." He noticed the time for them to leave the craft had arrived. "It's time for us to go outside. We may have time for questions out there unless we're in a rush to move and you'll be able to hear us talking. There will be two cameras along in case there's something to see."

Tippington got in the last word." I know the world will join me in wishing you the best of luck, and I for one will be sitting on the edge of my seat for the next few hours."

Armstrong wondered idly when Tippington was appointed the spokesman for the whole world, as be heard the audible click that told him the connection with the newsmen was broken, and the non-committal voice of mission control came through.

"You are a go for egress, Eagle II…Mark time eleven forty-six A. M.…. Go get 'em."

It seemed to be about the same time on Kadakas IV as Armstrong took a last look out the port, before sealing his mask, and undogging the hatch. The others fastened their masks, and the rectangular hatch swung easily upward, aided by its spring loaded mechanism. Armstrong half expected the same view he had seen the first time he opened the hatch, the sight of ground miles below, and he was relieved to see smooth grainy light gray sand less than three meters away. They fastened the ladder in place and he put his foot on the top rung. He eagerly stepped the rest of the way down, but stopped on the bottom with his left foot poised ten centimeters above the sand long enough to be sure that the camera Benton was manipulating on an extension was in position to record this historic moment. His faint smile could easily be seen through the faceplate as he placed his foot deliberately on the ground and pronounced.

"In 1969, another Armstrong said. 'This is one small step by man…One giant leap for mankind.' *This* step is equally small, but its import to mankind is so great as to make it impossible to compare to leaps, or even voyages."

"Congratulations, Eagle II." The celebration in the control room came over the open microphone.

"We have the president on the line…Go ahead sir."

"Congratulations, men. The debt the world owes you can scarcely be repaid. As you said, Colonel Armstrong, this moment does indeed go beyond any leap. In fact it far surpasses any Earthly event, save the creation of intelligent life by the Almighty. May He guide you in your service to your fellow man."

"Thank you sir. We'll do our best."

"I only wish I were there with you. I cannot imagine a more exciting time. I'll not hold you any longer. I understand you have some urgent business with rising water. Good luck."

All of the crew except James, who would stay with the craft, were outside by now, and Armstrong was leading them in the direction of the water. Benton and

Devlin had moved off to the right and left with their side arms drawn protectively. Armstrong's senses were finely tuned to the environment. He couldn't remember the last time he was so aware of every minute detail. As on Earth, there was little differentiation of the beach sand. Here and there he noticed odd-shaped grains, maybe the carcass of some long dead shellfish. He made a mental note to study some of them more closely after setting the tide marker.

Everything about the beach seemed so familiar to him, but there was…something. He couldn't quite put his finger on it. White sand…probably some sea creatures…

Over there!

A movement!

His attention was drawn to a point about ten meters away where a multilegged whitish creature about two centimeters across was making its way in spurts toward a small hole in the sand. The rest of the party saw the *insect* or *crab*? At about the same time and Laird got a camera focused on it before it vanished into the hole. There was no keeping anyone's attention on the mission at that moment. Like little children, they were drawn to the spot where the creature had disappeared. Devlin dropped to his knees and began shoveling the sand away from the hole with his hands. Even Armstrong was briefly caught up in the excitement, but then he felt their vulnerability.

"On your feet Sergeant, and get back to your post," he snapped. "Captain Benton, we have been training too long to expect this kind of lapse in security. See that it doesn't happen again."

"Yes sir," replied Captain Benton.

Armstrong knew he wouldn't say anything to the sergeant. Everyone had let his guard down for a moment.

The group reformed and moved once again toward the water, startling more of the creatures on the way. Laird had the camera on them. They ranged in size up to nine or ten centimeters, and were mottled gray and white in color, blending almost perfectly with the sand. Their shape was more like a stubby sow bug than a crab; domed, with all the legs under the shell. As the men approached the shoreline they noticed the surf was as high as that on the Pacific Coast of America on a rather rough day. They spent no time examining the water but were all business in their procedure for measuring the tide. While the two security men kept watch right and left, Armstrong moved the numbered surveyor's pole to the point where the strongest wave lost its momentum, and placed it while Laird used the transit farther up the beach. He took three sightings, backing toward the landing craft between each, before finally giving the thumbs up signal to his commander. Laird had the stake in place by the time the others got to him. It remained only to check the stake in ten minutes, and if the bottom were awash, the craft would have been moved. They used the time to explore that general area of the beach. The little sow crabs were everywhere, perfectly still and invisible until one of the party got too close and sent them scuttling.

Armstrong still felt there was something missing. Everything seemed normal——the water, complete with foam; wispy seaweed in the water, numerous seashells, not only of the sow crabs, but also of other life. But there was something missing...Scarcely six minutes had passed, when the first wave brushed the stake, but it became obvious to Armstrong they would have to move the craft minutes before. They had scarcely three hours until waves would wash freely over its footings.

James already had the vast doors to the stanisplummer open, and they could see several girders and beams on the ground by the lander and more still in the stanisplummer, as they approached. They watched as he wrestled another beam to the door and dropped it on top of the disorderly heap where it would wait along with the others for assembly. The three security men had practiced putting the crane together numerous times before, but their fastest time had been slightly over four hours. Armstrong and Laird would have to help, and they would have to take some shortcuts, but Benton had assured them that it was possible to get it done within three. Of course they had to get it done in less than that, because the five tons of spacecraft would have to be moved within that time also.

They got right to it, heaving heavy beams like longshoremen. It took three stanisplummer loads before they had sufficient parts to construct the crane. But soon after that it began to take shape. The girders and rigging were on in less than an hour and forty-five minutes and Armstrong was optimistic. It remained only to lower the huge diesel engine into place and connect it. While the security men were doing that Laird and Armstrong, with the aid of jacks, attached long heavy braces to the landing struts to reinforce them and manhandled the four skids into place. They had just finished the last one, when the deep-throated roar of the diesel engine greeted their ears. Armstrong glanced at his watch, but he needn't have, for just then a particularly strong wave tugged at his ankles, and he knew they had only minutes remaining before they would have to abandon the rescue effort and hope to salvage a functional stanisplummer during the next low tide. Not only were stanisplummers sensitive and unable to take that kind of abuse, but the heavy surf and current would probably carry the craft beyond their reach. True, they wouldn't be totally abandoned without the main stanisplummer, the lander carried a smaller spare, but exploration would be seriously curtailed, not to mention the comfort of the explorers.

The prefabricated buildings could not be sent up in the small one, so they would have to make do with tents until a larger stanisplummer could be constructed.

Just then panic drove through his brain like a knifepoint. The *spare stanisplummer*! No one had thought to unload it! He could see the bulldozer being lowered by the crane, now as the waves washed almost to his knees. Should he divert the dozer to save the backup and hope they had time to save the lander afterward? He could see that saving the craft would be a near miracle if he did that, but they might not be able to save it anyway. The dozer was down now, and James was already on top of it, going through the motions that would start its powerful engine, while Benton and Devlin worked feverishly to detach the crane hook.

The decision would have to be made before they finished their task. There might still be time to save the backup stanisplummer if he gave the order now. Someone would have to get back aboard, attach the hook to the backup, which would be wrenched from its tie downs and outside. Then they would have to go back for the generator that powered it, hoping it was fueled and ready. It was clear to Armstrong by now that if he chose to save the backup, there would be no saving the lander.

The water would be so deep as to drown the engine of the bulldozer by the time they got back. His *indecision* made the decision for him, and he felt a fleeting relief, partly with the knowledge that the dilemma was past him and partly with the realization that was his choice anyway. His training had taught him the mission was of paramount importance. The two landing pads on the near side of the craft were lifted clear of the sand by the crane at the same moment that the engine of the bulldozer caught and sputtered into life. The three officers got their arms wet to the shoulders sliding the skids under the pads. Devlin lowered the craft while James maneuvered the dozer to the other side. It would have to be lifted with the dozer blade because the crane was not mobile. They managed to horse the skids under on that side despite heavy surf that made footing treacherous and twice sent waves breaking over the men's heads knocking them down as they bent over.

All that remained was to attach the craft to the dozer and tow it to higher ground. Devlin was down off the crane by then helping the ground crew. James thought any moment would bring a wave that would wash over the cowling and drown the big diesel. It seemed to take forever to get the tow cable attached, and the men on the ground now had to hold on to the struts to prevent being swept away. The heavy surf was making it impossible to attach the third cable. Waist deep in the water between the waves, the four men fought a losing battle with the strand that had seemed to have come to life in the form of a giant python. Time and time again they seemed to have beaten the undertow and almost had it fastened, only to have a powerful wave batter it loose again. Finally Armstrong conceded that it would not work, and ordered the others to high ground, while he leaped over the tread to usurp James' position atop the dozer. As the four men struggled out of the surf, Devlin noticed the dozer was not following them. It was headed out to sea.

"What the hell is he doing? Committing suicide?"

"He might as well," someone replied, "we're all dead men anyhow."

They could all clearly see the dozer was on the other side of the craft with the waves breaking clear over the top of the engine cowling. Miraculously the engine continued to run. He was going to try to *push* the lander to safety.

"He'll break the thing into a million pieces." Devlin was a defeatist.

It was James who had the most confidence. "No, that thing is braced pretty well. He might make it, if the dozer isn't drowned first, and he can stay in the driver's seat.

"It's moving!" They could all see the drunken swaying of the craft, as it did indeed seem to inch toward them, and then came on steadily.

"With all that wave action, one of the struts will dig in and dump the whole thing in the drink." Leave it to Devlin to be the eternal pessimist.

The craft had moved about ten meters toward them, and he didn't look so certain.

"It's going to work!" Laird yelled triumphantly.

Just at that moment as if some malevolent god heard his exclamation, the lander tilted crazily toward them, and almost toppled before Armstrong could stop the dozer. He had gained a little against the tide, but now it began to look as if he'd lost. He frantically threw the machine into reverse gear, backed off, and moved around the lander. For a moment it seemed to the observers that he had given up and was fleeing for his life, but he turned abruptly, and lowered the blade into the water. They could see he was doing the only logical thing he could——try to dig out the front pads. He made two passes in front, and went around back again to resume the push. As he made contact with the spacecraft, it shuddered momentarily, and leaned as it fought the sand, but then broke free and moved toward the shore once again. This time it worked and the men cheered as the craft emerged from the surf and continued inland over dry sand. Armstrong did not stop until the craft was clearly above the high tide mark, and within five meters of the wood line.

This would be their base camp.

X

DOWN

Though eager to continue the exploration, the crew was totally exhausted, and Armstrong put General Janakowski's suggestion into orders. It was late afternoon by then, and extensive exploration would take much longer than they had light left to them anyway. It was strictly forbidden for anyone to go outside after dark.

Except for James, who had drawn first watch, they all found space for a cot in the control room or engine room and quickly went to sleep.

Armstrong fought that sleep for about ten minutes thinking; first almost out loud. *Would Jack O'Niell have approved his performance today?* Jack O'Neill was the wisecracking phony colonel on that old television series *Stargate SG-1*. As a kid Armstrong had loved the series and, despite the improbability of its basic premise——Stargate technology had been stolen by a malevolent parasitic race of aliens who took control of human bodies and posed as the ancient gods of the Egyptians to control the rest——he continued to identify with the sharp-tongued colonel. He was pleased that his own race of humans had possessed the intellect to create its own stargate and didn't have to rely on technology stolen from some mythical ancient lost race.

He sought to get some of his initial impressions down on paper.

1. No footprints on the beach——washed away by the tide??

2. No creatures larger than sow crabs.

3. Camouflaged sow crabs. He underlined the word camouflaged three times, tearing the thin sheet on the last swipe.

Why are they the same color as the sand if there are no predators? He took a long look out the transparent blister that faced the ocean, while the feeling he'd had earlier returned. His eyes were forced by the feeling toward the surf, now barely thirty meters away. It should be pretty close to high tide.

He tore his eyes from the wild scene, breaking an almost hypnotic trance, and wrote on the bottom of the sheet in large block letters: *SOMETHING'S WRONG?* As if to emphasize that suspicion, he drew concentric ovals around the question as he stared at the two words.

At last he shrugged, rose to his feet and went to the bunk. He fell asleep almost immediately.

*   *   *   *

It was after dark when Benton woke Devlin for his watch. The sergeant's first thought was to get something to eat.

"Houston? This is Eagle Two. What's on the menu for tonight?"

The bored voice of the duty officer came immediately, as if he'd been waiting for Devlin to ask that question.

"Anything you want tonight. Benton and James got steaks from Sardi's. How's that sound?"

"Roger, Houston. That sounds great. That you, Jones?"

"Roger. What kind of steak you want?"

"Check and see what they've got good tonight. Okay?"

It took Jones about ten minutes to check with the restaurant, so Devlin used the time to make his first look outside. The night was extremely dark. There were stars, appearing not much different from how they looked from Earth, so it wasn't overcast. He supposed the moon hadn't had time to rise. He hit the toggle in front of him and the shock of the floodlights made him squint at first, but his eyes adjusted quickly. With the aid of the powerful lights, he could see more than a hundred meters inland and the same distance in either direction along the beach. He would have to go to one of the other blisters to see the ocean, but this one was determined to be the most critical. If there were dangers on this planet, they were expected to come from land. He had become so engrossed in his surveillance that he jumped when the voice of the duty officer interrupted him.

"Eagle Two? This is Houston. The New York cut is the one they're pushing tonight."

"Sounds okay. Make it medium rare with thousand island and sour cream on the potato. Thanks, Houston."

"Roger."

It was more than twenty minutes before the meal arrived, hot and steaming. He used the time to look through the other ports, but he couldn't wait to sink his teeth into the steak. It was as good as advertised, and he was sorry when it was all gone, but he pushed the dirty dishes into the trash bin, and made the rounds of the observation points again before settling down into the one facing inland. He spent the rest of his watch gazing through the transparent face of the blister and engaging Jones in small talk.

"You been to the Moon casinos lately?"

"Nah. I can't afford them, and the wife keeps me pretty well tied down at home."

"A bunch of us went there last night. Those places get better all the time..." He told about his visit, richly embellishing the details. *He* had rejected the blond; the vacuum cleaner had been *his* idea and if they hadn't gotten caught, he had three women waiting to spend the night with him. Oh well, they would just have to wait until he got back. He had gotten so caught up in his story, that when the dark shape moved quickly across in front of him, he had been slow to switch the lights on.

"Whoa! There's something out there!" He was too late to see what it was, but he got a distinct impression of something large, flying and *scary*.

There was no point in waking the others, so he entered a brief report of the sighting in the log, and left the lights on until he was satisfied the thing wasn't going to return.

✶ ✶ ✶ ✶

Birds! The thought jolted Armstrong wide-awake. He had been dreaming about being on a beach, and the air had been filled with gulls wheeling and emitting their mournful cry. Somehow his dream had become connected to his conscious thoughts about the present situation. He suddenly knew what was wrong with the beach on Kadakas IV. *There were no birds*! The low gravity here should have invited some kind of creature to fly. It was much too simple to reason that birds had not evolved here, for if that were the case, why were the sow crabs camouflaged? Freak of nature? He knew better than that. The odds against that happening were astronomical. Animals developed survival mechanisms by natural selection. The ones with the right coloring were safe, while others were not allowed to live long enough to mate because some predator would eat them.

It didn't make sense. There were no tracks on the beach made by ground-dwelling predators, and even if they did exist the camouflage would do no good against them. There had to be birds here! Or at least something that flies and eats crabs! He decided he'd leave that puzzle for the scientists to sort out, and got up and went to the observation port where Laird was lounging doing his watch.

"Got the log, Jake?"

The sudden noise startled Laird, but he reached the notebook to his boss.

"How soon do I go on?"

"Another fifteen minutes or so. Couldn't sleep, huh?"

"I did rather well until a few minutes ago, when I finally figured out what's wrong with this place."

"What do you mean? I didn't notice anything wrong. This planet is beautiful." Laird had a puzzled look in his eye.

Armstrong ignored the question. "Let me bounce something off you. I was going to wait until Stauffer came up before I went any further with it, but it's really got me puzzled. I don't know very much about evolution, but it seems to me that there has got to be some kind of bird here that eats those crabs, because their camouflage is so good. But that's exactly what bothered me about this place. No birds anywhere around. Have you ever been to a beach where there were no birds?"

"Now that you mention it, no. That doesn't mean anything though. There could be any number of explanations for that. Maybe they fly in flocks, and this just doesn't happen to be their time for this part of the beach." Laird grinned slightly before he went on. "Or maybe they only come out at night. Look at this entry in the log." While he was talking he riffled the pages of the notebook, and his finger came to rest on the item that was initialed by Devlin.

Armstrong's brow knitted as he read the two scrawled sentences, and he scratched behind his ear before he ventured a query.

"Have you seen anything?" The obvious answer hit him as he asked it. If Laird had seen anything he would have said so right at the beginning.

"Not a thing. And I've been straining pretty hard to see out there, but as far as I know there is nothing out there but sow crabs." He reached his upturned palm toward the bubble in an expansive gesture.

Armstrong followed the movement with his eyes and then deliberately reached across Laird with his left hand and threw the switch to the floodlights. The two men stared in silence for a few minutes and Armstrong turned the lights off again.

"You might as well turn in, Jake. I would have only ten more minutes rest anyway."

Laird was so tired he welcomed the suggestion, and immediately left the commander staring into the darkness. The blackness of the night began to soften, and he expected that was due to the rise of the moon. The source of the light was to his left, so he got to his feet and went to the north observation port. The moon had already risen half its diameter by the time he got there. It was full and magnificent, and seemed to be much more than twice the size of the one he was familiar with.

"There you are, beautiful and twice as big as life," he murmured through slitted lips. "You make everything seem safe and serene. Is that your way of trapping us, Kadakas IV? Double everything: the beauty, *and* the danger."

* * * *

The entire crew was up and had breakfast out of the way at first light, ready to put in a full day. If they intended to have comfortable quarters for the following night it *would* be full. Clearing a large area for a compound, construction of three prefabricated buildings and a watchtower, fencing the compound, waste disposal pits, power supplies, and stanisplummers.

After breakfast Colonel Stark and the two other security men joined them on the planet to aid in the numerous projects. Everyone was aware of Devlin's sighting of the previous night and had put that information together with Benton's from the day before. They all assumed that *something* did exist, and the more they talked the bigger and more frightening it got. Fuel was added to the fire when someone had badgered Benton enough that he finally released the image he had in his mind.

"Well, it seemed to be large," he ventured. "Maybe like a great dane——gangly looking legs like that too…"

He hesitated until he was prodded on, and he shrugged and whipped out. "Well. Kind of like a gargoyle."

No one laughed, so encouraged, he continued. "You know one of those things that are half lion and half vulture, or something in the medieval legends, and are perched on a lot of old buildings."

No one spoke for a long time.

Armstrong broke the chilled silence. "We've got daylight. Let's go outside." It was thirteen hours and actually the sun (Alpha Centauri?) was just beginning to break the eastern horizon.

Time had been modified on Kadakas IV because of the different length of the day. With a nineteen point eight hour rotation period, the twenty-four hour Earth clock was unsuitable to schedule work by, so they had settled on a twenty-hour clock, and decided to run it in reverse, so that they would have a quick reference to sundown. Sundown was zero hours or twenty hours and the seven-hour period of darkness made it thirteen at daybreak. The hours were the same precise length as those on Earth and each crewman's digital watch could be converted to Greenwich mean time at the touch of a button. Every three days the watches would automatically be set back an hour to make up for the difference.

Outside the work became routine. They had to build another crane. Although the tide had gone back out and left the first one on dry ground, its engine was flooded and sand had invaded its crankcase. In addition, the receding tide had undermined and toppled it over. It would be much easier to build a new one and salvage the old one when they had time. Once the crane was in operation, another bulldozer and a trailer were brought up to transport heavy parts to the base site some one hundred meters inland. James was already using the original dozer to clear the two hundred meter square that would be necessary for their compound. By lunch time (seven local time) one building, the men's bunkhouse, was complete. It looked exactly like a doublewide mobile home without wheels——which is essentially what it was.

Stark ached to go exploring, but he knew it was going to be several days before he would be allowed to do that. This day was warm and beautiful, and if it hadn't been for his military training, he probably would have long since lost his vigil, and been caught up in some daydream. He checked the air tank he'd brought with him. Plenty left until Laird relieved him in an hour. He felt himself looking forward to that relief, knowing the afternoon labor would make time go faster, bringing him closer to adventure time. He glanced to his left and saw that the vegetation was a little more diverse, and the ground less even. To the northeast he could see a low mountain that seemed to have vegetation all the way to its summit, and a few other less prominent hills.

Catching slight movement on the ground about ten meters away, he disconnected the hose from the large air tank, and moved to investigate, more out of curiosity than concern. The source of the movement was readily apparent. There, going in and out of a quarter-size hole in the ground, were many ant-like creatures. They had segmented bodies, like ants, but only four legs. They even seemed to fill the same ecological niche for eight or ten of them were valiantly straining to haul the dead body of another four-legged insect into the hole. Stark found himself staring, fascinated by the colony, when he remembered the camera he'd left by the main air tank. He stepped back for it and revealed his find to mission control.

Just then, as he bent to get the camera, the most God-awful sound he had ever heard pierced the background rumble of the construction machinery. It was a cross between a screech and a moan and was much more chilling to him than anything heard in a horror movie. The noise seemed to come from all around him, and he looked frantically to the right and left for its source. *Was it his imagination? Maybe someone else heard it? Probably not mission control, because my mike is inside my mask.*

But he had to ask! "Houston, this is Eagle II. Did you hear that?"

"This is Houston. That's a negative. We didn't hear anything." Armstrong's voice came through then, sounding concerned.

"What's wrong, Jim?"

"I thought I heard a strange noise." His hand was trembling.

"Did you hear anything?"

"With these diesels running over here, I doubt I could hear anything if you sat next to me and screeched in my ear. Bob, you hear anything?"

There was a crackle and a pause as if Benton was trying to activate the toggle to the microphone. "I didn't hear anything either, but if it was near Stark, the engines would drown it out for me, too." The captain had sentry duty on the south side of the compound.

During this exchange, the panic Stark had initially felt subsided somewhat, but his eyes and drawn gun still roamed the panorama in front of him with more frequency than before.

After ten minutes or so, the sound had lost much of its frightening quality in his memory. *What would be the reaction of someone who heard a screech owl for the first time, or for that matter, the protest of a housecat when its tail had been stepped on?*

He hooked back up to the main tank and continued his surveillance without incident until his relief. That relief came at six, just after noon. As he walked back to the compound, he could see that the work of constructing the buildings was proceeding much faster now that everything had been unloaded and the whole crew was free to assemble parts. They had nearly completed the construction of the second building——-the mess hall and female bunkhouse——and it looked liked they would finish on schedule. It would only depend upon the tests that he would do this afternoon to decide whether the scientists could come to the planet in the morning.

Stark first went to the landing craft, where he and Miller lowered a four-wheel-drive pickup truck to the sand. A medium sized stanisplummer in the bed was transported and unloaded inside the bunkhouse. There would be several more of these later——one for each of the buildings, and several backups. These had specially designed interiors that would be used extensively for local transportation from the helicopters and HUMMVEEs that would come down later. But today they would be used to transport furniture and test material. Stark sent Miller outside to work with the rest of the crew and set to work himself.

The first breathing arrivals were the two rhesus monkeys that Stark thought would be the most important test. It was simple. They were put outside to live or die. The other experiments involved soil, air, water, plant and animal samples (he had managed to capture two of the sow crabs and some of the insects). Earth samples would be exposed to these, and the results recorded. Stark did not really know what results were expected. His instructions were simply to mix the samples in various strengths, and write down changes in color and texture every ten minutes or so. Biologists on Earth would analyze these observations.

While he made his observations, Stark spent the waiting time making the bunkhouse livable. Ten by fifteen meters, the room was an open bay, which had showers and lavatory on one end in the manner of a one-story army barracks. Enjoying physical labor of a kind he hadn't engaged in since his college days when he'd worked part time as a mover, he soon had all the crewmen's bunks and lockers into place. It didn't look much like home, but it would have to do for at least a month. Periodic looks out the windows told him that work on the rest of the camp was progressing at a pace better than expected. The other two buildings looked complete. The women's quarters and mess hall was directly across about ten meters of freshly smoothed earth (or should it be called kad?), and the lab——probably the most important building-was east of both of them by more than thirty meters. Within that thirty meters he could see the cinder-block foundation of the watchtower that would go up later, and beyond the lab Devlin and Caglin were driving metal posts into the ground next to the great rolls of chain-link fabric that would soon surround the compound, topped by six sharp strands of barbed wire.

Stark glanced at his watch and saw that he had a few minutes until the next checks. Breathing an audible sigh of relief, he lay down on the nearest bunk and closed his eyes. The sudden inactivity allowed his mind to return to the scare he'd gotten earlier, and he couldn't shake the foreboding that came over him. He reasoned, as he thought earlier, that it probably came from some benign creature whose only defense was that chilling cry——probably like a skunk with a vocal odor. At any rate, he thought, if it is dangerous, the fence will keep it out. They would be safe. But he couldn't shake the image of something with vicious rending fangs, and he was glad when it came time for checking the experiments again.

He made those quickly, reported his observations to mission control and left the bunkhouse. About thirty meters of fence was up, and he could see Benton supervising the construction of the guard tower. Twenty meters tall, it was made entirely with prefabricated sections. When it was finished it would look like a miniature version of an airport control tower. The work had progressed so satisfactorily that they had finished everything they'd had planned for the day with time to spare.

Armstrong gathered everyone except James, who had drawn the first shift in the unfinished watchtower, together in the bunkhouse as the light began to wane.

"God it's great to get out of that damned mask! Why don't we just stop wearing those things, Colonel, I noticed those two monkeys outside seem happy as larks, and I haven't felt sick or anything from the air I breathed while we were landing. In fact I never felt better in my life."

"I agree with Devlin, Skipper. Those masks are a pain in the ass. I'm starting to get a rash around my chin." Although Miller outranked Devlin, he had an unreasoning respect for his junior, and usually followed his suggestions.

"You're right. They are uncomfortable. More than once I wanted to rip the thing off, but we've stood it for two days now, and we can manage it for the rest of the time. This is not Earth. Remember, no matter how safe it looks, this place is totally alien to us. If we take off the masks now, we may be all laid up with allergic reactions that could kill us. Let's give it the required time and let the experts tell us when it's safe."

"But that doesn't make sense. Colonel. No disrespect intended. If there is something in the air up here that can kill us, they're not gonna let us come back to Earth and spread it down there. I, for one, would rather die now, than have to wear one of those goddamn masks for the rest of my life. Especially knowing that some time the germ or whatever it is will get us no matter how we try to prevent it." Devlin was adamant.

It's during times like these, thought Armstrong, *when the democratic system shows its greatest weakness. The Russians have the right idea. They wouldn't have to contend with this. Their soldiers are trained to follow orders without question.* Devlin's argument would be hard to counter, and Armstrong knew the rest of the crew was waiting to see how he handled the situation. From long experience, he knew this discussion was not about the comfort of the masks; it was a direct challenge to his authority. He was also aware that Devlin knew he was within bounds in making the challenge. It was a time-honored U. S. military tradition, and Devlin seemed the type who had succeeded in the ploy before.

What Armstrong said now would make the difference whether he could really be in control, or in name only. To carry the discussion further would only prolong the challenge, with Devlin gaining strength and allies at every turn. To summarily put him down could have a similar effect. All of this was in the commander's mind, but he paused only a moment before replying.

"I understand what you are saying, Sergeant Devlin, and it makes sense. But I'm going to wait for the judgment of the experts on this. Now let's get on with the reason for this meeting." He paused poignantly, meeting Devlin's eyes with the message that clearly conveyed: *Say anything more and I'll rip your heart out.*

Armstrong hoped he got the message. "Let's have the progress reports. Jake, you first."

Laird was doodling on a note pad. "You saw how far we got, Colonel. The whole compound was fenced and secured less than a half hour ago. All the buildings are up, but this is the only one finished on the inside. Everything went exactly the way it did in the practices."

"Benton."

"Same to report, sir. The guard tower is up, but without all the electronic equipment and sensors we will have tomorrow, and there are only three floodlights on the perimeter so far. The fence will be electrified tomorrow."

"Stark."

"Tests all concluded with the data given to mission control, and you see how it is in here."

Armstrong got to his feet, more because the small of his back began to hurt from the exertion of the day and the lack of a back rest on the bunk, than to create a presence.

"Well, gentlemen," he said after a moment. "Our training has paid off, and we're right where we are supposed to be. Now I think we need to spend a little time talking about the sound you heard, Jim. Can you describe it?"

Everyone had been waiting for this, and though the room had not been noisy before, the silence seemed to thicken while they waited for Stark to speak.

"It was like no sound I ever heard before. Sort of a cross between a moan and a screech, and it seemed to have come from everywhere at once." He paused for a moment as if trying to collect his thoughts and then leaned forward placing his elbows on his knees. "The sound seemed to go right through me."

No one spoke for a minute, and the foreboding grew to almost intolerable levels, when it was broken by Armstrong's voice.

"There's not much more we can say about that. It may or may not be connected to the creature Benton and Devlin saw. More than likely it belongs to something as small and innocuous as a raccoon."

The silence remained.

"Well congratulations on a day well spent. Let's turn in."

The meals were again ordered from mission control, and they sat on the edge of their bunks and ate. There was some small talk. But none included discussion of gargoyles. It was as if they had made a tacit agreement, and with that agreement came the hope that whatever they had on the planet with them would simply disappear.

*   *   *   *

That sound! Armstrong sat bolt upright in his bed. Had he dreamed it? Just then the stab of brilliance hit the back of his eyes as someone turned on the light, and he realized that everyone was talking at once.

He hadn't dreamed it! The others had heard it, too!

"What the *hell* was that?" Devlin's voice was the first discernable among the confused babble. They all quit talking and looked at Stark inquiringly.

"Yes, that was the sound I heard," Stark said rising to his feet. He glanced at his watch——fifteen fourteen.

"Who's on watch?"

"Caglin relieved me at fifteen hundred," put in Devlin. "Do you think he saw the thing?"

Armstrong went to the intercom on the table near the main door without bothering to put on a robe. He pushed the toggle and said into the air:

"Caglin? This is Colonel Armstrong, did you hear that?" The wait seemed interminable, and when Caglin didn't answer, Armstrong depressed the switch again and repeated his question with more urgency. Caglin's voice came through almost immediately, to everyone's obvious relief.

"Sorry to take so long to answer, Colonel. I thought I saw something near the fence, and I didn't want to lose it. I guess it was nothing though."

"What do you mean?"

"When the scream came, I was so startled I didn't do anything for a minute. When I turned on the floods, I didn't see anything and I still don't. Except for the shape on the fence. It's out of the light some, and hard to see. Probably just a bush."

Armstrong got the location of the object from Caglin, and he and Benton dressed to go outside. They walked cautiously in the direction given them by Caglin. They were still more than thirty meters from the fence when the portable light Benton carried showed clearly what the "object" was. A hole in the fence! One and a half meters high by a meter wide, and the broken wire was bent *outward*.

XI

GARGOYLES

On Kadakas IV it was almost daylight, but to General Frank Janakowski in Houston it was nearly midnight when the insistent ring of the telephone prodded him awake. He knew immediately it was something about *Project Icarus*. Most likely bad news or they wouldn't call him this late. All his senses became alert as he picked up the receiver.

"Janakowski here."

A voice he didn't recognize came through from the other end. "Sorry to wake you up, sir. This is Captain Arnold the duty officer. Something's happened on Kadakas IV that I felt you'd want to know about."

The pause made the general impatient.

"Well?" he barked.

"Sir. I don't know exactly what, but apparently they've come upon some kind of creature on the planet that could be very dangerous. Colonel Armstrong says he doesn't think we ought to send up the scientists until he's found out more about it."

"What happened? I thought they had all the fencing up. That should keep any kind of animal from threatening them."

"They do sir, but whatever it was went through the fence."

Janakowski ended the conversation, got dressed, and not wanting to take the time for his usual ride in the car, went to the stanisplummer. By the time he arrived, scientific members of the expedition had already assembled. They had been briefed about the delay, and there was fire in their eyes. *Why must people like these, Janakowski wondered, be so willing to endanger their own lives when confronted by something like this?* He had no doubt, that if asked point blank to volunteer to become a guinea pig with a ninety nine-percent probability of mortality, none of them would refuse. Now that they were about to be denied that dubious honor, though some showed visible relief, most had their backs up and were ready to fight that decision. Maybe it was a sense of false bravado, but he felt sure that the major reason was suspicion that if they didn't go now, some excuse would surface for them not to go at all. Some of them may have even harbored the thought that the crisis was *made up* just to prevent their adventure.

Stauffer was the first to speak, and as usual, he said exactly what was on his mind.

"General! We are being told that we may not be able to go up on schedule, because there is some kind of dangerous animal up there. I'm a *biologist*. A biologist *studies* animals! If you didn't expect there to be animals up there, why was I supposed to go at all?"

Janakowski was frank, his face showing faint amusement.

"If this animal is dangerous and we send you up there, you might end up studying him from inside."

Stauffer was not deterred, and hard defiance etched his features.

"All the more reason to send me. I have a great deal of experience handling dangerous animals. I have been in Africa, Asia, and South America, and captured the worst known creatures."

The general's response was quick and confident. He had felt the entire expedition should have been military and had little use for the undisciplined scientists, so felt little need to salve Stauffer's feelings.

"That's the key, Doctor. *Known!* What we're dealing with is very unknown. Those soldiers up there are best qualified to deal with the unexpected. Perhaps when more is known about the creature, you will be just the man to deal with it. First we've got to find out what we are dealing with, and if we have to fight it, then we can choose our weapons wisely."

Stauffer was about to retort. He opened his mouth slightly then closed it again when he realized he had no counter to Janakowski's logic. The ensuing silence was broken by a feminine voice at the rear of the group, calm and steady.

"If you expect to fight this thing, then you must expect casualties. None of the men up there are doctors, and you can't bring the injured back to Earth for treatment."

Janakowski had already thought about that, and his answer was ready. "That is very true Dr. Yeager, but we will not put you up there until there's a need. You will be able to respond from here just as quickly as you would from base camp on Kadakas IV, but be ready to go on a moment's notice."

She nodded her head satisfied and Janakowski looked at the other faces for argument. They hadn't softened much from the way they looked when he first entered the room, but they had either run out of arguments for the moment, or just decided he wasn't listening. He hoped it was the former, because he needed the full cooperation of these people.

* * * *

On Kadakas IV, the mood was one of excitement and foreboding. It was like the primitive feeling of expectancy that our ancestors must have felt when preparing for the hunt——like Indians going out for deer, but not knowing whether they would be attacked by a rival tribe or grizzly bears. This modern hunting party would have an advantage in that they would be mounted on all terrain vehicles and have the ease of instant escape.

The vehicles were designed especially for the mission. They were fully enclosed four-wheel drive HUMMVEEs, equipped with winches to pull themselves out should they become bogged. The interior was a stanisplummer, so that with the flick of a switch, they could be at base camp should danger threaten. The HUMMVEEs would be used exclusively for close-in transportation, while the longer distances would be covered by stanisplummer equipped UH-60 Blackhawk helicopters. The helos would have to be assembled, however, because they were too large for the freight stanisplummer whole, and they would not be ready for a day or so. Armstrong felt the puzzle of the creatures must be solved as soon as possible so he decided to go out that day with two HUMMVEEs, while the remainder of the crew assembled the aircraft. Armstrong himself would take James with him and head almost due north, and Benton and Caglin would go northeast. They would travel slowly, keeping in constant communication with and ready to support one another. At dusk they would stan back to base camp, leaving the HUMMVEEs secured where they were. It was not quite full light yet, but they had already finished breakfast and were lingering over coffee engaged in that sort of foreplay that precedes an adventure, some wishing they were going along and others wishing they weren't——both hiding their feelings so well.

"You guys are probably not going to see anything all day long and be bored to death. Here, at least I can do something worthwhile. We get those choppers together, we can really see something of this chunk of rock," went one argument. Its rebuttal was just as negative. "I got dirty and sweaty for the last two days, and I'm happy not to add greasy to that. You guys have fun playing grease monkey."

But when there was enough light and Armstrong gave the cue, they all rose from the tables, and pausing only to dispose of dirty utensils and put on protective suits, trudged to the landing craft and began unloading the HUMMVEEs. It took less than ten minutes before the hunting party had checked the vehicles and were outside the compound.

Both HUMMVEEs went first to the hole in the fence. Perhaps, they reasoned, there would be some clues as to what they were looking for. Benton left the HUMMVEE and joined Armstrong who was already kneeling, examining something on the ground. He could plainly see what it was: Footprints! There were six unmistakable prints clearly etched into the bare ground, surrounded by scraping marks. Whatever it was that had made the hole, had apparently fallen to the ground before regaining its feet. It must have flown away, because there were only the six prints in the soft soil. Surprised, Benton couldn't keep the excitement out of his voice.

"Boy! That thing is sure big!"

The prints were a lot like dog tracks, but there were six toes on each foot, and they were more than ten centimeters across. Armstrong went back to the HUMMVEE where James waited with the engine idling and took a plastic case and camera from behind the front seat. He walked beck to where Benton waited, carefully avoiding the prints and put down the case. He thumbed the toggle on the right side of his mask.

"Houston? This is Eagle II. We've found some footprints from the thing that made the hole in the fence. Are you ready to receive some video?"

"Roger Eagle II, send away."

Armstrong had already mounted the camera on the tripod and was carefully focusing it on one of the prints. He took long exposures of each then zoomed it back to take pictures of the group, and finally the hole in the fence. When mission control was satisfied, he retrieved the plastic case and held it out to Benton.

"Here. Take a plaster cast of these," pointing at the prints. "I'm going to look over here."

When Benton took the case, Armstrong walked thirty or so meters further away from the fence, looking for more animal signs, but found nothing. He returned to the HUMMVEEs just as Benton was repacking the case.

"Well, this is where we separate. Good hunting." James put the vehicle in gear, and it began moving along the fence line until it reached the beach. There they stopped and Armstrong looked at the digital satellite photomap displayed on an LCD panel on the vehicle's dashboard. The photo was a real-time image updated constantly from a satellite that had been left in geo-synchronous orbit about the planet. The new compound stood out clearly; a dime sized brown patch jammed between the white line of the beach and the unbroken green of the woods. The map had been overlaid with one-kilometer squares in the manner of Earth topographic maps as an aid to navigation and location. The grid square in which the base camp was located was designated as AA0000, with the number designations growing larger as one moved east and north. Armstrong strained his eyes looking for landmarks on the map that he could recognize if he saw them on the ground. Hills would be useless until he actually reached them, because the digital satellite photo had no indication of elevation. In fact the map would be of little use at all by itself. The use of POS-NAV GPS instruments, which were based on gyro and inertial microprocessors, complete the accuracy of the map data.

Though the forested area was almost uniform green, he did find a faint off-color region about thirteen kilometers to the north and made that his first goal for the day. He decided to just follow the beach for ten kilometers or so before turning inland. That would guide him well and give him maximum speed. He poked the touch-screen, marking for James the first waypoint, took one last look back at the activity around the landing craft and told James to drive on.

* * * *

Benton was less concerned about orientation, and he and Caglin pointed their vehicle in the general direction of northeast and drove off. Progress was slow because vegetation was thick; they had to make their own path by running down the lower bushes.

They had gone less than one hundred meters when they flushed one of the furry creatures that had run from under the dozer blade quite often on the previous day. These little animals behaved a lot like squirrels, but looked nothing like them——a furry beanbag with legs. Greenish-gray, they blended perfectly with the bushes——another example of the wonderful camouflage. They had no apparent external organs, no head, no tail, and no ears or eyes that could be seen. Miller had tried to capture one on the previous day but was unsuccessful. They had no time for that now, but Benton thought it would be easy to set a trap for them. He wondered how they managed to get along without eyes or ears. As they drove they flushed more of the furry little creatures, and at each stop they saw more different types of insects of the kind seen by Stark on the previous day.

But there was no more evidence of the monstrous creature they were looking for. The two men became more and more relaxed as they progressed, until it seemed as if they were out for a Sunday drive in the country.

All of a sudden there it was! The largest animal Benton had ever seen outside of a zoo, and to his horrified eyes the most menacing thing he'd ever seen. It was five meters high, with a row of half-meter long deadly looking spikes that seemed to grow out of its spine, and a cluster of those same spikes at the front and back of the animal. Four thin-looking legs supported the animal's body three and a half meters above the ground. Under the body was an appendage——which had no immediately apparent use——dangling almost to the ground. The animal was a paradox: dark brown in color, and in no way camouflaged. As soon as Caglin saw the thing, he hammered his foot on the brake, almost sending Benton through the window.

"Look at that thing!" His hand clutched the gearshift lever so firmly Benton could see the whiteness of his knuckles, ready to put the vehicle in reverse and escape. The captain had drawn his gun, but he needn't have bothered, because as soon as the creature saw them it emitted a bleat and galloped over the nearest hill away from them. The men could hear more bleating over the hill, but before they followed to investigate, they collected themselves and got their descriptions together for the report.

"Rover One? This is Rover Two. I've got a new kind of animal over here, and *what* an animal!"

"This is Rover One." Armstrong was slow to answer, or Benton was over-anxious. "What kind of an animal?"

Benton described the thing: "Big as an elephant with legs like a giraffe. It made a bleating sound and ran away from us. Those things never evolved eyes or ears——at least I didn't see them. That should be an advantage for us if they are dangerous." It was more a wish for reassurance than a logical deduction, and he was noticeably disappointed with Armstrong's reply.

"I don't think it logically follows that just because these animals don't appear to have eyes or ears, they cannot see or hear. This thing saw you or at least knew you were there, didn't it? And it made some kind of noise. It stands to reason that if they make sounds, they can also hear them. Or maybe they have some other way of perception like bats on Earth do. That doesn't make them any less efficient than us."

The ICT was silent for a moment, but before Benton could say anything, it buzzed back into life. "Go ahead and investigate this animal more fully. It may be a grazer and harmless, but be careful, and do not leave the HUMMVEE if there is any danger at all. I'll be waiting for your report."

Part of Benton was curious, and another part wanted nothing to do with the terrible creature waiting over the hill. He reminded himself of the ease with which they could escape if the things were a real menace. *Just push the button on the dashboard and I'll be back at base camp.* He couldn't reassure himself, and it was with great apprehension that he told Caglin to move to the top of the rise.

Caglin hadn't noticed before, but the landscape had changed somewhat from the low bushes and flat character around the base camp. Here, the terrain was more rolling and rugged. The bushes were spaced further apart with a kind of gray-green moss growing between them. Here and there were large rocks exposed above the ground. There was a rather large one of these on the crest of the hill. He pulled the HUMMVEE to a stop behind it and the two men stepped quietly out of the vehicle. As they approached they could hear the bleating sounds more plainly, and they drew their guns before they topped the rise. They weren't prepared for the sight that greeted their eyes in the valley. There must have been more than a thousand of the creatures grazing peacefully in bunches of fifteen or twenty with eight or ten of the animals separate from the others in the manner of the first one they had seen. Most of the animals were smaller than the one first encountered, but they remained huge. Like an elephant's trunk, the appendage underneath the animals was used to grasp the moss, and lift it to the mouth, which they could now see directly beneath the body. After they had watched for a few minutes, they could discern smaller animals underneath the groups. These had not yet developed the spikes and were assumed to be juveniles.

Benton became aware that their preoccupation with the herd had left them terribly exposed to danger from the rear when he felt a prickling feeling at the base of his neck. He immediately ordered Caglin back to the HUMMVEE, and he followed closely on his heels. They pulled the HUMMVEE up on the ridge, and began taking pictures while Benton made the report to Armstrong and mission control. Afterward they made a wide circle around the herd, coming into sight of the animals only once more. Then when they noticed some of the solitary animals begin to edge their way, Caglin gunned the engine and moved away faster than was probably prudent. The HUMMVEE continued on by dead reckoning in the same general direction as it had before. At about two thirty they came upon the badly decomposed remains of one of the animals they had seen earlier. It had been horribly mangled, but was still recognizable as one of the juveniles because the back spines were just beginning to emerge, and it was much smaller than the adults.

What happened to this thing? Benton wondered. Obviously, it didn't die of natural causes. It looked as if someone had slashed the thing repeatedly with a machete, or it had been run over by something like an outboard motor; only the slashes weren't so regular. Part of the animal was missing. *Eaten by something? Gargoyles?* Benton did not even want to think about that, and he made his report quickly, anxious to put the grizzly sight behind him.

Nothing else of significance turned up that day for either party, and as sunset approached both halted where the HUMMVEEs could be hidden. While Caglin was cutting foliage for camouflage, Benton checked the navigation instruments for a final reading——actually this would be his first. Not as familiar with the instruments as Armstrong was, it took him longer to get accurate readings, but he had them well before dark.

*   *   *   *

Everyone was waiting expectantly as Benton and Caglin stepped out of the stanisplummer in the bunkhouse. They had all seen the pictures and reports they had made and were anxious to discuss them in debriefing. Besides a few landmarks, some new species of plants and small animals, they had found nothing extraordinary.

"We need to attach names to things we've discovered, at least temporarily. I find it really awkward to refer to them as 'the thing that Benton found.'" That was Laird, but they all found themselves nodding their heads in unison, and Armstrong followed him up.

"Agreed. The sow crabs have already been named," said Armstrong, "but anything new will be named by the person who sees it first. Make the names short. I don't want them named after you; that would be just as confusing as it is now."

The last statement evoked a titter of laughter. The furry squirrel-like creatures became *skeeks* by vote, because no one could remember who had first seen one. The slow moving, larger beasts Armstrong saw today were christened *slogs*, and, with a chuckle, Caglin named the huge spiked creatures *bennies*——not because Benton had found them, but because, he said, they looked like the captain.

Nobody mentioned the gargoyles. They still hoped——contrary to evidence——there was no such animal. After dinner, the videos of the day's activities were shown again, and teams were assigned for tomorrow. During the segment of the video showing the close up of a lone benny, Benton noticed something he hadn't seen in person.

"Stop the video! Right there!" he blurted.

Devlin, who had the remote, froze the frame and Benton walked closer to the screen.

"Look at this!" he exclaimed, pointing to the benny's back. "Those are scars, not stripes. It looks like this benny has tangled with the same creature the dead one did, only he was luckier." The video showed clearly that they were indeed slash marks, some longer than twenty centimeters.

"Roll the video back. Let's look at some of the other animals in the herd a little closer," put in Armstrong. It took only a few minutes to comply, and Devlin zoomed the picture in, so they could look closely at some of the individuals. Zooming had made the pictures grainy and less distinct, but they could see plainly the unmistakable marks on the backs of almost all the creatures, some of which were so fresh, blood still welled up and streaked the sides of the creatures.

There was little question now. There must be gargoyles! And they were dangerous! *Had they been attacking the herd of bennies and been chased off by the approaching HUMMVEE?* Benton had to fight off the ensuing panic, as the thought seared his brain. They kept the frame showing the slashes displayed for a long time, as if wishing to make this evidence of danger disappear. When it was finally clear to everyone that it wouldn't go away, Devlin flicked off the image, and they turned to the task of organizing tomorrow's expeditions.

The completion of a helicopter made possible some changes. Armstrong would pilot it, taking Miller with him, and James would replace Caglin in Benton's HUMMVEE. The rest of the crew would construct a second helicopter.

With the advent of the helicopter, systematic exploration of the surface would really begin. Armstrong would go north, first stopping to pick up the HUMMVEE and move it some fifteen kilometers, where they would also deposit a large stanisplummer. Every thirty kilometers or so thereafter they would leave another booth like a rectangular egg. This line of stan booths would provide instant transportation from and to these points. These would be especially useful when the scientists arrived. Armstrong was to pick the locations for the booths with an eye to finding something interesting at each. The scientists had sent up a list of likely locations.

* * * *

Almost immediately after they took off Miller spotted a large herd of bennies to the east, and Armstrong changed course to fly directly over them. In less than five minutes they were there, and they could see the herd was agitated. The little bunches with the calves clustered tightly together, rows of vicious spikes pointing skyward like beds of wicked nails. The lone bennies (bulls, he presumed) began to move rapidly in the direction of the helicopter as if to attack. Armstrong maneuvered the craft to hover directly over some of them for a closer look. As he edged closer, a sharp thud reached his ears as he felt the craft shudder. *Those things could really jump*! They were jumping more than six meters straight up, and he frantically worked the controls fighting for altitude. He felt two more hits before he was beyond their range——if he'd been less quick to react, he realized——it was possible they could have knocked the craft out of the sky. As it was, the bottom of the helicopter probably looked like a sieve. After his nerves had settled sufficiently, he maneuvered back over the herd, being careful this time to stay out of their range. The bulls again moved to get under them, while the little bunches did not move at all. He edged over one of these groups, and some of the adults began jumping. Miraculously they did not fall when they returned to the ground, nor did they seem to land on the helpless calves underneath. They seemed uncannily able to drop precisely back into the hole they'd come from.

It didn't take long before the men had grown tired of the show, and Armstrong once again rose to altitude and turned the craft northward in the direction of the HUMMVEE. No more than ten minutes later they had it located, in precisely the same spot where they had left it. Not that he expected the vehicle to be moved, but it was a comfort to know something unknown hadn't destroyed or moved it. Still. Armstrong was cautious. He slowly circled the vehicle in the air three times before landing in the open area more than thirty meters away. Miller stayed with the helicopter and covered him with the machinegun while the colonel moved to the HUMMVEE.

He took great care with every step. All of his senses were tuned to take in anything in the vicinity of the HUMMVEE——even the slightest stirring of the leaves in the early morning breeze. As he neared the HUMMVEE he became even more cautious——step. step, step. Pause to listen. The closer he got the more convinced he was there was something there. Nothing but the wind? Step, step…step. Pause to listen——wait, listen again. He was within five meters of the HUMMVEE. Step…

All of a sudden the whole world seemed to explode in front of him. His training served him well, for he was immediately prone, with his heart in his mouth, and his gun tracking the moving form of the skeek that had apparently used the HUMMVEE for it night shelter. Humbled, he allowed himself a quick sigh before rolling onto his back. He sat up and an embarrassed grin involuntarily etched itself on his features as he met Miller's eyes. Armstrong scrambled to his feet and moved to the HUMMVEE. Less than five minutes later it was loaded in the cargo compartment of helicopter, and he was back inside the cockpit.

As he started the craft, he threw Miller a glance that clearly conveyed to the sergeant that his life would be much easier if he were smart enough to say nothing about the incident. In fact he felt better served not to speak to or even look at the commander for a while. He finally steeled his nerves about fifteen minutes later.

"Anything bother the HUMMVEE, sir?" he said, forcing his voice to be matter-of-fact.

Armstrong replied tersely, and in a tone that told Miller he was still not ready to talk. "Not a thing."

They flew without speaking for the next twenty-five minutes, Miller observing to the right and Armstrong to the left. Neither of them saw anything unusual.

The only real landmark was still the low mountain well to the northeast. Armstrong finally broke the impasse.

"That clearing over there looks like a good place to put our first stan booth."

He banked the craft to the right and began to descend. They went through the same ritual they had before landing at the HUMMVEE and put down like a feather. There didn't seem to be as much flying dust and debris on Kadakas IV as on Earth. Armstrong supposed that was due to the nature of the vegetation——the branches were not nearly so long as those on Earth plants and the low moss seemed to anchor the soil——or man hadn't been here long enough to loosen everything. Miller drove the HUMMVEE out of the cargo bay while Armstrong checked their precise location on the helicopter's GPS map display. It turned out to be almost exactly thirty kilometers from base camp in grid square AA0329. That number would designate the stanisplummer left here, and would also be the code one would use to get there. Once he had reported the location to base camp and mission control, the two men watched the orange box that was the stan booth materialize in the cargo bay of the helicopter. It took them only five minutes to operate the extraction mechanism and be airborne once again. Armstrong circled AR0329 twice while he gained altitude and then aimed the craft on a beeline to the north.

*　　*　　*　　*

It was much more difficult for Benton. He would not have the luxury of circling his HUMMVEE a couple of times, and then moving upon it with drawn weapon. He and James would simply appear inside the vehicle.

What if there was a gargoyle perched on top of the HUMMVEE, just waiting for their arrival, licking its lips at the thought of an anticipated meal? Worse! Maybe there were two or three of them and they had already gotten the top of the HUMMVEE open! It was slim consolation to Benton that if that were the case, all they had to do was press the button on the dashboard and they'd be back in base camp. Stanisplummers had been known to fail before——in fact, quite often. They were sensitive instruments. Benton watched the helicopter carrying Armstrong and Miller fly away over the trees and waited long minutes staring at the spot where it had disappeared. Finally, on rubbery knees, he turned toward the building with a wave of his hand at James.

"Let's go to work," he said with an enthusiasm he did not feel. The two moved directly to the stanisplummer in the bunkhouse, drew their weapons, and seated themselves on the bench placed to match the seats in their HUMMVEE. Benton's heart leapt up forming a knot in his throat as be leaned to press the switch that he felt certain would plummet them into the jaws of Hell. *This is it!* he thought while his teeth ground together threatening to crush one another. Nothing. There was nothing there and Benton was almost disappointed at the serenity of the scene that greeted them. The breeze was stirring the bushes slightly, and the dew made the low moss seem diamond studded in the early morning sunlight. The two men got out of the HUMMVEE and for a few moments just enjoyed the scene. Off to their left a skeek was making tentative movements away from his protective tree, not knowing whether they were a danger to him.

The scene reminded Benton of the early morning excursions to Boston Common he used to take on special Saturdays with his mother. The only things missing were the birds singing and the concrete walkways. James began moving quietly toward the spot where they had last seen the skeek, and could still hear movements in the undergrowth. He holstered his pistol as he took cautious steps forward. This action, Benton knew was to free his hands to catch the furry little animal, but he doubted whether there was any chance of that.

I probably ought to call him back so we can get started, Benton thought casually. *Nah! Let him have his fun. What's it going to hurt? It'll give me time to check the HUMMVEE before we go anyway.* He didn't go to the HUMMVEE immediately, but continued to enjoy the morning where he was. Idly he watched James continue his stalk, until he disappeared behind the nearest tree. Only then did Benton turn back to the vehicle.

He had been checking under the hood for no more than a minute when a shriek and burst of shots in quick succession pierced the still of the morning. Benton immediately panicked and was inside the HUMMVEE ready to push the stanisplummer button, when rationality fought its way through the red veil. He forced himself to get out. He remained stationary on shaky legs for a long moment, before advancing reluctantly in the direction James had gone. He glanced down at the gun in his badly shaking hand and doubted it would do any good, but he forced his legs to move him onward.

When he approached the tree where he'd last seen James, he slowed his pace and peered around the fringes. He saw nothing, and before moving away from the protective foliage, he called softly.

"James? Are you there?"

The answer was swift. "Yes, sir. Over here."

The answer was so calm that in spite of still shaky knees, Benton knew everything was all right. He moved briskly in the direction of the voice, almost immediately seeing the sergeant just down the hill, no more than fifteen meters away. He saw something else, too. A still and lifeless bundle on the ground about as large as a medium-size dog.

"That thing had a lot more guts than brains. It attacked me. Did you hear it yowl?" He was bending over the dead animal prodding it with the muzzle of his gun.

"I sure did. I don't know about it having more guts than brains. It probably would have gotten you, if you hadn't been quick with the gun. Maybe it mistook you for a benny calf…Well you found the ugly critter. What' you going to name it? You're lucky it's not naming you."

Benton found the talk masking the queasy stomach he still felt and wanted to keep on.

"I don't know. It's sure ugly," said James grasping a wicked looking forepaw and rolling the thing to expose the mouth, which, as with the bennies, was underneath the creature. This thing had the same six-toed paws as the prints they'd seen outside the compound, though nowhere near the size. The green-gray hair was short and on this creature they could see four orifices, spaced evenly on the forward hump. On close examination, these orifices revealed themselves to be small eyes and ears, similar to those on terrestrial animals. The mouth was a surprise——huge for the creature's size and jammed with rows of deadly looking teeth. That thing was obviously dangerous. and James did not have to think long before settling on the name *lobo*.

They brought the HUMMVEE to where the dead thing lay, and after contacting base camp, stanned it back to the lab for further study. Most of the rest of the day passed uneventfully for both crews. Armstrong and Miller had placed three more stan booths: AA0261, AA0l90, and AB0322. They had just lifted off from the latter and noticed they had finally gotten as far north as the mountain. It was directly east of them now and judging from the distance they had already traveled, much larger than they first supposed. Armstrong decided that the mountaintop must be that brown patch on the map in grid square BB1116. As they headed generally north, Armstrong's attention was drawn and held by the mountain, although it was technically in Miller's sector. Like a magnet his eyes continuously returned to the peak, and Miller also began paying it more attention.

Then he saw it! "Colonel, look! There! To the right of the mountain! Do you see it? No! Three of them!" Miller was excited and he startled Armstrong.

It was three or four minutes before his eyes found what the sergeant was yelling about. Finally he could discern the three flying figures just above the horizon. When he did see them, he immediately banked the helicopter and flew directly toward them at top speed. They looked close but seemed to get no closer for the next ten minutes or so. The way the birds were flying seemed to indicate they were flying in one place. Now and then, one of them would dip below the trees and reappear to join his comrades a few moments later. Then Armstrong saw why they didn't appear to get closer——they were extremely large! *Gargoyles*? He didn't know; they were still too far away to see the features clearly even with the binoculars.

As they closed the distance, the birds grew in size, and it became more and more probable that they were indeed gargoyles. That suspicion was confirmed more than two kilometers from the big flyers.

Gargoyles! That term was extremely descriptive——except for the lack of a head, which seemed to be common on this planet, they were almost identical to the mythical Earth beasts. The lack of a head did not make the gargoyle look any less fearsome than its namesake. The mouth was located in a similar position to the lobo's, and if anything had *more* teeth. The creatures were huge, with a leathery wingspan of more than fifteen meters, and their maneuverability quickly proved to be awesome. The helicopter had gotten no closer than one kilometer when Miller noticed through the binoculars that the gargoyles seemed to have seen them. The creature's first reaction was to divert their attention from the herd of bennies on the ground, and hover in position for a moment, as if trying to determine whether the helicopter was dangerous. Apparently they decided so, because the three turned as one and flew away.

Armstrong increased his speed in pursuit of them——the indicator read one hundred sixty KPH and they were barely closing the distance. The chase went on for five minutes or so before the animals separated. Armstrong followed the one in the middle that, rather stupidly he thought, made no attempt to evade. When he was within twenty meters of it he slowed slightly to match its speed so they could study the creature. The two men watched in awe at the rippling side muscles under the silky brown fur, which propelled the huge wings.

"The tail is just a thin membrane suspended between the rear legs, but they are not like bats, because they have both wings and forelegs. How can they fly? They're too damn big!" Armstrong put into words the thoughts he had been harboring ever since he'd seen the hole in the fence the day before.

"Maybe they have hollow bones like birds," Miller said tentatively." Even so that thing has got to weigh three hundred pounds. It must be incredibly strong."

Centering their attention entirely on the one gargoyle had taken it away from the other two, which they'd assumed to have just flown off. Armstrong realized his mistake when he felt the thump and tremendous jolt as something struck the side of the craft like a giant hand.

Miller broke through the noise of the rotors with an excited yell.

"They've circled and are attacking from behind!"

At the same time, Armstrong cursed himself for not being more careful and immediately began taking evasive action. Both of the gargoyles had come in from the side, and now he could see the third turn with remarkable agility and join its comrades in attack. Miller was frantically trying to bring the machinegun to bear on one or the other, but he was having difficulty because they were too close. Armstrong knew that the only way they could be certain of safety would be if they could outrun them, no easy feat, because no matter which way they turned there was the specter of another gargoyle and he didn't relish getting one of them caught in the rotors. He concentrated on avoiding them and looked for an opening between them. He heard the harsh burst from machinegun and saw one of the beasts hit, but there seemed to be little effect. It flew off to the side for a moment before resuming the attack.

Miller shot it again, and it tumbled over and fell spiraling to the ground. He heard Miller cheer and watched the thing fall for a moment, but looked up just in time to see one of the others try to dive on them through the rotors. The contact took off one leg and the left wing, sending the creature plummeting planetward after its comrade. At first Armstrong thought the helicopter had not been affected, but quickly saw that was wishful thinking. The rotors became more and more unbalanced, and he realized that the creature had probably bent one of the blades. Vibration grew steadily, and he knew that it would continue to get worse until the craft simply shook itself apart. The other gargoyle seemed to hang back, perhaps taking a lesson from the fate of its comrades.

They may not be attacked again, but Armstrong noticed they were losing altitude at an increasing rate. He fought the controls. Maybe he could bring the craft in for a safe landing before stanning back to base camp. That would save them from having to construct a new helicopter. Replacing the rotor was a relatively simple operation, and took considerably less time than assembling a complete craft. They were descending more rapidly now and Armstrong tried to call base camp on the ICT to be prepared to receive them should they have to depart in a hurry.

"Base? This is Rover One. We may have to ditch."

If it hadn't been for the sound of the protesting rotors, and cabin vibrations, the silence would have been ominous. No answer. He tried again with the same results. He finally reached the conclusion that the instrument was broken, maybe from the battering they took from the gargoyles. He decided to play it safe and abandon the helicopter.

"Hold on, Miller. We're getting out." He leaned slightly forward in his seat, pressed the toggle, and braced himself for the stanning sensation.

Nothing! They were still in the helicopter! Armstrong quickly hit the toggle again, and a startling thought hit him with the realization that the stanisplummer wasn't working. *The bennies!* The wiring for the stanisplummer and the ICT runs under the cockpit. The holes the bennies had made in the bottom must have sliced a key wire. Unwilling to accept it he pressed the toggle over and over, fighting the controls of the craft at the same time. The thought briefly crossed his mind that they could go out through the cargo stanisplummer, but he quickly crossed that off as being futile. It would take too much time, and with no one at the controls of the craft it would go down twice as fast. Staying at the controls, maybe he could maneuver it to safe landing. The last few seconds seemed to float by as if in a dream. The ground seemed to swim up at him, as he looked over the entire scene, including Miller's tense white face. He remembered trying the stanisplummer button several more times, but it was as if it wasn't happening to him at all. He was merely an observer.

This couldn't be happening! There were too many precautions taken to prevent it. Simultaneously they hit the ground with a grinding thump and the rotors hit a tree. Armstrong remembered looking up at the blades as they seemed to explode. And then...blackness.

XII

DEVLIN

Immediately after hearing base camp had lost communication with the helicopter, Benton and James secured the HUMMVEE and stanned back in. The primary concern was to organize a search party. They all knew the procedure, having been through the drill at least thirty times. Benton would take James and another HUMMVEE to the last stan booth put in place and begin the search. When the new helicopter had been completed and tested——more than an hour's work still remained on it——Stark would take Caglin and join the search from the air.

Urgency showed in their faces. Armstrong had plenty of time to report the contact with the gargoyles and had described the big carnivores, There was little hope that the stanisplummers were still in working condition, because the routine check-in period had long elapsed. Regulations were clear——any time there is a break in communications, explorers must stan back in immediately.

Stark, commander in Armstrong's absence, held a brief discussion with Benton before the latter joined James in the HUMMVEE that was already awaiting transport.

"Communications with them," the major was saying, "went out less than twenty-five minutes after they reported the establishment of stan booth AB0322, here." He emphasized the point by jabbing a finger at the large LCD display on the wall. "That should limit them to a seventy kilometer radius from there. I want you to begin looking about thirty klicks north of the booth. If the ground is not too rough, you should have almost an hour of daylight for search, otherwise we may have to delay the search until tomorrow."

"Even with the new chopper completed on schedule, we will not be able to get that far north to do any looking today. Benton, if you can't find them today before dark..."

His voice trailed off as both of them realized the consequences. *Night! Without the protection of the buildings, compound or even light. With who knows what out there! And very real flying gargoyles that were all teeth——the flying version of the great white shark!*

That fear was not voiced, though both men were painfully aware of it. The very fact that neither of the lost men had appeared in the bunkhouse alive, probably meant they were both already dead. However, even if there were not a regulation that made the search mandatory, neither would abandon the lost men.

Before Benton left, he and Stark examined in detail the latest GPS display. There was a chance that heat from a helicopter fire would show up, if the satellite cameras had been directed toward the crash area. The study was to no avail, so without any more discussion, Stark accompanied Benton to the booth in the center of the compound. Benton punched the code and was gone along with the HUMVEE and James.

Stark looked at the empty booth for a long moment before striding toward the west end of the compound and the partially constructed helicopter. As he approached, he could see that Devlin and Caglin were engaged in a rather intense discussion. He heard the end of the exchange before the two noticed his approach and turned back to the unfinished aircraft in silence.

"...doesn't matter." Caglin had been saying. "I think he does know what he is doing. Anyways they have a lot more training in these things than we do, and we probably should listen to them." He spoke with little confidence, and Devlin shot a contemptuous look at the young sergeant and began to reply.

"Just because they've been to *college*," He emphasized the word with a sneer, and continued, "doesn't mean…"

Stark felt a small disappointment that be hadn't heard more but proceeded as if he'd heard nothing. *Just like soldiers* everywhere, he thought uncertainly, *always griping*. He tried to dismiss the incident from his thoughts, but it remained in the back of his mind for a long time. *Was it curiosity about what they had been saying?* Stark honestly didn't know. It wasn't until the helicopter was ready to go that the incident was forgotten.

Stark and Caglin got aboard the helicopter at one hundred hours and headed north at top speed. Even so, they arrived at the place where Benton and Caglin had completed the day's search just *after* the sun had set.

✸   ✸   ✸   ✸

No one had seen any sign of the ill-fated helicopter, and the evening meeting was held under a pall of gloom. Laird was the first to speak.

"We have already got most of the parts for another helicopter up here, but with only two of us working, it will take more than two days to put it together. Do you think we ought to send only one search party out tomorrow, and keep four men working in camp? That way we'd have two choppers for the next day's search." He was clearly not relishing the thought of two more boring days of helicopter assembly.

"We need to keep all available people engaged in the search."
Stark replied quickly. "I can't imagine spending even one night out there, let alone two. No, we need to find them tomorrow if there's to be any hope for survival."

Laird was not going to abandon his argument easily, and reasoned, "That jeep is not going to cover much ground. In fact it probably won't do any good at all, but with *two* helicopters, we could find anything that's out there. Leave Benton and James, and we'll really put on a search day after tomorrow."

Stark paused for a moment and they could see indecision written all over his face. He was about to reply, when Devlin, emboldened by his superiors' hesitation, broke in.

"Why are we looking for them at all? We should be defending ourselves from those monsters. We all know that Colonel Armstrong and Miller are dead, or else they would have called in, or stanned back. If those gargoyles can take out a helicopter with machineguns on it, we shouldn't be puttin' another chopper out there for them to take out."

He waited for that to sink in before going on, and when none of the officers seemed inclined to stop him, he continued. "Instead of going off half-cocked, and keepin' people in danger flyin' and drivin' all over the place, we need to defend ourselves."

Stark opened his mouth to say something, but once Devlin had an audience, he was not about to relinquish the floor.

"Sittin' ducks! That's all you are out there! Those things are huge! You all heard their descriptions, and they can fly faster than the choppers!" His voice rose and grew intense, as he realized he was vocalizing the fears everyone had in the back of his mind.

"Tell me this," he asked rhetorically, "why didn't Armstrong and Miller escape? Or at least report their attack? Those escape mechanisms are supposed to be foolproof. Why aren't we getting a homing signal from the black-box in the helicopter?" He stopped again, long enough for emphasis, but not long enough for one of the officers to break in. "I'll tell you why!" He was almost yelling at them. "They couldn't, that's why! Those gargoyles attacked them so suddenly that they didn't know what hit them! And here *we* go blithely doing the same thing they were doin'! It's only a matter of time before someone else gets killed, too! And for *what*?"

"If we find anything, it will be bare bones, picked clean. I tell you, we've got to bring the chopper back here, and have mission control send up some weapons that we can use to defend ourselves with."

The ensuing silence lasted a long time. The officers looked from one to the other. It was hard to argue against the logic that Devlin presented, but they all felt a small loyalty to duty. Finally, Laird, forgetting his own negative comments spoke to the defense of the interim commander.

"First of all we don't *know* that they are dead. There could be any number of explanations for their not being able to return. Stanisplummers and ICTs are not foolproof, in fact they are rather sensitive instruments. You all know the wiring harness for the stanisplummers and ICTs are in the floor of the helicopters, and we knew they might be vulnerable there, but that was the only way to construct them rapidly up here. It wasn't expected to be a problem because crew should be able to get out before any crash. Maybe the gargoyles hit the bottom of the craft, and took it all out at once."

The idea was so farfetched that even as he said it, he wished he hadn't.

"What would you say were the odds against *that* happening, Colonel Stark?" The smirk that creased Devlin's features was blatant. Stark ignored the look and answered the question.

"Not very good, but that's not the point. It *is* possible, and we will proceed by the book until that possibility is exhausted."

Encouraged by his previous success, Devlin, pressed on, "When will your *professional* judgment tell us that possibility is not possible?" His tone when he said the word professional, bordered on insubordination, but Stark again chose to ignore the disrespect.

He held the sergeant's gaze and said: "We'll stay with the search until we find wreckage which proves there are no survivors, or until we've thoroughly covered the search area. If we don't find it then, I think we can assume they chased the gargoyles northwest and crashed at sea, We will take all actions necessary to protect ourselves from the gargoyles, but I don't believe we need to be unduly alarmed about them. That could just lead to panic."

He looked at the others and continued, "Tomorrow, Benton and James will continue to sweep the area they began today, and I'll take Caglin with me, and we'll look further north. If we are not able to see the wreckage from the air, perhaps they will hear our rotors and send up a flare,"

Devlin was not ready to give up, "Dead men are *really* gonna send up flares," he gritted sarcastically.

Stark realized at that moment, he could *not* let the comment go, or the sergeant would continue to become more and more belligerent.

"That's, enough Sergeant!" he snapped, and after the ensuing lull that demonstrated there would be no further challenge, at least for now, he went on.

"The danger from gargoyles and other animals like the lobos James saw is real, but if we take the proper precautions we should be able to deal with them. The new lightweight M-80 machinegun will be with all the searchers. Any potentially dangerous situation will be dealt with immediately and ruthlessly, Benton will not be more than ten steps from the HUMMVEE at any time, and if anything unusual happens at all, stan back to base camp immediately."

Devlin was not subdued, but he was smart enough to know that now was not the moment to continue the fight. And that is precisely what it had become—a fight for power. One that Devlin knew he could win. Caglin had already been intimidated that afternoon, and he knew that Benton would go along. The rest were not sufficiently strong to oppose him, but for now he would bide his time.

The meeting broke up shortly after that, and Stark ordered them all to go to bed, while he took the first shift as lookout. He wanted the time to think. Although he knew from the start that as second in command, he might have to take charge at any moment, the reality had not yet sunk in. His mind reeled from one side to the other.

One side agreed with Devlin, that search was futile, and probably dangerous, while the other could not believe that Armstrong, a man he idolized, was gone. He *had* to be out there, against all odds, surviving, and would be back at any moment, ready to take charge of the mission.

Stark, in his normal state of mind, would not have been challenged by a man like Devlin, and after a few minutes alone to settle things in his mind, he knew the sergeant would be no threat in the future. The only reason he'd let the man go as far as he did, was the shock of losing Armstrong. By the time he had to wake Caglin for the night shift, he had assured himself that his was the proper course of action, and after a few lingering thoughts about the safety of Armstrong and Miller, and the organization of tomorrow's, search, he drifted into peaceful sleep.

* * * *

Benton looked up into the unreal deep blue of the sky just in time to see the formation of at least a dozen gargoyles diving as one, directly at him. His first thought was, *My God! I'm at least twice as far from the HUMMVEE as I should be!* At the same moment he pictured the machinegun right where he'd left it leaning against the passenger door of the HUMMVEE. Time flowed in slow motion! His feet seemed to be mired in thick, gluey mud as he turned to run, but the action served to emphasize the uselessness of fleeing. This time the panic refused to come, and he remained terrifyingly aware of exactly what was happening. The grinning teeth came closer, and he gave up, allowing himself to fall into a sitting position on the ground, he threw his arms in front of his face, longing for the familiar red veil which would render him insensible, *But it wouldn't come.* Then they were on him, and he felt the cruel claws tear into him as they shook him like a rag doll, His mouth formed into a grotesque shape as the scream tore from his tortured throat.

"NOOOOOOOOOOOO!" The scream ripped his throat like a dull chain saw.

The unexpected noise woke everyone in the bunkhouse, and Devlin jumped back from Benton's bed as if he'd been stung. The room became filled with the buzz of inquiry and complaint. Benton was the first to recover, and he sat up on the bunk, chagrined.

"Nightmare. Sorry. They get pretty real sometimes."

The rest of the men settled back to go to sleep, and Devlin said under his breath, "Wow! That was something! Don't mind telling you, you scared hell out of me."

"I was being attacked by gargoyles. I was pretty scared myself."

The captain sat up on the edge of the bed and pulled his pants on. Devlin turned to go back to the watchtower, until Benton got up to relieve him.

"I won't be a minute," was cast toward the receding back.

"No hurry sir. I doubt if I could sleep very well now anyway." Devlin answered as be disappeared through the door."

* * * *

Minutes later Benton was inside the tower struggling out of his protective gear.

"I sure will be glad when we don't have to wear these suits anymore." He remarked conversationally.

Devlin had been about to put on his own gear for the short walk back to the bunkhouse, but he hesitated after the remark. He looked at Benton noncommittally for a moment, but didn't say anything to him until be was out of the suit and had seated himself on the high swivel stool which gave the best view of the compound.

"I'm not really tired," he said clandestinely, "and I doubt if I could sleep. Do you mind if I keep you company for a few minutes, Captain?" The sergeant had kept his voice matter-of-fact, so as not to betray his real purpose prematurely. He'd learned that there had to be precise timing for everything, and though he was pretty certain Benton was ripe for his bill of goods, he didn't want to scare his quarry away by making it seem planned.

Clearly aware that the regulations required all personnel not on watch to be sleeping between fifteen and nineteen hundred hours, Benton felt he needed the company. The dream and the incident with the lobo still had him on edge, and he had an unclear premonition of ill.

"I'd enjoy talking to you for a few minutes, but no more than that."

Devlin knew then that he had his fish hooked. Even that slight violation of the rules should be enough to demand his cooperation provided that subsequent violations grew only slightly in severity. Devlin had a nose for weak men, and now he was ready to exploit this one to the maximum. But not too fast: he had to play his fish expertly. "You're right about those suits. They're a royal pain in the ass. If it wasn't for the regulations, we could be out of them already. Especially since those damned monkeys are doing so well. I bet we could put that helicopter together twice as fast without them tomorrow. Well shit! Nobody listens to me anyhow."

Benton didn't seem inclined to reply so the sergeant continued after a moment. "It's like I said yesterday. What good are they doin' us anyway. If there is something in the air, we might as well get it over with, because they're not gonna let us back to Earth anyhow."

"They will if they can find an antidote for it," Benton countered uncertainly.

"Are you kiddin'! They won't find an antidote, and even if they do it'll be too late. We won't even know if there is something until we take off these masks. How're they goin' to know that it'll kill us until we try it? I know those monkeys are not foolproof; a lot of sickness don't affect them and *does* us. But that doesn't matter anyhow. We've already breathed air here and we're still 'kickin'. I say we quit playing the games and get out of the suits. Especially now when we need to have that other chopper to find the Colonel and Miller."

"You think they're still alive out there?"

"Now that you mention it, there's no goddam way. All *you're* gonna find out there is a crunched helicopter and two burnt bodies——unless the gargoyles ate them. If that happened, you'll only find a crunched copter. If you ask me, we should be stayin' here at base camp, and finding a way to protect us from the gargoyles, instead *of* makin' more targets for them. Maybe install some radar guided antiaircraft. Them babies would knock the bastards down, and they're probably the only things that will."

The captain grew visibly edgy. After he let Devlin ramble on for a few minutes, he reached for the control that doused the floodlights and ventured a timid rebuttal.

"That's pretty much already settled. Colonel Stark sounded pretty definite, and it's probably not a good idea to belabor the point. Besides you should really be getting some sleep, shouldn't you?"

Satisfied his fish was well hooked, Devlin decided not to jerk on the line. In the morning he could make some prods to keep the line taut. *I probably could get a commitment from him tonight,* he mused, *but no sense in pushing it. Plenty of time in the morning.* Vocally, he conceded that Benton was probably correct and began to climb into the rubber suit. He could not resist one parting shot just before he covered his face with the plastic mask.

"Colonel Armstrong was a hell of commander, and I'm not so sure the other two can cut it. It's too bad someone with *your* experience doesn't have seniority."

* * * *

It was bald flattery, and Benton recognized as much, but he could not help but feel a tiny pocket of satisfaction come bubbling to the surface. *I do have a good record, and the incident in the Iranian War would have gone the same way despite anything I could have done, except maybe kill myself. Even the brush with the lobo would not have changed, had I acted differently. My career has been a good one. I know what I'm doing, and I probably could do a better job than Stark.* He knew that most of the Major's service had been on staff. *I know I can do better than Laird, an Air Force flying bus driver.*

* * * *

Devlin pressed the attack quickly in the morning. As soon as they had gathered for breakfast, he blatantly muttered his doubts about the success of the search.

"Those gargoyles are so fast, they can probably knock down a chopper before the pilot knows what hits him. Must have made a hell of a mess of the Colonel and Miller. Not meanin' no disrespect, Major, but I still think we ought to take…"

"Why don't you just shut the fuck up!" James cut in contemptuously, "The Major's got enough to worry about without all that garbage you're spoutin' out your asshole."

Devlin was about to retort, but the glare in the senior sergeant's eye warned him off, so he just shrugged and said no more.

XIII

SURVIVAL

What is happening to me? He tried to scream; tried to force movement into his tortured limbs, but they remained dead. Torrents of swirling clouds spiraled around him. He was deep in the heart of a raging storm of light and color that refused to abate. *If I concentrate…I…can…do…anything.* He had to force his mind into focus, and the effort just to complete the thought was totally draining. For a moment he thought he was going to succeed, but just then inky blackness swallowed him up. On the brink he felt terrible panic as his consciousness drained into the awful pit.

Awareness again! This time he had a greater grasp on consciousness, but the pain in his shoulder, and to a lesser degree in his leg, almost made him long for the soothing blackness again. Almost. Somewhere, deep in the gray matter that was his essence, there anchored a drive to remain conscious, which far outstripped his aversion to the pain. A flood of blinding light assaulted his brain, panicking him once again, until he realized that he had merely opened his eyes and was looking directly into the late afternoon sun.

Where am I? His mind was working a little better, but the last thing he could remember was climbing reluctantly into the roller coaster car next to his cousin Peter during the family outing at Disneyland. They were just beginning that agonizingly long ascent of the wild ride.

But the sunlight? He was puzzled. Space Mountain was indoors and almost totally dark. *Why does my shoulder hurt? Did the ride collapse?*

Suddenly the large indistinct blotch of brown in the center of his vision resolved itself into the grotesque image of a huge winged, headless thing, sitting placidly not ten meters from him. Armstrong recognized the creature immediately and with that recognition, the memory of events leading to the crash flooded back into his brain. The proximity of the gargoyle gave him immediate cause for concern until be realized that he was still inside the wreckage of the helicopter and the creature could not reach him. At least that was his fervent hope. At any rate, the creature made no move toward him, and Armstrong ignored it for the moment. The more pressing priority was to take stock of himself and his injuries.

He raised his right arm slightly, and though he felt the pain in his shoulder increase slightly, it didn't seem to be that badly injured——probably just a sprain or bruise. With his uninjured arm, he explored the pain in his leg and was relieved to find that it was obviously only a bruise. The whack on the instrument panel had been hard; he rubbed the knot it had made on his forehead, but it was probably only a slight concussion.

Satisfied that he was basically intact, he turned his attention to Miller who, still strapped to his seat next to him, was not conscious. It took little investigation to determine that he was dead. The window next to him had shattered on impact, sending a dagger-like shard deep into his brain. When Armstrong discovered the wound, an involuntary shudder wracked his body, but he quickly recovered and began making arrangements for his own rescue.

After satisfying himself that the ICT and stanisplummer were indeed non-functional, he dug into the survival kit for the homing beacon, which he set and leaned back for a moment to assess his situation. The sun seemed to be in about the same place in the sky as it had been before the crash, so he couldn't have been unconscious long, and a brief glance at his watch confirmed it to be only ten or fifteen minutes. On reflection, knowing the craft carried little fuel was a comfort. With little danger from fire, there was no need to go outside and face the horror there. Armstrong found and took an aspirin, and closed his eyes long enough for the drug to take effect.

Though he purposely held his body immobile, his mind raced a hundred miles an hour, categorizing and filing away new knowledge he'd gained about the planet, particularly about the gargoyles. He supposed they had attacked the helicopter because they perceived it to be a threat. But why was that creature hanging around out there now?

Just then he got his answer unexpectedly. The craft lurched to the left as he felt a tremendous jarring. Eyes startled open, revealed the cause. The gargoyle had left its previous perch and was sitting directly on top of the cockpit, tearing at the shell with powerful forepaws. Through the transparent windshield he could see the huge tooth filled maw not twenty centimeters from his face. The claws were shredding the titanium hull like tissue paper and feeding the bits into its mouth. It apparently didn't like the taste, because the mouthful was spat out immediately, spreading metal and saliva all over the windshield. It must have smelled something it liked, for the bad taste didn't deter the rasping, digging claws and in no time it had carved a hole the size of a basketball in the roof. Armstrong had to duck back quickly to avoid the same fate as the hull.

The new development froze him for an instant only. He scratched frantically, for the M-80 he had suspended in the chest holster, scarcely noticing the pain it caused the sore shoulder. When the gun was pointed in the general direction of the beast on the roof, he squeezed the trigger and held it, sending a burst of twenty or thirty rounds into the creature's breast. It emitted a high, ungodly screech, not unlike the sound Stark had described the day before. The gargoyle hopped away from the craft and sat much as it had when Armstrong first saw it, scarcely seeming to notice the wounds it must have suffered. Waiting only a moment, he took careful aim at a spot on the center of the forward hump of the beast, midway between the eyes, and squeezed the trigger again. This time the animal folded into an empty, lifeless bag on the ground.

Trembling, Armstrong stared at the corpse for a long time, with the sights of the gun trained on the same spot, half expecting the thing to rise and threaten him once again. If the creature so much as twitched, he intended to add to its load of lead, but finally he realized the gargoyle would never move again.

It was ten or fifteen minutes before Armstrong's mind again relaxed to the point where he could think rationally. He discovered presently that the aspirin must have taken effect, because the headache was all but gone, his shoulder was bearable, and no how much he flexed it, there was no pain in his leg. He looked around carefully for signs that the gargoyle he'd killed might not be alone, and breathed an audible sigh of relief when he'd satisfied himself that it was.

My God those things are strong! He stood up in the cockpit, feeling around the edge of the jagged hole, half expecting the metal to crumple as easily for him as it had for the gargoyle. The fleeting thought that the alien atmosphere had somehow weakened the metal was disproved quickly as a sharp edge cut through the rubber glove and slightly into his right index finger.

He relaxed for a moment, letting the fear drain away, before making a quick assessment of his situation. *It's about one hundred hours now, so the new helicopter should be finished and following the homing beacon to me. It should be overhead in less than an hour. Before dark. Even if there is a hitch, I should be safe here for the night. If the gargoyles come back, I have enough ammunition to fight them off.*

He knew he was trying to cheer himself up and wasn't quite feeling the security he professed to himself. Logically it was true; he should have little to fear, but there was a little voice inside him that prevented everything from being perfect, saying, "WHAT IF???"

He dug the flare gun out of the survival kit and was ready to fire one through the hole the gargoyle had made in the roof. At *least that thing made it so I wouldn't have to go outside*, he thought with a wry grin. The observation was made just as the graying sky signaled the beginning of twilight. It was rapidly becoming apparent that he was not going to be rescued that day, and he was becoming alarmed again. Even if the helicopter had not been completed, a HUMMVEE should have had time to reach him by now. His mental calculations told him that he was no more than sixty or seventy kilometers from AB0322. *Unless there was a canyon or some other obstacle?* His mind hung on that unlikely thought as the darkness became complete. He hadn't paid much attention to the terrain when they had been following the gargoyles, and it was possible that the ground was impassable for the HUMMVEE.

He set about preparing the inside of the cockpit to be his bedroom for the night by moving some of the wreckage and equipment that had been upset by the crash. He was not very comfortable, knowing he'd have to sleep next to Miller, but he didn't want to put the body outside for fear some scavenger might desecrate it.

Armstrong slept fitfully during the night, waking at least six times in the uncomfortable sleeping position, but at long last dawn began to soften the blackness of the eastern sky. He was up immediately, anxious not to miss the searchers. It was entirely possible they would take off before dawn to arrive here at first light. He would have done so, had *he* been in charge of the rescue. He scanned the horizon until his eyes ached, but there was no sign of a helicopter. Once his heart had done a quick flop, when he thought he saw something in the distance, but it had taken only a few minutes to discover it was only another of the gargoyles. It frightened him momentarily as it seemed to be headed in his direction, and he was quite relieved when the creature veered to the south and disappeared from sight.

When his watch showed zero and he had still not heard the familiar whopping of whirling rotors, he knew there had to be something wrong. The logical place to start was the homing beacon! It was inconceivable that if it were working, he would not have been found by now. He used his pocketknife to pry the top off the instrument, and stared bewildered into the empty shell. *There was nothing inside.*

Nothing!

"*How can that possibly be?*" He voiced the despairing thought out loud. *These things are supposed to checked two or three times before we get them.* He felt raging anger at the negligence of the person or persons responsible, but he transferred his rage to the trees and bushes around him.

"You think you're going to get me don't you! Well you don't have a prayer!" he exploded defiantly. "I didn't come all this way to be humbled by the likes of you!" Now he was outside the helicopter for the first time, demonstrating his contempt for the planet and its denizens.

"I'll get out if I have to *walk!*" The last sobered him somewhat, as he realized that he indeed *would* have to walk. He didn't know precisely where he was, but he knew the probability of being found by any search party for a long time was slim or *none*. He was outside the logical search area. They'd be looking for him in the north, but he had turned almost southwest in his haste to follow the gargoyles.

His first step was to use the GPS to find his exact location. It was AB5110, more than fifty kilometers from the nearest stan booth. On Earth, with good hiking equipment, trails to follow, and no dangerous animals to worry about, he could make that distance in one day, but here, to press that fast would surely be suicide. Besides the continuous need to ensure he was headed the right direction, he would have to move with extreme caution, lest he become dinner for some local beast. It would take him at least two Kadakas IV days, maybe three, to get to AB0322.

He required less than a half hour to get ready, once he decided to abandon the wreck. Taking only essentials, he even shed the rubber protective suit, knowing that he could only carry enough air for a half hour at the most. He did keep on the mask with its filter, assuming it might do him some good, but he had walked less than a kilometer before abandoning that, too. It was much too hot. It wasn't difficult wearing it while sitting, or even working, but the extra exertion of the walk made it impossible. Besides, he rationalized, the mask's curved plastic lens had impaired and distorted his vision somewhat. Most of his load consisted of the two M-80s and a generous supply of ammunition for them.

It was slow going——the moss and low shrubs provided little resistance to the HUMMVEEs, but the ankle-deep growth seemed to grasp at his boots every step of the way. It was as if the vegetation were in league with the gargoyles to slow him, and maybe, he thought apprehensively, eventually to hold him for them. Not anxious to expose himself for aerial observation by the gargoyles, be kept close to the trees whenever he could, paying special attention to the thicker copses. He didn't relish the thought of being surprised by one of the lobos James had described. The skeeks were abundant, and it was logical to assume they would be less active if predators were around. He was somewhat relieved by that thought.

His continuous meandering made progress slower, and he had to make frequent readings with the GPS to prevent traveling any farther than he had to, but he felt the extra time an acceptable tradeoff for safety. Early in the afternoon he came upon a swiftly flowing stream, no more than five or six meters across. Only a few centimeters deep, with a bed of eroded rock, it was no obstacle, but it served to point up another crisis——he was thirsty. The exertion and the relentless sun beating on him, made the delicious looking water even more irresistible. He realized that he should be able to complete the trek easily without taking water for the duration, but, he rationalized, his reflexes would be faster if he had plenty of water. And he would certainly be more comfortable. Thirst might possibly even impair his mental function. The water may contain something toxic, but the tests taken at base camp had turned up nothing as yet. The odds were that the water was too dangerous to drink, but the logic faded with the flow of the stream across his field of vision. Simple human need triumphed, and he energetically scooped the cool liquid into his mouth with his hands.

When his thirst had been slaked, he continued his march, and as the sun's rays began to slant more and more to the west, his apprehension about the night ahead grew. He considered and discarded a plan to continue on through the darkness. The constant drag from the vegetation tendrils had exhausted him, and it was quite clear he was too fatigued to go on. When he found a thicket of trees suitable to shelter him for the night his watch read two. That gave him two hours of light to improve the shelter, and gather firewood. He collected a large supply of two to three centimeter thick branches and constructed himself a rather sturdy lean-to in the lee of a large boulder that jutted out of the copse like a squat obelisk; not strong enough to stave off gargoyles if they came, but enough to make him less conspicuous and allow him a certain amount of warning.

He took a final reading with the GPS as the sun sank to a bloody hemisphere in the west. AB3ll6——he had remained on course, and traveled more than twenty-two kilometers——*not bad for half a day*, he thought proudly. *I should be able to make it easy tomorrow.* His spirits buoyed briefly before the darkness closed in over him like a shroud. The brightest star, *Proxima Centauri* in the northern sky was a brilliant beacon but didn't begin to soften the harsh blackness. That would wait for the rise of the moon. Right now the brilliance of the star only served to emphasize to Armstrong that he was a long way from home. The setting of the sun pulled the temperature down with it what seemed to be more than ten degrees. Armstrong knew that it was merely an illusion, but he pulled his jacket close about his shoulders and inched closer to the fire.

The night on Kadakas IV, as on Earth, brought out its noises, each carrying its own sinister message for the listener. Here a rustle, there a hoot——not quite like an owl——in the distance (seeming closer) the unmistakable screech of a gargoyle. Armstrong huddled inside the rude shelter, dozing fitfully on and off. The pain in his head and shoulder had returned with a vengeance, stubbornly resisting the soothing aspirin——but he had kept the fire burning, and the night passed without incident. What little sleep he'd been allowed had taken the edge off his fatigue, and the rest had allowed his tortured muscles to recover somewhat. He was eager to go. Long habit made him scatter the ashes of the fire and he did not begin the trek until the last ember was completely out. *Smokey would be proud of me*, he chuckled as he shouldered his load on the uninjured side and started off to the west.

XIV

FUEL TO THE FIRE

Devlin seethed. The mundane work assembling the helicopter allowed him a lot of time to think. The tasks were almost automatic——lower the component into place with the crane, line up the holes, insert the proper bolts, tighten to the proper torque. Laird, working with him did little to break the monotony. The pilot rarely spoke, and then only about the craft they were assembling.

By midday the disgruntled sergeant could take it no more." Major, I gotta go take a crap. Be back in a few minutes." *Maybe a short break will clear my mind and make the rest of the day bearable*, he thought caustically, as he move toward the bunkhouse.

Laird said nothing, but gave an offhanded wave of his left hand to acknowledge Devlin's comment.

Devlin sensed there was something wrong as he waited in the entryway for the decontaminating spray to complete its dousing of his suit. As soon as he entered the main building the feeling proved correct. Benton was sitting in the stanisplummer, seemingly in a trance. Devlin thought he must have just arrived and was initially surprised the captain hadn't warned them he was coming in, as was usual. It made him think there was some kind of an emergency, but if that were the case, *where was James?* He addressed Benton cautiously.

"What's happening, sir?"

He repeated the query twice when there was no response, before finally realizing that the man was completely insensible. He went to where the captain sat stunned and helped the man to his bunk. For obvious reasons, no one else could use the booth while someone was inside. Benton was pliantly cooperative; he rose to his feet and followed the sergeant to his bunk, where he sat docilely and blankly. Devlin made no further attempt to communicate with him, nor did he inform Laird of the incident. Instead he entered the stan booth himself and punched the code of Benton's HUMMVEE.

In an instant Devlin found himself in a small valley surrounded by trees larger than any he'd seen on Kadakas IV. There was no sign of James anywhere in sight. Attracted by sounds of scuffling, he cautiously got out of the vehicle and climbed to the top of the nearest hill about fifteen meters away. There, on the other side, a scene greeted his eyes that he would never forget. Three gargoyles were fighting over something with playful intensity, while a fourth lay dead in a heap a few meters beyond. At first Devlin did not recognize the object of their attention, but there was no question, although thoroughly mangled, it was the body of James or what was left of it.

Devlin's body rebelled at the sight, and though he tried to suppress it, the vomit came in deep, agonizing spasms. Luckily, the three gargoyles kept their attention on their victim, and he was able to stumble blindly back to the HUMMVEE. By the time he'd returned to base camp, his composure was completely regained, and his mind had devised a plan to turn the situation to his own advantage. He had already surmised Benton's role in the situation. All he had to do now was confirm it and get it to work for him. Benton remained where he had left him but had regained his senses somewhat, although he was still highly disoriented.

Devlin knew Benton would have to be questioned intensely before the captain regained control, and he attacked directly into the heart of the matter.

"Captain, what happened to James?" he hissed brutally.

"God! They're so big!" Benton almost screamed. "Got to get away! My God!…My God!…So big…Somebody stop them! Aaaaaaaah God!" The captain began to babble incoherently so Devlin steeled his nerves and slapped his superior's cheek hard with the back of a ham-like hand.

"Benton! Get ahold of yourself!" he exploded, and the captain's screams subsided into sobs."

Devlin was more direct then. "How did James let himself be taken by those monsters?"

"They were right over us before we had a chance to react. We both looked up at the two above us and James shot one, but then two others came at us from the side, low. I ducked, but James didn't see them coming. The thing must have knocked him out immediately, because the impact was tremendous, and he bounced down the hill. As soon as he was down, they all went for him. There was no chance: They were too fast. I had to get away!...I had to——Don't you see? They'd have gotten me, too if I hadn't gotten away!"

Devlin disgustedly realized then that the captain hadn't even tried to rescue James. He'd simply run. The sergeant reached for Benton's holster and withdrew the M-80 machinegun. A quick sniff of the barrel confirmed that the weapon had not been fired, and he walked quickly to the stanisplummer booth, dialed the number and was back inside the deserted HUMMVEE. He started the engine and drove to the top of the hill overlooking the carnage. The monsters had finished with the human and had turned their attention to the dead comrade. He aimed and fired the weapon without leaving the vehicle. Two of the beasts fell dead, and the sergeant returned to base camp purposely leaving the other alive.

He went directly to Benton, handing him the weapon. "Listen Captain. I'm going to go get Laird, and here's what you have to tell him. You and James were attacked by three of those things, and they got James down after he shot one. You shot the other two, and checked James. He was dead, so following regulations you came back here. You got that?"

Benton mumbled something that was unintelligible to Devlin, but he nodded his head, subdued.

"We'd better make sure you've got it. I shot two of the others, and left the other alive so there would be a reason for the missing body. I gotta make sure that you've got the story straight. You'd better repeat it back to me."

"We were attacked. James shot one. I shot two. James was killed, and I came back here." The captain was clearly ashamed; he refused to look up as he recited the script, and Devlin hoped he would tell the story convincingly.

*   *   *   *

He needn't have worried. Benton had told so many stories to cover for his cowardice he was an old hand. By the time Laird returned, the captain had rehearsed it in his mind so many times, he was sure the story Devlin had concocted would hold up under the closest scrutiny. *This* situation was not so "old hat" as it seemed, however. This time someone shared his secret. *Why had Devlin gone to the trouble to give him a cover? Certainly not because he still harbors admiration for me? Or, maybe he does? Sure——anyone can have an occasional failure—— So that's what Devlin thinks this is.* He knew it was not the answer, but it was comfortable and safe for now, and he decided to accept it. He would have time to reason it out later, but just then Laird and Devlin entered the room.

Laird asked only a few cursory questions——apparently Devlin had already filled him in on the details, before he raised the microphone to the ICT, which would allow him to talk to both Stark and mission control simultaneously. Thumbing the button, he said almost matter-of-factly,

"Houston? This is Eagle II. We have more trouble." Stark would be monitoring the conversation, so he didn't bother to use his call sign. Stark and Caglin were back at base camp in less than five minutes.

"Benton, take me back to where James is." The acting commander was all business and his tone startled Benton. Especially since he knew that the body was gone, and the other gargoyle might still be there.

"Do you think that's a good idea? There might be other gargoyles there. We probably should wait awhile to be sure."

"And let them eat James? No way! Let's go." He stepped back into the booth and waited for Benton to join him. The action left the captain no choice but to follow, and the two men were in the HUMMVEE facing down toward the three gargoyle corpses, and one live one still there blissfully feeding on the remains.

"My God, look at that disgusting thing!" Stark wasted no time dispatching the remaining gargoyle with his machinegun from the HUMMVEE. He watched for a moment, making sure it was dead, then started the vehicle's engine and turned to his companion.

"Show me where James fell."

He put the HUMMVEE in gear and began inching it forward down the hill, still wary of any movement.

"He was right down where they are, but I don't see him now. They probably ate him." Benton realized his slip as soon as it left his mouth. He'd used the word *they* when there was supposed to be three dead gargoyles when he'd left and the other one had come afterward. Stark didn't look as though he'd picked it up, however, because he kept the camera trained on the carnage in front of them as they approached, and Benton breathed an inaudible sigh of relief.

"I hope not. Maybe he's beneath one of the bodies? No. I guess that's not possible, because you said you saw him before you stanned back. Right?" He didn't pause long enough for Benton to answer. "Well, let's get out and take a look around. These monsters are too big to load in the HUMMVEE and stan back to base camp. We'll have to study them here. Whoops——What's that?" About five meters ahead of the HUMMVEE there was a small dark object on the ground. As he bent to pick it up, Stark recognized it as a piece of rubber suit. He held the scrap of shredded material up for a moment, before wrapping it in a handkerchief, and put it in the pouch on the bib of his own rubber suit." Looks like that's about all we're going to find of Sergeant James."

They searched the site half heartedly for a few more minutes, finding two more bits of rubber, before Stark decided any further attempt was futile, and they returned to base camp.

All five of the remaining members of the expedition sat quietly where they had gathered in the mess hall. Someone had put on a pot of coffee, and the perking sound was all that could be heard.

At last Stark broke the silence. "Tell us exactly how the gargoyles attacked you, Benton." he began quietly. "The rest of us may need that information sometime."

Benton thought for a moment. "The first one we saw was hovering over us. James hit that one, but our attention was distracted, and when it fell it almost landed on top of him, he dodged out of the way. The one that neither of us saw came from the side and knocked him down. We were standing on top of that hill, and the impact carried him clear to the bottom where you saw the bodies. The third one came at me just after the one hit James. I had warning enough to duck, and I don't think I was hit, but I could feel the air disturbance as it went by. It lost interest in me and joined the other one, which, by the time I got back to my feet, was already on top of James. I settled my nerves and killed both of them."

"When I checked James, it was obvious he was dead; probably since the time the thing hit him. It must have been traveling over two-hundred. I guess the one that was there when we went back ate the body."

"The hard plating on the front of those things," Stark added grimly, "must have evolved for precisely that purpose. One hovers, while the others fly in at great speed from the side, and batter the prey to the ground, where it is vulnerable. I wonder if that implies some intelligence to cooperate that way?"

"No way, sir! Not if they were eating each other! They can't be intelligent." Devlin was indignant at the thought.

Just then a voice not present in the room boomed from the wall speaker.

"Even us supposedly highly intelligent humans have all shown many examples of cannibalism." Everyone recognized the voice as belonging to Sean Kelly the ecologist. "But I don't believe," the gravelly voice continued, "that evidence of cooperation in the hunt indicates any modicum of intelligence. Lions and wolves here on Earth cooperate extensively, and no one would accuse them of being unduly intelligent, at least not on a par with humans. No, it sounds to me like your gargoyles have simply adapted to a method that works for them. The spines on the backs of the bennies are formidable weapons, especially when the animals spring into the air. A winged predator would not last long if he attempted to leap onto the back of one of these. Whereas the technique you described would work admirably Colonel Stark. Decoy them and knock them down from the side. Very adaptive."

Stark frowned and responded, looking in the direction of the screen upon which the red haired ecologist's likeness was displayed." What should we do to defend ourselves from them, Sean?"

"Well, you know more about security in general, but the first thing I'd do is to see if the horny plate can be penetrated by bullets, in case there's another immediate attack. No sense having impotent weapons."

"The real defense, however, doesn't involve killing them at all. I would stay near trees, which should discourage them from flying too low, and as soon as one is spotted overhead, assume one is coming from the side. Hit the ground immediately, and try to find the direction it's coming from. If you stay low it probably won't hit you. They should be used to much taller targets, like the bennies."

"Excuse me, Doctor. This is Sergeant Caglin. I don't know as much about biology, and all that, as you do, but I just thought of something. What happens if the gargoyle that's hovering over us sees us laying on the ground? Won't he think we're hurt and come after us?" The transmission came through as if Kelly were in the next room, because of the lack of distortion over the ICT, but it took a few seconds, as if the scientist was considering the reply.

"That is a consideration. You need to be concerned about that, and certainly keep the decoys in sight. Opinions on how to deal with the gargoyles flew from all quarters for the next fifteen or twenty minutes, but nothing was really resolved, except a consensus that the creatures were extremely dangerous.

Finally, General Janakowski himself ended the nonproductive talk by requiring the party to practice the technique proposed by Kelly with one addition. As soon as the threatened group threw themselves on the ground everyone had to shoot at the decoy.

Benton was the obvious one to notify James' next of kin, and he went to the isolation ICT booth at the entrance of the mess hall, while the remainder of the group, except Caglin who was on watch, stayed in the mess hall lingering over coffee and discussing the turn of events. All thoughts of continuing work that day were suspended, and they had broken contact with Earth to have a little while to themselves.

Devlin broke the gloomy silence." We should stay here, except for one more trip to study those dead monsters. We've got to find ourselves a way to defend ourselves from them. I said that *before* James got himself killed, and *now* it's the only thing we can do. Finish the other helicopter and arm it with some heavy weapons, so we can fight them. We can fly the two choppers together to support each other the way they did in the Iranian war. With that kind of firepower, and knowing what the gargoyles do, we couldn't be beat."

"I agree with him, Jim." Laird was clearly not happy with his position of supporting the sergeant against the colonel, but he added, "Armstrong's lost by now, even if he did survive a crash, the gargoyles or lobos have got him. Any further search is useless and dangerous."

Stark by then, was even finding himself thinking the search should be called off. He was fighting back periodic stabs of guilt over James' death and was right on the verge of going along with Devlin. The other two men stared at him, waiting for some kind of response, but he couldn't bring himself to give up. Somehow he couldn't shed the thought that Armstrong was out there somewhere waiting. He glanced out the west window at the afternoon sun dipping lower toward the expanse of ocean. *Two hours of daylight left, he thought, and I'm wasting it!* He got to his feet without giving them an answer.

"Devlin," he commanded, "Go up and relieve Caglin. Tell him to meet me by the stan booth in the bunk house." With that he walked toward the rack where his protective gear was stowed, put it on and left the building.

After he'd gone, Devlin turned to Laird and sighed, "Well what can we do? He's determined to kill himself and the rest of us tomorrow. I tell you, sir. We're really gonna come up short if he keeps it up. Sooner or later those damn gargoyles are gonna come here for us. We've got to be ready for them!"

Laird was not ready to commit himself, and he gave the sergeant a cold look and shrugged. "You'd better do as he says and get Caglin."

Devlin rose and ambled toward the door, but as usual he couldn't resist a parting comment. "Meaning no disrespect, sir, but that man is obsessed, and he's gonna have to be stopped."

Stark and Caglin continued their sweeps for the remainder of the day without results. They did see two gargoyles in the distance but didn't pursue them, and they flew off. Stark knew he was in for more of the same kind of dissent from Devlin when he returned, and he harbored strong suspicion that the rest of the men were in sympathy with the caustic sergeant. *The only way I can calm them down is to find Armstrong,* he thought, *but where is he? God dammit! The wreckage ought to be down there somewhere!*

The disappearance of the last crescent of the sun over the horizon finally confirmed his fear that they were going to come up empty, and before the waning light faded entirely, he located a safe landing site and set the craft gently down. Before he reached for the stanisplummer switch, he voiced his concerns to Caglin. "None of the others are with me, are they?"

"Are you talking to me, sir?"

"You know I am, Caglin. Answer me. You are all on Devlin's side, aren't you?"

"Is this off the record, sir?"

The major sighed in exasperation. "Whatever the hell you want. Just give me an honest answer.

"Well, sir, I really don't know which course is best, but it really seems like a big waste of time going back and forth over these forests. We probably couldn't see nothin' anyway. Devlin does make a lot of sense. If those things attack base camp, we should he able to defend ourselves."

"Oh for Christ sakes, Caglin, those gargoyles are just dumb animals. They're not capable of...Oh hell! What's the use?" He snapped. Frustrated, he flipped the switch on the control panel with a disgusted forefinger.

There *was* more of the same from Devlin, and the silence of the rest confirmed his suspicion. Stark didn't blame them,—the man could be extremely persuasive, and he himself was having doubts. He *wasn't* concerned about attacks by battalions of gargoyles—that was pure poppycock—but his confidence in the possibility of finding Armstrong was beginning to waver. Certainly he would be in a better position with the men if he were to give in—even if he allowed them to make a fort out of the base. *But what about the men lost out there?* The worst thing for him to shake was the notion that he was continuing the search for personal reasons—Armstrong had been a personal idol to him. *Would he have been so adamant if someone else were crashed out there?* He felt that the answer was affirmative, but he couldn't be *totally* sure.

There was an easy way out of the controversy. All he had to do was tell General Janakowski the situation, and let him make the decision. In that case, however, there was a chance *that* would make the situation worse. There was the possibility that the men would perceive it as a weakness. *Oh come on Stark! You know that would reveal weakness, or you'd run to the general in a minute!*

XV

THE PLAIN

Armstrong stuck rigidly to his policy of staying near the trees for most of the morning, but after the sun had lifted well above the horizon, he came to an area that was flat and wide open except for the low mossy growth. It was a huge meadow more than five kilometers across. It looked to be almost twice that in length. He had a choice. He could go boldly into the open where the walking would be easy, but he felt sure he would be vulnerable, or he could stick to the trees and add more than ten kilometers to his trek. He sat in the cover of a rather tall tree for a long moment, weighing the possibilities. A bold skeek——probably curious about such an obviously helpless creature as he, out unprotected——cautiously moved in little spurts to a spot no more than ten meters from him.

"Hello, little friend." The sudden noise startled the little creature, and it scuttled half way up a tree until curiosity held it there frozen, emboldened by the fact that Armstrong had made no threatening moves. When the skeek came back toward him in the same manner as before, Armstrong took care not to startle it and in a soothing voice spoke again.

"What should I do, little friend, go across or around?"

The skeek emitted a chirp that sounded much like a finch on a summer morning, and moved so close to the man that if he had reached out his hand, he could have touched it. The sun was warm and pleasant, and for a moment Armstrong closed his eyes and deferred his decision. The pain was still there, but resting had made it a great deal less intense.

"Well, the thing to do," he muttered to himself, "is to see whether I am close enough to the booth that the detour will not take too much time and get me there after dark."

Digging into the sack on the ground next to him, he found the GPS. Checking his watch, he told the skeek. "Seven twenty-two hours, and located at AB 2418. I've got a little over twenty kilometers to go if I go across. Ten more if I go around. Going around will take a lot more time because I'll have to wade through the bushes, while it doesn't look like I'll have to if I go across.

"Let's see how long it'll take each way." He did some mental calculations, and then looked longingly across the open plain. "I took five hours going the fifteen klicks this morning. I should be able to cross that plain in less than an hour, even as crippled as I am, but if I go around, it'll probably take three hours longer." The fact that the long way would put him there after dark, confirmed the decision he'd already made. The walk across the meadow would be easy compared to the progress through the woods, and he looked forward to not having the extra weight of thousands of bushes hanging around his ankles. He forced himself to his feet and was shouldering the sack, when a movement to his left caught his attention, and he dived for the cover of the tree again.

Whatever it was, he knew it was no skeek——it was much too large——but he hadn't gotten a good enough look at it to tell. He waited in the lee of the tree for more than a minute, watching alertly, when it trotted into full view. A benny, and a large one, more than five and a half meters tall. Armstrong froze. The huge animal was not more than a hundred meters from him, and remembering the size of the herd from two days before, his heart pounded when he realized it was unlikely that the creature would be alone!

His fear was correct, for on the first one's heels trailed two more, not quite as large. On some instinct, Armstrong pulled himself up on his knees, and hugged the tree as closely as possible. He was none too soon for, as if on cue, the bushes stirred behind him, and looking around he saw two more of the creatures coming directly toward him. He tried to become part of the tree. Climbing it would do no good, it was scarcely ten meters tall, and he felt, power from even one of the bennies was sufficient to uproot even the strongest tree. He got great opportunity to see them close up. They passed within three meters of him, and he could clearly see the small eyes set in the front hump, the protruding chin under the body, and the elephant-like trunk. The animals were obviously herbivores.

A parade was passing him now——all sizes——some calves no taller than his own waist, walking directly underneath with mother's trunk caressing and guiding. None of the bennies seemed to pay the man any attention, and Armstrong presumed that they didn't see him. *Poor eyesight from small eyes*? Or just didn't care about him because he posed no threat to them.

It took more than a half hour for the herd to pass, and when it finally did, it stopped *en masse* with the nearest animal only thirty meters away, and began to graze placidly.

What do I do now? He thought. He glanced at his watch. Six forty-eight. *Should I take a chance that those things will leave me alone?* He decided that he had to do something. There was no telling how long the herd might stay here—— maybe days. What shape would he be in by then? He suddenly felt extremely hungry and thirsty. A man can get along without food for a few days and water for something less, but waiting for the bennies to move along…*No! I've got to chance it*!

Untying the sack again, he found the flare gun he had brought with him on the off chance the searchers would come near him. He checked the load, shouldered the sack and holding his breath, began moving slowly and cautiously along the edge of the wood line. He looked like a mime pretending to walk on eggs. When the bennies seemed to take no notice, he walked a little faster, keeping the flare gun trained in their direction. Finally he was walking his normal dragging gait, much relieved that the animals continued their peaceful eating. The open plain was tempting, especially since he'd lost so much time waiting for the herd to pass. Each tendril of bush that caught his legs threatened to throw him to the ground and made it seem more inviting, despite the fact the bennies were grazing as far as he could see.

Finally he muttered, "What the hell!" and recklessly he took tentative steps onto the plain.

He felt naked, and kept glancing behind him, expecting something to leap on him at any moment, but the nearest bennies still paid him no attention. His senses were trained completely on the animals as he approached, his legs wound like springs, ready to run. His direction of march would take him through the herd on a path as far as possible from any of the bennies. Their long legs looked as if they could move the at tremendous speed, and he was certain that if they took a sudden dislike to him, he would have no chance to reach the safety of the trees. As he approached within twenty meters of the first benny, the animal stopped eating, turned so that its eyes were fixed on Armstrong, and raised its trunk toward him.

Armstrong froze once again, scarcely wanting to breathe, and waited until the beast lost interest and dropped its trunk to the moss. Two more steps and the thing became aware of him again, and he stopped, not as long this time. Step…step…step…Now he was past the first one and his attention went deeper into the herd, but the prickling sensation at the nape of his neck and upper back told him that he was still aware of the first one, and he glanced back periodically to reassure himself. In the midst of the herd, directly to his front, he could see the way blocked by a mother and calf. If anywhere in the herd were dangerous, Armstrong knew this would be one, but there was no choice. Any direction he went would send him toward a calf or deeper into the herd, so he continued on. Step…step…step…Suddenly he knew he was going to get a challenge.

One of the smaller bulls began moving, almost nonchalantly in a direction that would place it squarely between the mother and Armstrong. His heart thumping like a trip hammer, the man stood where he was and waited, with the flare gun outstretched before him, for the bull to make its move. At this moment he felt more impotent than at any time in his life. He wanted to break and run to the trees. He had the flare gun, and two of the most up-to-date machine guns, but what good would they be here? His only chance, if they decided to attack, would be if a flare could scare them off. If it didn't, there wasn't enough ammunition to kill them all, even if he used only one round for each one——and they were big enough that one round would not kill one. *Do these things have a vulnerable organ like a heart? Where would it be?* He would die in the middle of a pile of benny carcasses. The bull stopped five meters in front of him and pawed the ground with pad like feet. It made no other sound, but Armstrong knew it was telling him to go no closer to the calf.

He edged slowly to his left, and the animal matched his movement. If he could continue far enough the beast might let him pass by the mother. He moved again to the left with the benny keeping pace. Step…step…step. It was as if the two were doing a well-choreographed dance routine, and despite his fear Armstrong allowed himself a slight chuckle.

Abruptly, he was aware of a growing crescendo of rumbling. Tearing his eyes away from the bull in front of him, he saw the entire herd seemingly in motion. Not in the same direction, but at random, in the same manner a disturbed anthill seems to crawl in dissonance. Alarmed, he snapped his attention back toward his main concern and saw that the cow was moving off to his right, with the small bull giving him a parting snort (if that's what it was) and following her. For an anxious moment he thought the animal was coming toward him, and he nearly pulled the trigger on the flare gun. The fact that he didn't probably saved his life. He became aware that the activity was *not* due to his presence in the herd, for several other of the huge animals passed him closely without seeming to notice him. *But what was it?* His alarm metamorphosed into a cautious curiosity once he satisfied himself that he was not in danger.

Then he saw the cause of the herd's behavior.

Gargoyles! Three of them! Hovering over the herd three or four hundred meters from him. They were still pretty high, so the bennies had not begun their springing tactic. None of the herd was near Armstrong by now, and he began looking for a place to hide. He found one, which didn't seem to be very satisfactory at the time——a mere depression in the ground——but it was all he had, so he dove for it.

When his curiosity had overcome his fear, he peered over the lip of the hole toward the drama unfolding to his front. The three gargoyles had maneuvered themselves over separate small groups of bennies and were almost hovering—— actually he could see they were flying in tight circles, alternately going low, then higher. They were baiting the bennies to jump, and in the group closest to Armstrong, they did. A large swift shadow passed directly over the startled colonel, and he looked up just in time to see a new gargoyle flashing toward the jumping bennies. Its timing was bad; all the jumpers were down as it flew harmlessly above them, but off to his right he saw another coming, and *it* didn't miss. The hapless benny was caught at the apogee of its leap, and the impact carried the victim out of its group where it hit the ground rolling. The gargoyle that hit it also went down in a heap but scrambled up immediately before the bulls that converged upon it could present a danger. The hovering gargoyle dropped like a rock onto the upended victim, slashing both hind legs with powerful claws before taking to the air.

The benny, dazed, struggled to its feet, and limped back to the group from which it came. Apparently the winged monster had not been successful in dispatching it; it wouldn't leap for a while, but unless infection set in the wounds or it bled excessively, it would probably survive. The hunt continued for another half hour, with some of the gargoyles being more successful than others.

Armstrong counted three dead bennies, and one dead gargoyle——it had gotten too low as a decoy and had been impaled on the spikes of a rather large bull. As soon as the beast was on the ground and helpless, it was repeatedly gored and trampled by all the bennies in the area. Almost as if that had been a signal, the attack broke off and the gargoyles flew off.

Armstrong found himself immersed totally in the spectacle and had let his guard down, when he became aware of a shadow that blocked the sun, he knew what it was before he looked up and saw the hovering shape. The gargoyles had found a straggler and were closing in on what they thought to be easy prey. His reaction was swift: he fired the flare gun directly at the waiting belly. He missed. The sudden flash of light from the flare deterred the beast only momentarily, and it floated over him again like a huge greenish-brown hang glider seeking thermals. Armstrong rose up slightly to unsling the machinegun from his shoulder and lay back down just in time to feel the violent gust of air disturbed by the swiftly flying gargoyle, which came from the side supporting the one above him. If he had not been in the depression, the diver surely would not have missed. The one above him was growing bolder, and descended within ten meters. The down draft from its wings seemed to be like a hurricane, hammering bits of the moss into his face and eyes.

The cruel eyes on the forward hump seemed to glare right through him, and he could have sworn the jagged maw watered in anticipation of the delectable morsel. Armstrong shuddered and loosed the first burst from the M-80 directly into that maw. The animal's wings folded and it dropped like a rock on the lip of the depression, rolling onto Armstrong's injured leg. Pain exploded in his brain like a buzz bomb. How he remained conscious, he didn't know, but it was clear that if he stayed there, either the supporting gargoyle would finish him off, or worse the bennies would attack the downed gargoyle and trample him in the process.

The other gargoyle had already landed on the corpse of the first, and unsheathed glinting claws seemed to be reaching for Armstrong's exposed throat. Through the fog of the relentless pain he was aware that he had somehow aimed the machinegun, and a neatly stitched row of holes appeared on the fearsome creature's chest and it toppled over backward. Armstrong closed his eyes tightly to momentarily grit back the pain in his leg.

With superhuman effort he tugged his leg from under the oppressive weight. The relief he felt almost made him pass out, but he fought it off and opened his eyes to see yet another gargoyle hovering over him. He raised the gun and routinely shot the beast, taking care this time that it would not fall on him.

Resting watchfully for a moment, he planned his move away from the carcasses. He could see that none of the bennies were making any move in his direction, so he felt certain he would not have to worry about them. He rose to a crouching position and tested his weight on the injured ankle. Pain once again stabbed through him, revealing that it was either badly sprained or broken. Resisting the temptation to sit down again, he forced himself to hop away from the pile of corpses, for fear it would draw more gargoyles. He was right: no sooner had he moved, than two more of them landed on the carrion and began to feast.

They paid no notice of him, and after remaining still for a long time, he hopped laboriously back toward the woodline from which he'd come. It took him at least twice as long to return as it had coming out on the plain, and he was drained from pain and fatigue by the time he reached the relative safety of the trees. He lay under the nearest tree and rested for more than two hours, before he was able to think clearly.

What to do? A skeek came out of the tree to his left and regarded the man, but this time Armstrong was too fatigued to notice. All of his concentration was focused on finding a solution to his dilemma. The manufacture of some kind of a splint or crutch was going to be necessary in order to continue his march.

A quick look at his watch showed that even at full strength and going across the plain, he could not make it to the booth by nightfall. Less than four hours of daylight remained, and unless he could rig something up in a hurry he would have to remain here for the night.

I guess that's the best course now, anyway, he reflected glumly. *If I wait until morning, maybe some of the pain will be gone. I should be able to make it that far if I can make some kind of a crutch.*

Using the semi-rigid sections of bark and strips of rubber suit, he constructed a passable cast for his ankle, and while rummaging around in the trees for firewood and materials for a shelter he found a strong, thin stick, that he modified into a crutch. Thus, twice as hungry, and extremely thirsty, the man settled in for his second (and he hoped last) night in the wilderness of Kadakas IV.

XVI

THE PLOT

Morning arrived at base camp in much the same manner as it had for Armstrong. The air was filled with tension. Devlin was poised like a tiger, waiting for Stark to make the move that they both realized was inevitable. The men talked and joked as usual while they ate the morning meal, but there were undercurrents of edginess, and everyone watched the acting commander carefully while laughing too much at unfunny jokes and listening too carefully to uninteresting conversation.

When Stark finally did speak, the sudden silence caused his voice to echo hollowly from the walls. He made the exact statement everyone knew he was going to. "Caglin will go with me and continue the search, and the rest of you will remain here and complete the new helicopter. Jake, if you complete the 'copter before dark, you and Devlin come out and join the search."

No sooner had Stark closed his mouth than, as if following a tennis match, all eyes went to Devlin, but the colonel had his eyes there first. Devlin was sullen, but he said nothing. He had been aced. After the two searchers left, however, the mouth came unlimbered.

He was working with Benton connecting some circuits under the left skid of the helicopter, while Laird took the first shift in the watchtower——they had decided to keep someone there for fifteen minutes every hour as a precaution to salve their fears of gargoyles.

"Laird agrees with *me*, and I'll bet we could get him to call mission control and get those missiles up here, if we talked to him together."

The comment bordered on mutiny, and Devlin controlled his tone of voice so that he could claim he was joking if the captain protested. But Benton either didn't recognize it as such or was intimidated by the fact the sergeant knew his secret. His voice was edged with caution, as he responded tentatively.

"Colonel Stark would hear the transmission and be back here or tell them to cancel."

Devlin took the statement as license to dig a little deeper. "It'd be an easy matter to wait by the stanisplummer, and take the good colonel under control when he comes in for lunch. Then we could legally declare you as the new commander. Laird, being a pilot, is not really qualified to command."

His voice was still bland, as if sharing some incidental matter that had just occurred to him. Benton recognized the statement for what it was——blatant mutiny——and at first was indignant. He was about to fire back a silencing command at the sergeant, but he felt just the slight edge of the red veil slide down before the retort could pass his lips. *This man knew his secret.*

What *did* come out was so ineffectual as to only urge Devlin on. "No one will back you."

"The hell they won't!" Devlin growled, no longer tentative. He now knew that Benton was completely his, and he pressed the argument home. "They all know Stark is obsessed. Mission control would accept the argument in a minute. Every time Janakowski asks Stark whether the situation is under control, he feeds him that bull about everything being okay. You heard the transmission last night. They asked flat out whether they could send us help when James' death was reported. What did Stark say?" He paused rhetorically and went on before Benton could break in. "You heard him. Of all the ramblings of an idiot! 'No thanks, everything's under control.'"

"What the hell's under control? We've got three men dead! Unless we can get some heavy weapons, probably five more any minute." The sergeant stopped breathless, and Benton finally got the courage to say the word.

"You're talking about mutiny." he commented almost inaudibly.

"Not no! But *hell* no I'm not!" Devlin gritted challengingly. "Stark's gone crazy. Obsessed with saving some dead men, and leaving our guard down. Some orders are illegal, like the Mai Lai incident in Vietnam, and the Prescott incident in Iran. That sergeant——what the hell was his name? Wilson. Yeah. He had the guts to refuse to obey his platoon leader when ordered to a frontal assault on that strongpoint. The court martial backed him up——they said the order was suicide ten times over and served no purpose——that lieutenant was crazier than a loon."

"In Vietnam they gave Calley a life sentence for *obeying* an illegal order. We've got the same thing here, and if mission control knew all the facts, they'd *order* us to take over."

The sergeant was beginning to look wild-eyed, but Benton gave it no notice. He hung on every word, and with each second the ramblings seemed to grow more logical. The captain stopped listening to the words, because they were becoming redundant, but he rolled the half-baked logic around in his mind until it seemed well done. If Devlin could convince Laird, he would go along also.

Just then they saw Laird coming down from the tower, and Devlin stopped his tirade. He turned to Benton and said in a low voice," I'm gonna get the next shift in the tower; you loosen him up and get him to see what we are talking about."

This was a hitch. Benton realized that Devlin was counting on *him* to get Laird on their side, and he was about to decline the responsibility when he thought the major was already in earshot. The three men worked in unnatural silence until it was time for Devlin to take watch. He departed with a sullen comment to Laird, telling him where he was going.

Alone with the major, Benton wondered if he dared broach the subject. He now knew that he was stuck with the job, but how did he get into it without totally repelling Laird. He cleared his throat loudly and was about to make some asinine opening statement, but he realized the major paid no attention, and he lost his courage. He worked in silence for the next ten minutes, his hands automatically going about the task of plugging in the wiring for the stanisplummer into the cockpit of the almost complete aircraft.

It was Laird who broke the silence and took Benton off the hook. "Bob, do you think Jim's right to go on looking for Armstrong?"

"What do you mean? It's in the regs that he search for two complete days."

"I think we both know he'll go on searching tomorrow, and the next day and the day after that. He's like that. He'll probably have *us* out there looking, too, and we'll keep going over ground that's already been covered. Devlin might be a little fanatical in his concern about the gargoyles attacking us, but we do need to find a way to defeat them. There's no way anyone can settle on this rock if they're still a danger. I want to get out of here sometime, and the longer we take looking for the wreck, the longer we'll be stuck here. We've got a hell of a lot to do!"

"I liked Armstrong as well as anyone——he was a hell of a brave man, but *was* is the key word. Both he and Miller are dead. I don't think anyone doubts that by now, and there is no sense wasting valuable time on a wild goose chase."

"You think we can convince him to give up the search?" Benton put on a show of sounding dubious.

"Frankly, no I don't." He emphasized his doubt by dropping the ratchet wrench he was holding clanging against the floor of the helicopter.

"I think we're going to have to relieve him of command."

"Do we have grounds?" Benton still looked incredulous.

"It's not cut and dried, but I think we can convince mission control of the necessity. First we have to be sure everyone here agrees. Devlin and Caglin will go along for sure. Devlin has loudly proclaimed his opinion, and Caglin will go along with anything he says. The only one left is you. What do you say?"

"This is a pretty big step, Jake. I'm going to have to think about it. If mission control doesn't back us up, we'll be up for mutiny charges, and even if they got wind of this conversation, we'd be charged with conspiracy."

Benton stopped work and tried to scratch his nose, an effort he abandoned as soon as his finger touched the plastic faceplate. "Maybe we should wait and see if he decides to give up the search tomorrow. Then we won't have to take such drastic action."

"Come on, Benton!" Laird exclaimed. "You saw him this morning. He's determined, and he's not going to give it up or listen to anything anyone has to say opposing him. He's closed himself off to reason. Devlin's shift in the tower was up and the two officers watched as he climbed carefully down the stairs and crossed the intervening fifty meters of bare brown ground, kicking up little puffs of dust with his heels. Without a word he picked up the spanner wrench, climbed the scaffold and began tightening access plates on top of the craft.

*   *   *   *

In the helicopter far to the north, Stark knew that he could not cancel the search tomorrow. It was possible that the two lost men could survive for more than a week. The weather was good, so exposure would not be a problem, and he was convinced they were out there somewhere. The problem was comparable to looking for a needle in the proverbial haystack, but anything can be found if you look long enough. With a slight temerity, he understood the real obstacle would *not* be how tough they would be to find, but how he could keep the men from mutiny. *That damned Devlin! He's got everyone all charged up about those gargoyles invading base camp.* The monotony of the search had inured him to the passage of time, and he was surprised when he felt the pang of hunger rumble through his innards. Desperation made him resist the urge for more than an hour, straining his eyes to see what wasn't there. Finally, Caglin forced him to make a decision.

"Sir, I don't know about you, but I'm pretty damn hungry."

Reluctantly, Stark acknowledged the implied request but just then had an idea." Sergeant, you go on back and get something. I'm not really hungry. I'll stay here and search! If you don't mind, bring me back something to snack on."

It was heresy, but he was desperate to have as much time for the search as possible.

"But sir, it's against regulations for you to fly alone, and as much to eat while this thing is in the air."

Stark was adamant. "I don't need you to tell me regulations, Caglin. This is an emergency."

"I can handle it, sir. I'll just stay here with you."

"That was not a request!" snapped Stark. "It was an order! Now get out of here!"

It was impossible to go by himself through the stanisplummer in the cockpit, so with some difficulty, he unsealed the hatch to the cargo hold, stepped through and pulled it closed behind him. When he was ready, he rapped on the glass port, and Stark hit the switch. Caglin arrived in the main cargo stanisplummer near the ship, and was surprised not to see anyone working on the obviously still unfinished helicopter. His alarm vanished quickly when he realized they were probably in the mess hall eating lunch, and he walked in that direction. Some caution told him not to blunder directly in, and he first peered through the window.

When the mess hall proved to be empty, he repeated the action at the bunkhouse. There they were. All three of them were facing the empty stan booth, and Devlin had an M-80 on his lap with the muzzle pointed directly into the glass-enclosed box. Suddenly it hit him with a shock. They were waiting for Stark to come in for lunch, and they were going to take over. Although he himself agreed with them in substance, it took all his self-control to prevent him from going immediately back to warn the major. For some reason, he didn't want to talk to the men in the bunkhouse either, and he went to the mess hall, threw two sandwiches together, grabbed some soft drinks, and left without alerting the others he had been there. He would aid the cause by staying silent, but if the plot went sour, he could claim no knowledge of it.

* * * *

The three in the bunkhouse sat grimly waiting, until they responded to Stark's routine report that told them they would not be seeing him until the end of the day. The tension and its subsequent release shook the resolve of the men in the mess hall, but none so much as Benton's. He took it as a sign that the plot was doomed to failure and argued weakly for its abandonment. But the others had determined their course of action and the decision was inalterable. They had the patience to wait until that evening, so they casually went back to work on the helicopter. Shortly before two hundred hours, Stark and Caglin made the final westward pass that completed the first sweep of the seventy-kilometer square search area. Stark had long since decided that this would *not* end the search. He intended to cover the square again, and even once more, if that was what it took to find the downed helicopter. He was certain they hadn't gone down in the ocean. It took very little deductive reasoning to conclude the gargoyles were not in the least equipped to be sea birds. Thus, they would have no reason to fly over open water. In fact, they would probably avoid it. As large as they are, they must have to land quite often. He couldn't see them being able to take off again from the water. He turned the craft directly south and followed the shoreline for more than a half hour before banking the craft again to the east.

One twenty-eight, he thought after a quick glance at his *watch*. *I can make three passes before dark, if I fly at full speed.* Just then Caglin was pointing out the orange rectangle that was stan booth AB0322 directly on a line between them and the low mountain in the distance. It was the same mountain he'd seen his first day on the planet, and it still fascinated him. The direction to it was slightly south of the seventy-klick box, but he continued to fly that direction on a hunch. *What the hell! We didn't find them north of here. Maybe they went this way. It's a long shot, but...* The stan booth slid beneath them, and they fell into the routine surveillance once more.

Caglin saw it first." We ain't seen nothin' like that before, Major. It almost looks like a cut in the ground."

In front of them was a long open area. From their vantage point, it looked like a lone divot on a well-tended golf course. They were headed right for it and in less than five minutes, it revealed itself to be a long open meadow. When they got closer, they could see it was not empty. There on the ground was a huge herd of bennies clustered toward the center and eastern side.

"Look sir, some dead gargoyles. There and there. Two of them must have died together, because they are lying almost on top of each other. D'ya think one tried to help the other out?"

Stark could see dead bennies as well, and he knew the gargoyles had made their kills, probably in a large pack, and they would probably come back to eat when the herd had moved on. Maybe they were a hunting pack and they had returned for the rest of the flock. No. That would imply a high level of intelligence. Something the gargoyles do not possess. He was interested, and almost succumbed to the temptation to land for a closer look, but the lengthening shadows reminded him of the mission, and he allowed the clearing to slip beneath the craft as they headed further east.

✳   ✳   ✳   ✳

Armstrong wanted to be sure he had enough wood to last the night, so he hadn't lit the fire yet, but he had constructed his leanto, and was resting as comfortably as possible on a mattress of gathered moss. He must have been dozing when he heard the familiar sound of the helicopter, for the noise was very clear when he first became aware of it. His initial impression was that it was a dream, and he remained immobile for long moments waiting for the sound to fade.

"It is a helicopter!" The bellow caused two skeeks, which had shared his tree, to scamper for their lives. Armstrong burst through the top of the shelter like an erupting volcano scattering sticks all around him. As he came erect, the motion threw him slightly off balance, forcing his entire weight onto his bad ankle.

AGONY!

Pain seared through his brain with such intensity that no mortal could cope with it. A pain that could only he relieved by unconsciousness or insanity! It was the former that comforted him.

* * * *

Stark saw the reflection first. "Did you see that? Light reflecting from over there…There it is again!"

He pointed his finger, indicating a spot some eight kilometers to the front and slightly to the south.

"I don't see anything, sir." This time they both saw it. It was definitely a reflection off some smooth surface. The only thing they'd seen on this planet thus far, capable of reflection was water, and that couldn't be it now. The sun was too low.

Ten minutes later they were on the ground next to the wrecked helicopter. Stark walked the few intervening meters to the mass of twisted metal and plastic, carefully skirting around the grotesque dead gargoyle. Even from their helo, it had been apparent there was only one body inside, and Stark confirmed it was Miller.

The colonel's mind worked rapidly. *Only an hour of daylight left. Which way would he go? Was he badly injured in the crash? Did he crawl off somewhere to die? That gargoyle was killed by an M-80. If he were badly injured, he wouldn't be able to do that.* His thoughts jerked rudely back to the way the gargoyles hunt. *Maybe the other one killed and ate him? No. Wouldn't it have at least partially eaten the other gargoyle?*

"Caglin, get your butt over here, and help me search." Stark shouted in a voice that got the sergeant there quickly. "I want a quick search around this area, no more than fifty meters radius. You go clockwise, and I go the opposite direction. Look for shreds of protective suit, like we found when James was killed. Go!"

The cursory search took about ten minutes and was fruitless, boosting Stark's morale. They quickly got back aboard the helicopter, and took to the air.

"Which way do you think he'd head? PE0322 is closest but not by much." Caglin was amazed the commander had managed to survive and was uncertain why Stark had failed to report it as yet. "Colonel Armstrong was pretty sharp. He would go toward the nearest booth, unless there was some tough terrain to cross, and we didn't see anything unusual except the clearing which ought to make…"

Stark stopped talking as if he'd forgotten what he was going to say next. "Of course! The clearing!"

He abruptly suspended the zigzag search pattern and pointed the nose of the craft toward the setting sun. "It has to be! Why do you think there were two dead gargoyles together off to the side that were not gored and trampled like the other one?" He directed the question at Caglin, but it was clear that he didn't expect him to have the answer.

"I don't…"

"THERE!"

Caglin followed the direction of the pointing finger, but could see nothing.

"I don't…" Caglin was cut off again.

"Because of an M-80." Stark chortled. "That's why!"

Caglin still had difficulty understanding what the colonel was talking about, but just then he saw what Stark continued to point at——a vertical, pencil lead smudge just to the right of the rapidly diminishing orange dome that was the setting sun. As they got closer and the sun sank lower, the eye could easily follow the smudge to the ground, and pick out the faint glow of the fire that Armstrong was building larger by the minute.

XVII

THE SCIENTISTS

Caglin was greatly disappointed that he was not able to see the looks on the faces of the men in camp as they saw Armstrong materialize in the bunkhouse booth. Prudence decided that the injured man go via the cockpit stanisplummer, even though he would have to sit up. Because there were only two places in the cockpit, Caglin had to wait until the other two vacated it before he could follow, so the surprise had dissipated somewhat by the time he got there. To the discerning eye, there were still signs, and Caglin made it a point to look for them. Devlin was carefully disassembling the machinegun on his lap for cleaning, and no one but Caglin noticed that it was still loaded, until the sergeant surreptitiously slipped the drum into the belt pouch. The two officers had obvious (to Caglin) sheepish-relieved expressions etched into their faces. Neither Stark nor Armstrong seemed to notice, but Caglin thought he glimpsed briefly what he took to be a look of triumph that the former directed at Devlin.

※　　※　　※　　※

The mood in the room was significantly different from what it had been that morning. Everyone (with the possible exception of Devlin) was wildly enthusiastic about the commander's return, and without the pall of gloom even the air seemed to be clearer. They talked to each other about the adventure for more than fifteen minutes, bombarding Armstrong with question, before Stark remembered mission control and moved to the ICT. Before he flicked the activating switch, he made sure the camera was trained on the colonel. The picture and voice those on Earth perceived seemed to come from the grave.

"Houston, this is Eagle II." Armstrong sang with obvious delight. "Long lost little boy reporting in."

"This is Houston." The sounds of celebration in the background were so great that the speaker could barely he heard. "Welcome back-"

Armstrong told his story in great detail then, and it was a half hour later that the gaiety subsided. When it had, Stark's expression changed, and he said somberly.

"Houston, I hate to put a damper on the merriment but we've got something serious. I think the colonel's ankle is broken. The doctor is going to have to come up, set it and look after him. The response was immediate.

"First we'll send up an x-ray machine and get a picture of it. If it's not broken, there's no sense risking the doctor yet."

Stark recognized the voice of General Janakowski, but was quick to press his argument. "Now that we know a little more about those gargoyles, I don't think they're as big a threat as we expected, and I think the colonel agrees with me. We can protect ourselves from them. All we have to do is maintain a close watch, and the procedures given us by Sean will work admirably. We shoot a few down over the compound, and they should learn to leave us alone here. True, we can't think in terms of unprotected children living here until we've found a way to deal with them, but I think we'll be a lot closer to finding it, if you send the scientists up."

There was a slight pause before the gruff voice of Janakowski came through.

"Is that your opinion, too, Scott?"

"I agree with Jim, one hundred percent, but let me throw in my two cents worth. I believe we can get rid of these abominable protective masks now. I lived for more than two days without the use of them. I even took a drink of the water yesterday, and I'm still kicking. In fact, except for the sore ankle, I never felt better in my life."

The general hedged. "We'll get back to you on that, but for now nothing's changed. Standby for the x-ray machine."

That ended the transmission to Earth, and everyone was up, eager to please the returned commander. Even Devlin volunteered to make the round trip to the mess hall for his meal, while the others helped him to shower and shave.

The x-rays showed that there *was* a break. Fairly clean, but the doctors decided it needed a pin on the left side and of course, a cast to be sure it healed properly. Katy Yeager and Sue Powell, who would assist in the surgery, were scrubbing in the latrine of the mess hall within two hours of the conversation with *Project Icarus'* director. The tables in the dining room had been moved to the walls, and an entire, well-equipped operating setup had appeared as if by magic in their place. Armstrong was already on the table, his ankle shaved (the three officers had cut cards for the privilege——Laird lost) and prepared for surgery. There was no real emergency about the operation, but they felt the sooner it was over the sooner it would heal, and he could be in one of those new lightweight plastic casts. He had already been warned by Janakowski and Doctor Yeager that he would have to stay off it for at least a week, but nobody really believed they could keep him down for more than three or four days.

The night passed quickly, and morning brought a jubilant group of six scientists into their midst. The population of Kadakas IV had grown to fourteen, and the newcomers were eager to get out into the bush to begin their jobs. In the mess hall the old-timers were bragging noisily about their expertise on the planet and how they'd narrowly escaped death, when Armstrong, completely recovered from the effects of the anesthesia, rolled out of the stan booth followed by Stark. The stanisplummer link between the two buildings was put in to get the commander into his own bunk without having to force his unconscious body into a protective suit, and the wheelchair was the only way they could prevent the willful commander from walking the distance on his own. Stark moved the chair to where it could be seen by everyone in the room——a mobile throne with right leg elevated and thrust out before him like a proud lance.

Since his rescue, his stature in everyone's eyes had taken on tremendous proportions. This was not the man they had grown to take for granted over the last six months. This was a superhero! One who had single handedly challenged an alien planet and won! Never mind that he had no choice, the accomplishment was everything. It was as if those in the room had suspended respiration simultaneously. Everyone's attention was riveted on the man in the wheelchair.

Armstrong hesitated, instinctively knowing that the pause would allow the worship to grow even deeper. Oh, the reverence would steadily erode in the future, as they had daily contact with him, especially in such a small group, but the deeper it began, perhaps the longer it would stay. Maybe long enough to complete the mission? He didn't know. He hoped so. Finally he rubbed his temples with forefingers and began to speak.

"This day begins an important phase of the mission." He paused momentarily to be sure everyone was listening. Trying to meet everyone's eyes, he went on.

"The advance party has been here long enough to determine that we will probably not drop dead any minute, and the animal life here, though dangerous, can be coped with. I'd like the word *cope* to be the key word in our study of Kadakas IV. We have been given *carte blanche* to make this planet suitable for people. We have a chance to begin with a virgin world. Unspoiled! Unpolluted! And not inhabited by sentient beings! Of course we don't know the last for sure, but we'll deal with that when the time comes, if we have to."

"The main thing I see here is: WE HAVE A CHANCE THAT WE NEVER HAD ON EARTH!" A dramatic pause here for exactly the right amount of time captured his audience completely.

"We have the opportunity to develop a planet, yes, even to exploit it, forewarned that lack of controls can produce disaster. Obviously, our just being here has changed this planet forever. I believe, however, that with prudence, those changes can he minimal. *You* have been entrusted with the task of determining what we can and cannot do. Today begins the day when we can cease wondering whether we can survive here; we already know we can do that. Now we must find out whether we can *co-exist* with Kadakas IV." They had all heard the pitch over and over again, but it took on new meaning for them here. They sat entranced, hanging on Armstrong's every word.

"You must understand, of course, we are here for the good of mankind, and we shall wrest from the planet living space, natural resources, arable farm land to feed the hungry masses, and provide employment. This will be a frontier which will bring prosperity the likes of which has not been seen since the closing of the American frontier in the early twentieth century. But this time it will be for the *whole* of humanity. Not just a small group of lucky European immigrants. This will be the beginning of a frontier that will last indefinitely——even infinitely, although we can't be totally sure of that. For some day, maybe thousands, or even millions of years in the future, we may run into another intelligent race that will compete with us for the universe, but it would be an unimaginative race that would not coexist with us in a limitless universe. There will be enough for everyone."

"But we don't have to do it at the expense of the planet. Indeed, we have it in our power to make Kadakas IV, with the sophisticated technology that now exists, polluters and despoilers can be detected in an instant and punished almost as rapidly. We here have a responsibility to be sure the first experiment is a clean one. Granted it would probably be much faster and easier to get a fleet of helicopter gunships up here armed with Hellfire missiles and hunt dangerous animals like the gargoyles into extinction, in much the same way our ancestors did with the American Indian. We could probably do the whole job in less than a month, and with less uproar than the Indian massacres caused, because the gargoyles are ugly as sin, and obviously not very intelligent. I ask you though, is that necessary, or even wise? Probably not."

"I think we can find an easier and better solution. One that is infinitely better for the creatures, and us. If, after a reasonable period of time, *that* is not found, extermination may be necessary, but let's find out first."

If anyone had been watching closely, they'd have seen Devlin's face visibly redden at these last comments. "The ecology on this planet, from the layman's point of view," Armstrong leaned forward in the chair and gave everyone the impression talk was for him alone, "is not nearly so complex as that on Earth. The life forms are not so diverse. In an area the size of the one we explored here, on Earth, one would encounter perhaps ten times the number of species. If I understand it right, a less complex ecology is a great deal easier to destroy than a more varied one. Our little party may not do it, but the numbers of human beings who will descend upon this rock in a very short period of time could do great harm, if not destroy it completely. If the balance *is* destroyed, it might take centuries to restore it again, if even that would be possible."

"One last comment before you go out there. While you take the great pains I know you will to prevent damage to the planet, do the same for yourselves. Never forget the gargoyles are extremely dangerous, and if you're threatened, shoot quickly. Do not wander off by yourselves. Remember two brave men died here already, and though their deaths helped us learn how to defeat the creatures, you are still vulnerable. Scientists, while you are working in the field, there must be at least two security guards at each site. I know we don't have enough for a lot of different sites now. Maybe mission control will send up some replacements, but until they do, no more than two sites at a time can be manned."

Eyebrows raised at the last sentence, because everyone knew three divided by two didn't come out even. There were only five able-bodied military men, two of whom would be in the helicopter extending the string of stan booths to the north or beginning a new one to the east. That left only three for guard duty. Everyone assumed that one would be left in base camp for security, and the others would go out in the field. Armstrong saw their surprise but wasted no time in explanation.

"Bob. You take Sergeant Caglin to one location——let the scientists decide where, and Jake, you and Devlin guard the other. Boris you, Hiro, and Katy have work to do here. I'm sorry, but you'll have to secure yourselves until we get those replacements. However we've had no evidence of gargoyles here since the hole in the fence, so maybe they're leery of this place already."

"Everyone, make sure you've gone through gargoyle drill at least ten times before you're allowed out in the field." Gargoyle drill had evolved into simply falling prone immediately, locating the creatures and shooting them down. The main danger was the prevention of hoverers from falling on top of them. Armstrong's experience showed them the hundred fifty pounds could do them significant harm.

The silence that ensued made it obvious to everyone that Armstrong had finished speaking, and they fell into discussion about where the first sites might be. The chatter approached the level it had been before the colonel came in. Hans

Stauffer approached Armstrong, who was engaged in a low conversation with Stark. He waited patiently for a few seconds until he was noticed, then began to speak, cutting off Stark in mid sentence.

"Colonel, I appreciate what" (his w's came out v's so the word actually came out vat) "you are doing, splitting your men so ve can haf two sites. but it seems to me zat will only slow down za vork, because ve will haf only za zree sites already zere. Shouldn't ve have someone in za helicopter setting up more?"

"That's just what Colonel Stark and I were talking about. "He scratched his temple with his left hand, and continued calmly. "We are taking the new helicopter directly east. In three days, we will give you a close look at the *hot spot*."

XVIII

THE HOT SPOT

During those three days the scientists were busy. The results were important discoveries. The geologists had discovered several oil and other mineral deposits in close proximity to the stanisplummer booths. The biologists had completed their initial environmental tests more quickly than they had anticipated, and based on those results, General Janakowski had given the okay for everyone to go outside without the protective gear. They sighed in relief as they tossed their suits into heaps and breathed in welcome gulps of Kadakas IV air.

No one had come close to the solution of the gargoyle problem yet, but fear of the big flyers was diminishing rapidly. Two of the groups had been attacked, but were able to defeat the creatures easily. The drill worked flawlessly. The only real danger would come if someone let his guard down. Armstrong and Stark had extended the string of booths almost fifteen hundred kilometers east, and they had discovered a greater variety of life with each landing. They had gone over a mountain range nowhere near as rugged as those on Earth and were beginning to encroach on a vast plain; the mountain slopes had larger trees and different types of animals. The most notable of these was a great bear-like creature, which was probably too large for even the gargoyles to tangle with. It was the size of a killer whale, with powerful fierce-looking claws, and they had given it a wide berth.

The discoveries were important but seemed unexciting and routine as they got closer to the hot spot. Located as it was on the high plains, it was an enigma and a favorite topic of conversation at mealtime. In fact Devlin had channeled his energy into a more positive line. He had become proprietor of a pool for which he took bets as each new bit of information was received regarding the cause of the spot. They were gathered for conversation as usual in the mess hall after dinner, where the hot spot had even greater focus of attention. Tomorrow they would reach it, because the last landing of the helicopter was only about seventy kilometers west of the phenomenon. George Barstow was repeating for everyone the reason why he felt it could *not* be, in his expert opinion, geothermal in origin.

"I've said this so many times, once more won't hurt. Geothermal activity is most generally associated with volcanic disturbances and is therefore located in the mountains. Not only is this spot *not* located near any mountains, I don't believe there is an extant volcano on this planet. It's so old and has revolved so many times, that the crust of this ball is almost uniform in its thickness. The topper is that it is so old that its core has probably cooled so much that, even if there were chinks in the crust, molten activity is so deep that it's not possible for any to reach the surface."

"But the tide…" someone interrupted.

"Just serves to add weight to my argument." Barstow continued. "The tidal forces are *very* great, what with two stars having strong influence and a huge moon to boot, and that would seem to cause rifts and upheavals. Not so."

"You've got to remember the crust of a planet is not brittle to the point of breaking. A ten millimeter thick pane of glass five centimeters long in a vise will shatter if it is bent only one centimeter, but if you flex a pane a meter in length, it will not only flex easily, but probably much farther than a centimeter. Like flexible modeling clay the more it is rotated and flexed the more uniform its thickness, the more flexible it becomes."

"There *is* a chance, but not very likely, that I am wrong, and there is a geyser basin. I'm not going to place any bets on it, though."

Six people in Devlin's pool *had* though, but the smart money was on the other major theory——radiation. Recent satellite imagery had shown the area around the spot to be defoliated somewhat, especially to the southeast. In that direction there was a swath of bare ground extending more than thirty kilometers, which was gradually less foliated as it approached the spot, like a giant shadow. At the very edge of the spot the ground was almost totally denuded. *Perhaps radioactive dust blown from the spot on the prevailing wind?*

That was Armstrong's theory, and he'd already begun to take heavy precautions for that eventuality. They had been monitoring background radiation for the past two days. So far there had been no change, but he fully expected tomorrow to be different.

There was a third theory, but it was so far fetched that no one but Joni Huntley——the author of the theory——would venture a bet on it. It held that the spot was residual heat escaping from a huge underground city, where they would find an advanced civilization, a sort of *Shangri-La*. The sheer lack of evidence that there had ever been intelligent life on the planet had taken this one completely out of the running, but that didn't keep Joni from extolling its virtues to anyone who would listen.

There were listeners now; two with amused grins on their faces——Hiro and Benton——and one who watched the female scientist with reverent attention.

Caglin probably didn't hear any of what she said but would defend it as gospel to anyone trying to dispute it. He had been hopelessly in love with the pert geologist ever since he first saw her.

"If that's the case, why are there no roads, or farms?" Hiro was interrogating the girl.

"There could be any number of reasons," she replied seriously.

"Maybe they're advanced beyond the need for surface transportation or even the need for food. Maybe they're not from this planet at all but from another star and using this as a base."

Doctor Yeager, who had just joined the group, cut in.

"Kind of a big base isn't it?"

"Yes it is big, and I can't explain that." She fidgeted nervously and leaned against the wall with her arms folded across her stomach. Caglin jumped to her defense.

"At least she's not afraid to say what she thinks. What do *you* think it is?"

Katy looked pensive and a little contrite. She *had* been jibing the girl a little too much. "You're right. None of us will know what it is until tomorrow. Maybe we'll all be wrong." She looked at her watch. They had less than five minutes to curfew, and she began looking around for someone to talk to. She wanted to escape the tense moment.

Just then Devlin helped her. "All right, ladies and gents," he blared. "Last chance to get your bets down. The latest odds are: geothermal three to one, radiation even, city fifty to one, and Major Laird's latest theory that it's a huge heated waterbed pays five thousand to one. Come on! You can't top odds like that."

Everyone laughed, and three or four moved toward the sergeant, but everyone was aware that the gathering was over for the evening. They all began moving in the direction of their beds.

In the morning there was an air of festivity, and everyone was there when Stark and Armstrong stepped into the stanisplummer. The colonel had become accustomed to the weight of the cast and moved with an easy grace. Before he settled on the rail that conforms to the seats in the helicopter, Barstow made him promise again that as soon as they landed in the hot spot, he would be allowed to examine it first hand. Stark pressed the toggle, and when the booth was empty, the other teams began to go to their own work sites. Stark had made the mistake of landing the helicopter facing east, so the first rays of the bright orange disc caught them full in the face. It made Armstrong's momentary stan dizziness even more pronounced, but he fought off the effects quickly.

"Jim we're going to have to remember to make it SOP not to park these things facing the rising sun. It's really hard on the eyes."

Stark squinted at the commander, his left hand on his brow shading his eyes. "I see what you mean."

He looked away from the sun at the unbroken plain that was around them. He couldn't get used to the flatness of it. As far as he could see there was nothing but the greenish-yellow moss like plant, except in the west where he could still see the misty purple of the mountains rising like the bumper on a billiard table.

"Reminds me of west Texas. 'You ever been there?"

Armstrong was preoccupied with the settings on the radiac meter he had in his lap. "Huh? Sorry, what'd you say?"

"This country reminds me of Texas."

"Oh, yeah. Well let's get going." He turned his attention back to the instrument, and Stark started the turbine. Armstrong yelled over the whine.

"Looks like no unusual readings over night." Reminded, he donned the helmet on the floor in front of him, so he could use the intercom. "That's kind of strange isn't it? If there *were* radiation out there, you'd think there would be some kind of reading here."

"Maybe not. The weather pattern on this plain probably has the wind blowing the same way nearly all the time. It may never blow this way at all."

They flew over undistinguished terrain for twenty minutes and landed to establish a stan booth PC5386, only thirty kilometers from the hot spot. The next booth, if they could approach the area, would be inside it. The meter continued to show no increase in radiation, but Armstrong was still reluctant to abandon his theory.

They took off quickly. Just after they were airborne, an interesting sight greeted their eyes. Armstrong saw it first. It caught his attention *only* because it was the only thing he'd seen the whole morning that was different; just a blotch of white on a field of yellow-green.

"Take it down over there, Jim, where that bit of white is." The helicopter banked right and lost altitude. The white came into focus——a gargoyle skeleton. "Okay, we don't need to see any more."

As the aircraft leveled off once again, Armstrong was aware of the same sensation that had troubled him on the night of the landing on the planet. Something was not quite right. *The gargoyle skeleton? No, they had to be common.*

"There, Colonel!" The excited cry made him forget his foreboding, and following a line from Stark's pointing finger he saw it, too. The slight change of color signaled the forward edge of the hot spot. It was actually very close to the same color as the rest of the prairie, with just a touch of brown mixed in. He glanced at the radiac meter, and the reading made him totally discard the radiation theory. There was no change in the reading. As they got closer, the ground was increasingly brown, until it became uniformly the new color. The GPS display told him they were now over the hot spot, but they could see no reason for it from the air.

"We're here. We might as well set this thing down and see what we've got."

At an altitude of about one hundred meters a curious sensation came over Armstrong as he looked down. The ground seemed to move! He attributed it to the movement of the helicopter at first, but when they got a little lower, he could see clearly that it *was* moving. At thirty meters he could see why——animals. The ground was teeming with life. Animals similar to the skeeks and about the same size were assembled in a herd. The helicopter landed easily in the midst of them, crushing several of them in process. Stark had hovered for the last few seconds, hoping to scatter them, but they seemed to show no fear or interest in saving themselves. The reason wasn't apparent to the men when they got out—— the animals could move and did as they continued to eat the moss. Armstrong had to take care not to step on the little creatures, because they seemed oblivious to him. Even when he stood still they kept bumping into his boots, and after picking one up he thought he knew why——they didn't seem to have either eyes or ears, although these may have been hidden by the long fur. They were similar to the other animals on this planet in that they were quadrupeds, they had no head, and the mouth that was filled with innocuous looking little teeth, was directly under the body. The mystery solved, the two felt initial disappointment that it was so simple and remembered the rest of the crew in suspense.

Armstrong thumbed the push-to-talk switch on the portable ICT on his belt and said with great gravity, "We have solved the mystery, and it is not dangerous, so we'll put in a new booth here and let you all come see for yourselves."

The response was immediate.

"I'm in the booth right now and on my way through the cockpit." It was George Barstow, and though Armstrong knew it was a breach of the rules, he relented.

"You're going to be disappointed, George, but come ahead." He saw Barstow in the helicopter almost before he quit talking and moved himself toward the cargo doors to remove the orange stan booth.

Stark, joined him, holding up one of the creatures, saying, "I wonder if these things are good to eat." They're about the size of small rabbits. Maybe they taste as good."

"We won't find that out for a couple of weeks, but fried rabbit does sound good." Armstrong's mouth watered as he thought of the rabbit dinner his mother had cooked for the family last week. *Was it really only last week? It seemed like a year.* The day turned picnic like. Everyone was there but Epilov, who wasn't interested in the mystery, and Barstow, who went back to work muttering to himself about how biologists have all the fun. Two of the soldiers had been placed on gargoyle watch——these furry little things probably drew their share, and Armstrong wanted to take no chances. The women were cooing about how cute the creatures were, and everyone was stroking the soft fur of one or two of them. Benton had picked up on Stark's idea of eating them, and some of the men were talking about how good they'd be with this barbecue sauce or that spice when Joni interrupted them, appalled.

"How can you even think of eating these cute little things? You're all a bunch of barbarians." There was a chorus of agreement from the other two women, with male support from Sakagowa, who was a vegetarian, and Kelly who didn't happen to care for rabbit, or other *rodents*. Even stoic Hans Stauffer was caught up in the interest in the creatures, but it was purely professional and in no way culinary. Not bothering to stop longer than the time it took to gather ten of the creatures for specimens, taking great care not to harm them, he followed Barstow back to the lab.

It took only ten minutes to find the atrophied organs that before eons of evolution had been eyes and ears. Now they were totally useless. But how did these fuzzy little creatures survive in such a hostile environment? That was the question that puzzled him. They should be easy prey for gargoyles, or lobos. They were extremely slow, had no way of fighting, and had no protective camouflage. How do they stay alive?

There were several possibilities. Maybe they don't taste good, or are even poisonous. Maybe like skunks, they emit some unpleasant odor, not to humans but to the predators here. *Well*, thought Barstow, I'll find out. The problem intrigued him. This is exciting——all of the other animals found on this planet fit neatly into niches and were easy to relate to Earth counterparts, but this…

After the first day, everyone forgot about the little creatures, except Stauffer. They were named *wuzzies* by Joni, and they were so cute and cuddly, several of the women had tried to keep a few as pets, but they would not stay. As soon as they were outside they wandered off. Finally the only ones left were those trapped in Stauffer's specimen cages.

XIX

A MORE PRESSING DANGER

Armstrong felt no hunger that evening and decided his self-conditioning was working. He had habitually eaten three meals a day on Earth. With the short day on Kadakas IV, however, to counter that threat of gaining weight, he made it a point to skip one meal in six. He hadn't bothered forcing that regimen on the others for they were expected to remain on the planet for no more than a month. Stark and Laird had followed his lead voluntarily, and he'd tried to get some of the others to do likewise. Benton and Caglin had given it a half-hearted try but had given it up, and Devlin had outright refused. His reasoning was, "If there's a chance that we might die up here, at least I'm going to buy the farm well-fed!"

When the colonel felt no urge to eat on the following morning, he became slightly concerned and went to Katy to see if he might be sick. She gave him a quick examination. Satisfied with her diagnosis that he was fine, he joined the rest of the crew in the mess hall. However, he still had no desire for food. It was a strange way not to be hungry. If he thought about food, he lost interest, but if he were thinking about something else, his stomach would growl, and he would feel a fleeting pang. He thought about forcing something down so he wouldn't feel too uncomfortable by noon, but he decided against it. His mind said *eat*, but his body fought it off.

By that evening, when he still felt no hunger it began weighing on his mind and he resolved to eat, regardless. The dinner for the evening was steak and it was done to perfection, just how he liked it. Normally he'd have no trouble downing it, whether or not he was hungry, but now he just sat and stared at the plate. It seemed the harder he tried to eat the more repulsed he felt. He was totally involved in his dilemma, otherwise he might have noticed the other untouched steaks on the table.

Just then Benton, who got up and headed on the dead run for the latrine, interrupted his thoughts. The captain didn't make it. After his third step he left a trail of greenish vomit behind him. They could all hear him retching, agonizingly through the open door. The doctor rose and followed him. It was a long time before he reappeared, haggard and wan. By then Katy had her black medical bag, and had latched onto his arm, escorting the captain toward the bunkhouse. The incident broke up the meal, and they all went about their business after several untouched steaks went into the garbage pit.

There was no change in the morning. By mid afternoon, Armstrong discovered, though he seemed to feel no worse, his mouth was exceedingly dry and his lips were chapped. He had the cap on the full canteen halfway off when a shudder carried through his body. The thought of taking a drink so repulsed him that he tightened the cap back on the container and put it away. *How long had it been since he'd had anything to eat or drink?* The thought was just in passing and carried no particular concern, but he could not remember the answer. *I'll force myself to eat something tonight.*

That evening's debriefing revealed that Benton was worse, and that Laird and Devlin were showing the same symptoms. The doctor reported that she had found nothing wrong with them, and she had simply prescribed plenty of fluids, and made them comfortable. However, the liquids would not stay down. They'd take one swallow, or even a sip, and the contents of the stomach would come right back up. The retching would continue for more than five minutes, until the men were totally exhausted.

"Mission control has people working on it," Katy was saying dejectedly, "but we've got nothing to go on. I've been able to find nothing in their bodies that is not present in the rest of us, and anything that is remotely alien has been tested in terrestrial animals in astronomical proportions. I'm retesting of course, but I'm as certain as I can be that all those samples are benign. I can't even replenish fluids expelled more rapidly than normal because of the vomiting and sweating due to the physical exertion of the spasms. Any attempt to introduce fluids either orally or intravenously simple causes the retching to recur. Benton is so dehydrated, that he continuously calls for water, but I'm afraid to give him any."

When Armstrong discussed his own lack of hunger with the doctor, it was determined he probably had the same illness as the other three, and that Caglin and Stark were also sick. It hit them then that all the original crew was sick, and *none of* the newcomers. *Had they taken off the protective gear prematurely?* Armstrong ordered everyone to again wear the suits when they were outside and required the scientists to suspend planetary research to concentrate on discovering a cure for the illness. Learning from the example of the first three contracting the illness, Armstrong required that himself, Caglin and Laird stay indoors where the air conditioning would inhibit the loss of fluids, and not attempt to eat or drink anything. They would simply wait and see if anything could he done for them.

It became increasingly clear on the following evening that something would have to he done for Benton. He was vomiting almost continuously now, and he had grown so weak that he was unconscious most of the time. Nothing had turned up in any of the research. Attempts to insert IVs seemed to make the retching worse. Katy thought they were just making him lose ground that much faster. Laird and Devlin were somewhat better. Though the vomiting sessions did come upon them periodically, the doctor had allowed them to relax and kept them continuously bathed in cool water. Unless a cure could be found, it was only a delay of the inevitable. Death by dehydration and malnutrition! Benton was close to death already, and Katy feared he would not make it through the night, but the other two might be able to hold on for a week. If Armstrong, Caglin and Stark did not attempt to eat, they would last for twice as long perhaps. Katy Yeager had never seen anything to compare with this.

Many times before there had been illnesses that other doctors felt were terminal, because they couldn't recognize the symptoms. Then she had almost invariably been able to match up one of the symptoms to some almost-forgotten memory, and, with some research, find a treatment. She had been revered as almost psychic in her ability; a notion she had decided was absurd. Now she knew it was false. *How can you treat something that is not there? For this there was no memory!* She had come as close to breaking down during the treatment of Benton, as she had her entire life.

Everything she did seemed to make him worse! Always before, when there was a wrong guess the symptoms did not accelerate——The treatments were simply not effective, and she would go on to something else. With this however, the more she did the worse it became. The worst thing for her, however, was the fact there were no symptoms except for the revulsion to food and water. There was no fever. No infections showed up on cat scans or other tests. No abnormal blood pressure. No blood vessel blockage…Nothing! It couldn't be happening.

But it was! The ecologists had joined with Kelly and Sue Powell in the attempt to assign a cause to the malady, but they were having no better luck. Blood samples from the sick men showed numerous local bacteria and viruses had already invaded them, but none were shown so far to be different than those in their own bodies. Using laboratory animals, they injected varying amounts of these new microbes with concentrations many times higher than those in the men. Not only was there no reaction from antibodies, but the animals showed no aversion to food. If anything they ate more heartily *after* the experiment than before.

Benton died that night, fulfilling the doctor's prophecy. The situation took on a new urgency. Gargoyles could be exterminated, if necessary, but this illness *had* to be overcome. Not just because this planet would be shown not suitable (*Project Icarus* had another landing scheduled for within the next half decade, not soon enough for thousands of poor.), but the kicker for the men and women here was——*they couldn't go home* even if they did avoid contracting the illness themselves.

After noon, Sue Powell joined Armstrong, sitting by himself in a corner of the bunkhouse. She had an initial pang of selfishness as she drew near to where he was sitting, but she shook it off. They hadn't talked alone since that night on the moon, fulfilling the agreement they had made not to allow their mutual interest to interfere with the mission. His spirits rose as she sat next to him.

"It's good to see you," he began, and she smiled, relieved that he was not upset with her.

"I was hoping you'd come, but I didn't want you to think I was weak by going to you." He looked her in the eyes for a moment, and his voice took on an indefinable tenseness. "I'm scared, Sue. Russians and gargoyles I can fight, but this…"

She put her hand on his shoulder. "I'm sure we will find a cure, Scott. The best doctors and scientists on Earth are studying it, and we have a lot of time now that we know not to give you food or water."

He was depressed and felt like being negative. "Those same high powered guys have been working on cancer for decades, and it's still the biggest killer ever."

She had no counter to the comment, and she just gave him a dejected look, eyes brimming with tears. "They *have* to find a cure, Scott. It *can't* end this way. The world so full of hope one minute, and to have it dashed to pieces the next." Then she controlled herself and reached for his hand. "Come on, there's no sense talking like this. Let's take a walk."

"Not very romantic with those masks on." His spirits rose as he got to his feet.

"I don't care, as long as you're there it'll be nice."

Neither of them said any more until they were outside near the western fence looking over the ocean. It was high tide, and exceptionally calm, so the water looked almost like a lake at his feet. Sue broke the silence, choosing a topic calculated to take Armstrong's mind off his problem.

"I had the strangest feeling the other day——almost as if something was trying to communicate with me telepathically. Nothing very strong, but it was there. Do you think it is possible that there are intelligent beings on the planet?"

She had been interested in ESP as a student and had once scored rather high on the Rhine tests for telepathy. It remained a passing interest to her, though she had been frustrated at her lack of progress. Armstrong had placed little faith in it, but realizing her interest, he had humored her. Now, however, he was in no mood to listen to what he considered hogwash and was about to change the subject when she went on. "Probably just a dream, but it was almost like there was a baby…frightened of being eaten by some terrible monster. It touched my mind for only an instant, then it was gone."

"It was a dream." Armstrong remembered Benton's nightmare with a shudder. "I've had them myself, especially since we found the gargoyles. Those ugly things are perfect for stimulating bad dreams."

She persisted.

"It wasn't a nightmare. In fact I seemed to feel pretty good about it."

Armstrong shot her a look that told her he wasn't interested in hearing any more, so she changed the subject. "Isn't the sea here beautiful? The greenish tint reminds me of the way it looks in the South Pacific."

They talked for about fifteen minutes before she began to feel guilty about the time she was taking out of work——she had been helping the biologist——and she left Armstrong alone.

Finally the realization that the combination of the rubber suit and the sun were making him sweat his life fluids away, he returned to the air-conditioned bunkhouse.

* * * *

A day later, while Devlin and Laird had grown visibly worse, the scientists had come no closer to a solution. In fact, they had given up in the laboratory. All the possible leads had turned into solid, unshakable dead ends. Armstrong had gathered them in the bunkhouse for a discussion to determine their next course of action——a last ditch effort. At first they just looked at one another with dejected looks on their faces, but Armstrong, talking through the gummy, dry orifice that his mouth had become, directed them to begin reviewing their research, from Benton's first symptom to the present. No one wanted to begin, so he did, pausing often to lick his lips in a vain attempt to moisten the cracked, bleeding edges. He hadn't attempted to salve them with Chap Stick after the first attempt sent him retching into the latrine.

"When Benton first got sick, I was already feeling symptoms. I was hungry and thirsty, but something prevented me from eating. That same day Major Laird and Sergeant Devlin began their bout…"

Barstow interrupted him at that point, the wiry geologist showed fear on his face like a mask. "Exactly one week after your landing here. That means tomorrow we should be feeling the same symptoms, and in a few weeks we'll all be dead."

The same thought had occurred to the others, but no one had voiced it until now, and if the mood was depressed before, it was desperate now.

Barstow was not finished. "If we go back to Earth, maybe the symptoms will reverse themselves, and we'll be okay."

"There's no need to be hysterical about this…" Armstrong found it difficult to say any more.

Devlin, whose gaunt face clearly displayed the debilitating effects of the disease, seized the opportunity. "That's our only chance. Epilov, you know all about those stanisplummers. You can get us back." He sank back on the pillow drained of energy.

Everyone knew that none of the stanisplummers here had the capability of dialing an Earth number. It was a precaution for just such a circumstance that presented itself now. The only way they could return to Earth was with the consent of Mission Control. With this illness that clearly was a threat to every person on Earth, there was no chance that approval would ever be given.

Armstrong began to talk again as if he hadn't heard the interruption, but many eyes found their way to the Russian engineer. "We can solve it here. Let's just think." The last came out like someone attempting to whistle with a mouth full of crackers. It was to no avail. The discussion netted little. There was too much fear in the air, and Armstrong's normally powerful personality could not fight its way out of the dry mouth. He recognized at that moment any further discussion would only add to the hysteria that was already lying heavily over them like a dark fog.

He was about to adjourn, when Katy Yeager's voice splashed through the gloom like a spray of icy water. "Major Laird has gone comatose!"

They all looked at the still figure on the bed with the useless I. V. tubes dangling along his sides like unnatural spaghetti.

Sean Kelly broke the ensuing silence with a flat statement. "I don't know about you folks, but I am going to make my last few days of life, if that's what they are, *worthwhile*. I'm going back to work to find as much about this planet as I can. To hell with it! Being depressed about something I have no control over is not what I hope to be remembered for. Maybe I can find something worthwhile to leave to the human race." He cast them all a defiant look. "If I've got to go, at least I will go with dignity. I'll feel a whole lot more comfortable about dying here than taking this damnable illness to Earth, and, perhaps, being the cause of the death of the human race."

"Besides, I'm just not interested in any more crises." With that, he turned on his heels and stomped off in the direction of the laboratory without bothering to stop long enough to put on his protective suit.

The rest, stunned for a moment as they watched his receding back disappear through the door, milled around and finally seemed to reach simultaneous decision. Those who wanted to try for a return to Earth gravitated toward Epilov. The others, like iron filings drawn to scattered magnets emulated Kelly and returned to work.

It took a long time for Epilov to convince those who wanted to abandon that if Earth did not want them to return, it was not possible to set the stanisplummer from this end to get them back. The booths here were not even compatible with any but the two that had sent them up. The leading agitator, Barstow, would not be convinced and kept badgering Epilov and Sakagowa. He eventually grew belligerent and threatening, but other than Devlin, who could not physically support him, he had no outspoken allies and was just ignored.

The following day they received two pleasant surprises. None of the scientists got ill as they were expected to, and Laird, in a coma, was being kept alive with a glucose solution fed intravenously. In desperation, Katy had tried the IV, fully expecting him to convulse and die on the spot. But he did not. After gaining the approval of Armstrong she tried the same solution on the rapidly failing Devlin. He was not so lucky. He immediately went into violent retching spasms, green phlegm coming from his lips. She could only stand and watch as he writhed, afraid to give him a sedative for fear it would be toxic to his weakened body.

Devlin died vomiting and screaming.

XX

HOPELESSNESS

Twenty hours later, Laird regained consciousness; his first words were to ask the doctor for water. The rest of the party somehow got wind of it, and by the time the doctor secured Armstrong's permission to give him the water, they were all assembled in the room. The major was handed the almost full glass with a most ceremonious aplomb. Without hesitation he drank deeply, emptying almost half of it. He lowered the glass in front of him, allowed himself a puzzled look around, as if not recognizing his surroundings and raised the glass to his lips once again. When the glass was drained he held it out to the doctor and implored her to give him some more. Katy took the glass and was turning to refill it when Laird spoke timorously.

"Why am I here?" The question left the watchers dumbfounded, and no one could think of anything to say for a moment.

Armstrong was the first to recover from the surprise. "What do you mean, Jake?" That question confused Laird even more and his eyes flashed around the room with greater anxiety.

"What is my name?" he inquired sheepishly.

The amnesia was complete. The pilot had no recall of anything related to the mission, or anything else in his career. It was as if his entire consciousness had been wiped entirely clean.

By that time Armstrong, Stark and Caglin were edging closer to the critical stage in the illness. Caglin had to be strapped to his bed to prevent him from eating or drinking something. They had been five days without food or water and fell into prolonged periods of delirium. Still, none of the scientists showed any signs of the illness.

As Armstrong's delirium extended to fill the day, it became necessary to place command in the hands of Katy Yeager, the only military member of the expedition still unaffected. Because the crisis was medical in nature, the choice of the doctor was well founded, but the frustration of the medical researchers was evident. There had still not been any modicum of progress, and although the work schedules were around the clock, the attitude of hopelessness throughout the base camp was rampant. Being the commander of the group added to her despair. With Armstrong alert, she had his strength to lean on, but now she had never felt so terribly alone. It was difficult for her not to feel personally responsible for the largest failure in history. Finally in desperation, she resorted to a long time Armstrong tactic, the group meeting. The previous one had been less than successful, but before that they had produced results, and she could think of nothing else to do. She resolved not to allow any negative comments to surface, if humanly possibly. It would be a slim hope, she realized. Hundreds of the best minds in the world had sorted through every detail of the data with negative results. But it was *something*, and it beat admission of defeat.

She addressed them reluctantly. "I really don't know where we go from here. You all know what we've looked at. We've been over that ground many times. Reviewing what we've done again would be a waste of time, so I don't want to do that. What we need is a fresh start. I want to hear your ideas, and they can include anything we haven't covered before."

Looking around the room, she saw that no one but Barstow seemed inclined to speak. She felt sure she knew what he would say and refused to acknowledge his waving hand. When she saw him begin to speak anyway she desperately cut him off before he could utter a sound.

"Someone *must* have an..." Just then she saw out of the corner of her eye a tentative motion of the hand of Saksgowa, and she turned to him with an eagerness that betrayed her willingness to grasp at straws. "Hiro?" Barstow gave her a look laced with venom, but he relented while the Japanese technician began to speak haltingly.

"Excuse me, Doctor Yeager." Sakagowa darted quick looks at the other people in the room as he spoke, as if trying to gage their reaction to him. "I do not know much about biology or medicine, so perhaps I should not be speaking at all, but I thought since everyone seemed to be stymied maybe..."

He stopped momentarily, looking for reassurance. He got none, but no one seemed inclined to stop him, so he decided to go on, now with more confidence. "I was with Toshiba Corporation before I was selected for the honor of accompanying you here——in the lower executive level. You all know that we created some of the complex electronics necessary for the development of the stanisplummer along with vital components for the computer industry. I have been in many such similar situations as this——*not*, you understand, related to medical problems, but involving technical ones. We have been in situations when solution seemed to be impossible. The answer eventually surfaced using a technique we called 'brainstorming.' Some of you may be familiar with the technique?" He paused again when he saw some of the faces light up in recognition.

Barstow broke in immediately. "I *know* the technique you're talking about. In fact I've been involved with it before. I also know that ninety-nine percent of the time it doesn't produce the solution for a given problem. Sometimes it produced a suggestion for something entirely unrelated, but how could that help us here?"

Barstow's tone was belligerent, and Sakagowa again looked around the room for support before responding. All of the faces seemed noncommittal, and none but the geologist appeared to be hostile.

"Doctor." He addressed Barstow directly. "I've read some figures for the success rate of brainstorming also, and it seems to me that failure rate for a specific solution is much lower than that. If the session is tightly controlled and the participants are prepared thoroughly, it's more like eighty-five or ninety percent. It *is* much better if the participants go into the session without an inkling of what the problem is, but that is quite impossible in this situation. Ten or fifteen percent chance of finding a solution to this illness is not very good, but I would be more willing to put my money on *that*, than on repeating what we've done so far."

Epilov had been listening carefully to the exchange, and when Sakagowa paused, he jumped in immediately. "The Russian Union has done extensive research for several decades in the area of parapsychology, not necessarily in the area of extra-sensory perception, but also in the area of mind enhancing drugs which have been used in brainstorming sessions. Remarkable results have shown failure rates of only on the order of sixty-five or so percent. This work has been done under the cloak of secrecy, because it was felt that it would give a marked advantage over the West if we could find answers that they didn't have."

The speaker in the mess hall barked into life with the hurried voice of General Janakowski. "I've heard about this technique, and the boys in the aerospace industry swear by it. Let's quit talking about it, and *do* it. What do you need?"

Everyone's eyes went to Sakagowa. Stuttering, the little technician spoke. "Toshiba has a room, dome shaped, with thick padding on the floor and walls. Participants take off their shoes, loosen tight clothing, relax and begin talking about anything that comes into their minds. The idea is to eliminate pressure and distractions. The entire session is recorded. Consultants listen to the tapes afterward, and glean useful information."

Things moved quickly then. Within two hours Janakowski had sent a suitable "*brainstorm room*" that would shield the members of the expedition from outside interference. Two more were installed in the auditorium in Houston. Those in close contact with the problem would participate in a simultaneous session and another group was hastily put together from members of several high IQ *Think Tanks*.

The only stickler was the acquisition of the mind-enhancing drug from the Russians. At first they denied knowledge of its existence. Only a threat to bar them from access to anything learned in *Project Icarus* pried it from their unwilling hands. Four problem-solving experts were called to Houston, arriving quickly thanks to stanisplummers. After a brief conference, they all concurred that the brainstorming technique would come closer to the solution of the enigmatic illness than any other. They worked together to come up with an orientation for the participants.

Precisely two and one half hours after Janakowski said, "do it" the three groups were relaxing inside the brainstorming domes, waiting for the drug to take effect. It was thought important to have Armstrong, Stark, and Caglin participate in the session, though no one knew whether they would be coherent enough to understand what was going on, let alone be rational in their comments. They were, of course, without the benefit of the mind-enhancing drug, for obvious reasons. Laird was also present in the padded enclosure. His memory had returned somewhat with his physical recovery, but he still had no recollection of anything pertaining to the mission.

The "Brain man" chosen as the spokesman began his instruction. "The idea," he said placidly, sounding much like the stereotypical mortician, "is to relax as much as possible. Lean back. More…That's it…Now, try not to think of anything. Close your eyes. Let your fingers hang loosely at your sides. Let your mind go blank. You should be completely relaxed. Fine."

"Now imagine your vocal cords are attached directly to your memory. Your memory must have a direct line out. Try not to think about anything. Just say what your memory wants you to. No matter how nonsensical it may sound let it come out. Some of the most nonsensical sounding ideas have been combined with others to form some very sensible concepts."

"There are only two constraints. One, do not speak while someone else is speaking. There is plenty of time, and you will be heard. Two, while someone else is talking, try to allow your mind to absorb their ideas. Do *not* listen to what others have to say or make judgments about it. Most important, make no reference to anything anyone else has said."

"Now, relax and begin."

He waited about five minutes and went through the spiel again then left them on their own. The session lasted four and a half hours and would have gone on longer, except the experts recognized the signs of fatigue and told the participants to sleep for four hours before resuming the session. They were already analyzing the results. As they left the think tank there was some off hand conversation.

Barstow, his voice overriding the others, still thought the idea was silly and made no bones about it. "We ought to be expending this time experimenting, not listening to a bunch of idiots, in some sort of a comfortable *encounter* session." He spat the word out like his mouth was suddenly filled with bile. "The next thing you know, they'll have us naked and yelling at one another, exhorting us to 'get it all out, it's good for you'."

He stomped off to the bunkhouse when nobody challenged him. Sue Powell didn't feel like sleeping, but she dutifully went to her bed taking with her a tape of the session, intending to listen to it. At first, she was inclined to agree with Barstow, but she was clutching at straws. She'd had great difficulty not listening to the others during the session. Although she sometimes forced herself not to listen, she was sure she would remember almost word for word. None of what she remembered would come close to solving the problem. It was all nonsense. Using earbud headphones so as not to disturb the other women, she listened for no more than fifteen minutes before going to sleep.

Sakagowa had started it off because he was the one with the experience. She remembered the disgust she'd felt at his inane comment.

Sakagowa: "Spring on Honshu is most beautiful. The cherry blossoms, the azure water…" (How could he waste precious time like that when Scott was dying?)

Caglin: "Flying is fun, but in a helicopter its like you're suspended from some great skyhook, hanging just above the treetops and when you turn…"

Huntley: "God! It's terrible that they're sick." (At least *she's* on the right track, even if it's no help)

Sakagowa: "Why would you want to eat them?" (What?).

Caglin: "Gee this planet is pretty. I've been here for a longtime now, and I'm never going home." (He must be delirious).

Stark: "I don't know what to say, but I've got to say something. Sow crabs are plain little things if you can even see them. They look exactly like sand."

Epilov: "I'm going back to the Russian Union when we go back. They can't be all bad if they made available the drug." (The drug must have gotten to his reason.)

A voice Sue didn't recognize: "None of the bacteria are harmful maybe it's bad air—vapors, like they believed in the Middle Ages? No, the chemicals have all been analyzed." (At least they were getting closer to the problem).

Powell: "Do you want to eat me?" (Was that really her own voice making that asinine comment? Somehow that made her angrier than the others' irrelevant statements).

Armstrong: "Those damned gargoyles are atrocious. They eat their own dead. Cannibals! I can see them now, eating bones and all. Waste not. Want not." (Oh God Scott, get well *please!*).

Stauffer: "I'm not hungry now. Why did I say that?" (I wonder? This is really a waste of time).

Yeager: "There is really nothing physically wrong with them. Why?" (That was obviously the largest error ever made. All you had to do was take one look at the emaciated bodies).

Caglin: "I bet they would taste good." (What a time to talk about food but I guess it's natural for him, as hungry as he is).

Stauffer: "Why are you taking them? Will they be hurt?" (What's he talking about?).

An unidentified voice: (unintelligible)…"where we can look now?"

Armstrong: "Bleached white gargoyle bones." (Is it a minstrel show or some kind of incantation?).

Powell: "Who are you, and what are you trying to tell me?" (This startled Sue fully awake for a moment, as she hadn't remembered making that statement either. Try as she might, she couldn't relate the comment to anything that made *any* sense. She missed part of the next statement because of her puzzlement).

Stark:…"killed by the gargoyles. The sow crabs and the skeeks are camouflaged." (Nothing important, although it would have been of professional interest to her if she could take her mind off the present crisis).

She didn't remember any more of the tape, because the next moment she was transported as if by magic to a wide yellow-green plain where she could see nothing but the same unbroken color in any direction, except the deep blue sky. There was a feeling of extreme peace and well being, as she knelt to the ground and began running her fingers through the soft luxurious moss that grew there. The moss excited her, as if it were the solution to all of the ills on this world. She lifted a torn handful to her nose. The smell was fresh and good, and she couldn't resist a small taste of the foliage. It was delicious, and she ate with relish. She continued eating and lay face down feeling the pleasure of the warm sun on her back. She lay that way for a long time, reveling in the sheer delight of it. Suddenly she felt incursions of alien thoughts at the base of her cortex, and she drew herself alert. Not her body, but her mind probed toward the strange outside emanations. Quite naturally her first concern was toward the sky, and somehow she perceived a tiny helicopter landing from directly above. She didn't "see" it with her eyes, which were still focused on the moss below her, but she was fully aware of its presence.

When it landed, it happened so fast she had no chance to move her fingers and the tiny craft landed on them causing a slight pain in those extremities, and her mind sharpened into focus. The helicopter seemed to recede from her, and grow until it was a hundred meters away and normal in size. The door opened, a man got out and came directly toward her. He hadn't taken more than a dozen steps when she recognized him, and there were no signs of illness on his face. Her heart leaped! It was Scott, and he was well! She jumped to her feet with a smile on her face and joy in her heart.

"Scott!" She heard herself cry, as she broke into a run in his direction, tears streaming down her face.

He was raising his arms toward her now, too and running in her direction, but as fast as they were both going, the distance remained the same. She recognized that and doubled her pace, desperate. He seemed to get slightly closer and her anxiety began to fade, but at the moment when it seemed they would touch, a change began. He was moving in slow motion now, and as he moved wings grew behind his shoulders and his head seemed to recede into his chest. His features took on terrible grinning proportions. He was turning into a gargoyle!

She stopped her wild run perplexed and unwilling to believe what she perceived. Tears began to flow more freely with a deep sorrow. She felt her mouth form words.

"Do you want to eat me?" She asked evenly, knowing the answer——an answer that filled her breast with a deep sadness. Sue awoke in her own bed just as she saw the grotesque animal recoil from her. It was a bad dream, but unusual, because she had felt no fear, although the monster was indeed fearsome.

Why? The dream had seemed so real and familiar: almost *deja vous.*

The recorder was still running, but she was too upset to listen to it for a few minutes.

When it did break through her preoccupation, she heard Armstrong's voice.

"…wuzzies taste like? Wuzzies are not camouflaged!"

Her pulse raced, as she knew what she had to do. She leaped from the bed and threw on her clothes. Taking the still running recorder she went into the mess hall, rummaged in Katy Yeager's black bag and stepped into the stanisplummer with what she'd found. Tears of joy blurring her vision, she could barely read the numbers as she punched the code PC8491.

※　　※　　※　　※

Less than ten minutes after she'd left, the first stirrings of life came into the mess hall. Although they had been told to sleep for a full four hours, daylight had broken full on the camp, and everyone was eager to get on with the brainstorming. After a hurried breakfast (downed rather guiltily in front of the sick men), they took their places in the think tank. Even Barstow seemed to realize that the technique was their last hope and was cooperating fully. As they squirmed around in the deep comfortable padding, listening to the pitch of the problem-solving expert, the mood was of cautious optimism.

The expert told them that there were some leads they would like to expand on, and everyone listened while an unidentified voice made the initial comment in the session.

"What are you thinking about eating?"

After a moment Armstrong's voice broke in. "Wuzzies might taste good."

It was the same thought that occurred to several of them, and they were confused. No one spoke for a long moment.

Armstrong startled them all just then.

"Where's Sue?" He exploded, realizing that he'd had a feeling something was wrong but was so intent on the session, he'd not been conscious of her absence until now.

No one answered, so he sprang to his feet and propelled himself to the entrance of the think tank. He could hear the turmoil behind him, as they realized his comment was not part of the brainstorming. He was already in the female quarters by the time anyone else had gotten out of the think tank. He found nothing there and returned hastily to the dining hall.

"Tell me what you suspect, hurry!" He screamed to the air.

The voice of the expert responded reluctantly. "If we tell you our suspicions now, it may prejudice the next session, and we may not be able to get any further information of value. We must carry…"

"God damn it!" Armstrong roared. "I don't have time to listen to that crap. Tell me what you've got!"

Janakowski's voice came through immediately. "What's the matter, Scott?"

"General, Doctor Powell is missing. I think she may have reached some kind of a conclusion about what happened to us and has gone off by herself to investigate. Tell us what you've got. Maybe she came to the same conclusion."

"What have you got?" This was Janakowski's voice, but it had dropped in tone, as if he were addressing someone sitting right next to him.

The problem solver answered. "It may be entirely wrong. If we had one more hour in the session, we could plant more ideas, and maybe…"

"We don't *have* one more hour. Sue Powell may be in trouble already." Armstrong was almost begging.

"Tell him." Janakowski's order was calm and those on the new planet listened intently for the answer, but the expert was not ready to give up so easily.

"But…"

"Tell him!" The command from the general stifled any further protest from the expert, and after a pause, which made the group think he was getting some papers together, he began speaking slowly and deliberately. "We think the illness is not physical at all, but psychosomatic." The statement was met with flat disbelief from those on Kadakas IV, and the muttering that could be heard showed their disgust with the brainstorming session. Someone said with heavy sarcasm.

"Right! Two men died from bad thoughts, and three more are wasting away."

"Hear him out!" Janakowski's commanding voice rang out again.

The expert's voice continued tentatively. "The overriding theme of all the comments in the first session, dealt with being hungry or aversion to eating something. That is highly unusual in these sessions, so we grasped that from the beginning…"

Armstrong interrupted him impatiently. "I'm sure the explanations and motivations are extremely interesting, but right now we don't have time for it. Just give us an outline, so we have something to go on."

The voice responded sounding harassed. "We don't know much more than that. We had hoped to get some specific details from the next session. We think the disease is psychosomatic, induced by something you saw or heard up there.

"Psychosomatic illnesses have been well documented as having caused deep disorders, even death." This was Katy Yeager, and they listened to her with more respect than they had the problem solver. "Here the symptoms are an aversion to eating and violent vomiting whenever anything is ingested. *That* was the cause of death and the illness. Of course! That has to be it! But how could it be possible that more than one person is affected by identical *psychosomatic* illnesses? More than that, why didn't the rest of us get it, too?"

"The illness was caused by something we saw or heard?" Armstrong repeated quizzically." What did *we* see or hear that none of the scientists noticed? That could be anything."

The distant voice of the problem solver returned. "Whatever it was had something to do with tasting good, or not. At least that is as much as we've been able to tell. We've edited some of the tape with cogent comments. We were going to play it at the subliminal level during today's session, but we might as well play it now at normal volume."

There came a scratchy sound as the recorder began. They heard a replay of their own voices.

"Why would anyone want to eat them?"

"Do you want to eat me?" Armstrong started at the sound of Sue's voice."

"I can see them now eating bones and all."

"I'm not hungry now."

"Bleached white gargoyle bones."

"They're so cute, why would anyone want to…"

Armstrong heard no more. Seemingly recovered from his illness, he bounded for the stanisplummer, pausing only to consult the chart by the door. He stepped inside the booth, punched the code and was abruptly in the center of the vast yellow-green plain. There were few wuzzies around him, but looking to his left he saw the main herd, which stretched to the horizon. He strained his eyes looking frantically around him while he was still in the booth, and for a moment his heart sank as he thought he had been mistaken——then he saw the girl away from the herd to his right, and when he saw what was standing next to her, he fairly sprinted toward her from the booth, despite the fact he was unarmed.

A huge gargoyle!

He was ready to do battle with the creature hand-to-hand: ready to sacrifice his own life for hers. As soon as he reached her, he realized there was no need. The huge birdlike animal had no inclination to fight. The stench from its vomit reached him as he approached, but Sue had to restrain him from attacking the beast as he drew near.

She caught hold of his arm and yelled at him. "No, Scott! It won't attack. It has the same illness you do, but it *is* capable of hurting you even in its weakened condition."

He stopped then and looked at her incredulously. "What are you doing here?" he demanded. His fear for her safety had turned into a towering rage.

Just then a burst from an M-80 sounded, and they looked around to see the gargoyle crumple to the ground, its last strength drained. The approach of the others allowed Armstrong's anger to dissipate, and he pulled her to him in a relieved embrace. She allowed it for a moment only and gently fought her way from his grasp.

"Listen, Scott! Can you hear them?"

"What do you mean?"

"The wuzzies! They...*it* is talking to you."

The statement was so ludicrous that for a moment he feared for her sanity, but her face was so earnest that he found himself listening. Then *he* heard it, too. No, *heard* was not the word. *Felt? Imagined? No! Perceived! That was it*!

He perceived that something was trying to communicate with him, but there was no sound. It was strange, but also familiar. He had heard that inquiry *before* in precisely the same manner. *Do you want to eat me?* The question was right inside his head. It shocked him as he realized the first time he heard it, he had been convinced it had been *his own thought.* A reaction to his being hungry, and he had looked around for something to eat. The first thing he'd come upon was the wuzzies. This time he formed a question in his own mind directed back at the inquiry.

Who are you? The answer came swiftly. *My body is on the plain all around you. Please don't eat me. We have much to talk about.* The request was plaintive, but there was no fear. Only a resounding sadness.

XXI

WUZZIES

As soon as Armstrong has assured the creature (creatures?) that he had no intention of eating it, he felt the "illness" fade from him, and he confirmed it by taking a long welcome drink from the canteen. The illness had been simply a post-hypnotic suggestion, induced telepathically by the collective intelligence of the wuzzies. The reason the soldiers had been the only ones to succumb was the scientists had revealed no intention to eat the animals. The biologists had been interested only professionally. Barstow had been too disappointed to display hunger, Sakagowa was a vegetarian, the women thought of the wuzzies as cuddly little pets, and Epilov hadn't gone to the plain. The individual wuzzies taken as specimens had no effect. The intelligence was collective and was powerful enough to communicate only in large numbers. That capability had been the sole reason for the survival of the furry creatures. They had no camouflage, nor other means of defending themselves. The mind would reach out to any creature venturing near the group, and if it showed any threat it would be neutralized.

It took only a few minutes of telepathic conversation to determine it was *they* and not *it*. Groups of up to five thousand or so of the creatures formed single individuals. They estimated the total population of these individuals at more than a million and a half. Early in their evolution they had been spread widely over the planet, but their recalled "history" had them moving together when they were able to communicate intelligently with another, little more than two thousand years before. All of them had been banded together where they could exchange ideas for the previous thousand years.

Recently, however, some of the dissidents had been thinking of striking out on their own, claiming resistance to new ideas by conservative elders.

The discovery of the intelligence on the planet was a two-fold blessing for the humans. First of all, it was clear there was not a dreaded disease present that would render the planet uninhabitable, but also because the wuzzies welcomed them. They had agreed to defend the humans from gargoyles and other dangerous beasts. They looked forward to nothing more than the exchange of new ideas. The only problem was time. It would take time for the wuzzy individuals to migrate to the places where the humans would settle.

* * * *

Unless humans can construct a stanisplummer large enough to contain five thousand of the furry little animals at once, or the creatures gain a total trust of the aliens, so that they'll be content to be transported piecemeal, we will have to wait. But that is for the future. For the present we can be content in the knowledge that man is a star walker.

ABOUT THE AUTHOR

This book was actually written in 1980 and 1981. I was unemployed at the time and hard at work trying to find a job. However, job-hunting is not a full-time job, so to fill time I took some computer programming classes at a local community college (I still had some eligibility for the GI bill). In addition I had an inkling that I could write, so I put down all the ideas I had ever had about what the future really could be like in my spare time.

I wrote initially with my scrawling block printing on the back of the green bar computer printout paper my programming assignments were printed on. I really enjoyed the writing and Kathy, my wife volunteered to type it for me if we could somehow get a typewriter. We bought a cheap (it might have been second hand) portable typewriter and we became a team. We imagined we would quickly become famous, turning down million dollar movie offers. Unfortunately, I knew next to nothing about writing and, as it turned out, even less about getting a book published.

Alas, I had to be practical and finally accepted a job as a schoolteacher in Houston. At the same time I continued my military career in the army reserve, from which I retired as a lieutenant colonel. I continue to teach a Klein High School here (Computer Science—the Community college programming courses paid off). During that time I wrote two more novels—one about my younger brother's true life adventure during the Tet Offensive in Vietnam and the other taken from my extensive knowledge of a European battlefield about a future war in that venue.

978-0-595-38296-5
0-595-38296-7